OUT OF TIME

OUT OF TIME

A Nick Donahue Adventure

CATHI STOLER

For Madison Grace O'Dare
the newest member of our family.
We love you to the moon and back a million times over.

Praise for Out of Time

"*Out of Time* by Cathi Stoler is a twisty, unputdownable thriller set in the world of horseracing, mobsters, and international conspiracy with a winning protagonist. Highly recommend this addition to the Nick Donahue series!"—Lee Matthew Goldberg, award-nominated author of *The Mentor* and *The Great Gimmelmans*

"*Out of Time* leaves you out of breath in the very best way! This pulse pounding, high stakes game could only be played by the deft hand of gambler extradordinaire, Nick Donahue. Underpinned by classic mystery elements dripping with peril, and comprised of an exceptionally engaging cast of characters, *Out of Time* is a delightful ride from start to finish."—Marie Sutro, award-winning author of the Kate Barnes Series

"Take one debonair professional gambler, add a sexy private investigator, an Arab billionaire, and an ISIS terrorist group, shake from New York to Kentucky to Dubai, and stir in lots of mystery, intrigue, and danger. *Out of Time*, Cathi Stoler's latest Nick Donahue mystery is a must read."—Catherine Maiorisi, author of the NYPD Detective Chiara Corelli Mysteries

"Stoler nimbly raises the stakes in this sequel that brings back urbane gambler/adventurer Nick Donahue in a fun, fast-moving caper."—Richie Narvaez, author of *Holly Hernandez and the Death of Disco*

"Smart, fast-paced, and infused with international intrigue. This crime solving duo is the new Nick and Nora Charles as they use their wit and subterfuge to prevent a deadly attack. Chandler would approve. Highly recommended."—James L'Etoile, award-winning author of *Dead Drop* and *Face of Greed*

"Cathi Stoler's latest Nick Donohue adventure, *Out of Time*, delivers on the promise of its title. The plot is swift-moving, the characters are on the run, and the luxury settings are breathtaking. When the story opens Nick is on top of the world—or, to be more precise, tethered to the top of the world's tallest building. How this charming and resourceful gambler happens to land there, and how he gets himself down, make for a riveting read. There are thrills aplenty in this suspenseful novel, but Nick's deadpan delivery and ironic self-deprecating manner leaven the work with laugh-out-loud humor. *Out of Time* is a 2024 must-read."—Lori Robbins, award-winning author of the On Pointe Mysteries

"*Out of Time* pushes all the right buttons with a rollicking plot, surprising twists, and a fascinating cast of characters who collide in this fast-paced tale of blackmail, world-class horse racing, and terrorism. And with the sizzling chemistry between charming scoundrel Nick Donahue and professional investigator Marina DiPietro, *Out of Time* is easy to dive into and almost impossible to put down. Perfect for fans of *The Thin Man*'s Nick and Nora Charles."—Mally Becker, author of the Agatha Award-nominated Revolutionary War mysteries

"Opens with a dizzying shot of adrenaline and never lets up! In *Out of Time*, Cathi Stoler takes the best of classic horseracing mysteries and international thrillers in a pulse-pounding new direction. It's a great ride, taking readers from the tony hotels of New York to the luxury oasis of Dubai, to the iconic track and stables of Churchill Downs, all with truly unexpected twists. And it has a wonderful heart, in a cast to love and root for, led by gambler Nick Donahue, his partner Marina, and his colorful family and friends. Whether you come for the ponies or the plotters, it's a terrific read, with an edge-of-your seat finale – and one last twist at the end. I'm counting the days—or the cards—'til the next one!"—Nikki Knight, author of the Vermont Radio and Grace the Hit Mom Mysteries

Chapter One

Just ask Marina.

If you want to know how I wound up tethered like a sacrificial goat to a flimsy spire swaying in the wind on top of the world's tallest building, maybe she can explain it.

She'd tell you I had a special knack for getting into trouble. And she'd be right.

From where I stood, the Arabian Gulf looked like a giant swimming pool. The water shimmered in a sensuous ripple. Its surface, blue and sparkling, tinged with golden light from the afternoon sun beating down from above. A sight that normally would have drawn a wow if I hadn't believed it would be one of my last.

A half-mile below, people scurried in and out of streets and buildings like the streams of black-bodied ants they resembled. Not one of them poked a nose into the air and noticed the man far above struggling against his bonds. Had the citizens of Dubai become so used to the Burj Khalifa in their midst, they didn't even glance at it anymore? Seemed so. The people who put me here hadn't even bothered to gag me. I could scream all I wanted, and not a soul would hear.

The Salafi thought I was their insurance, like a Blackjack player protecting his bet, while hedging that the dealer has twenty-one. They already had what they wanted. At least, I thought so.

Believe me, I was scared. Being trussed up and hung above the city was just the beginning. They were waiting to make sure the other player hadn't pulled a switch. Either way, I was sure they'd kill me. I wasn't going to be the one to tell them I thought he had, that what would happen if he had given in would be unthinkable.

The sun had almost dropped below the horizon, the water turning cool and steely, the wind picking up and creating ripples along its surface. After hours under a blazing sun, a night up here, when the desert turned frigid, was going to be even more brutal. Shivers ran up my spine just imagining it. I tucked my chin toward my chest and tried to conjure up warm thoughts. It wasn't working. All that came to mind was Marina, her green eyes wide with surprise, then anger, as that big black Glock pushed into her. Watching as they led me away, dumped me in the car, and drove off. My anger had been the equal of hers, my mind reeling with thoughts of what they might be doing to her. Was it possible she'd escaped and made it back to Adnan's villa? Or was she still in their clutches, desperate in some blistering desert wadi? The fear came later when they put me up here.

This was Marina's case. I'd just come along to keep her company, to be a sounding board when she needed one. Then, before I knew it, I was smack in the middle of things. So, if you want to know how this happened, I'm not sure either one of us could tell you. I just hoped we'd live long enough to try.

Chapter Two

New York One Month Ago:

We were in New York, our troubles with SuisseBank and the mob behind us, helping my brother Alex and his fiancée, Simone, prepare for their upcoming wedding. I was taking a few weeks off from playing blackjack at the casinos—gambling professionally was the way I earned my living. Marina, whom I'd met when she was working undercover for MI6 and had roped me into helping her, had left the agency for good and set up her own investigative firm.

There were several prenup celebrations scheduled before the big day. I was the best man, and Marina was the maid of honor. Simone had no family to speak of, just an uncle on a remote farm in a tiny Swiss village. She had adopted our family as her own, and the feeling was reciprocated. I couldn't have been happier for Alex. He deserved to have this tall, beautiful, and brave woman by his side and as much happiness as he could get. Especially after what he'd been through.

While the bride and her minions were slated for a few days of high-end shopping and luxurious spa treatments before Saturday's nuptials, I'd invited a few of Alex's school buddies for a bachelor party excursion to Atlantic City. Since I'd been living in London, I came back to New York infrequently and hadn't played blackjack in Atlantic City for a long time. With so many of the casinos closing or tottering on the brink, I didn't want to waste the opportunity to try my luck on my native soil.

But, no. There's always one spoilsport in the bunch. Her name was Mother. Our mother.

"Atlantic City?" she exclaimed and gave me "the look" when I attempted to explain my plan. You know the one: chin tilted up, eyes looking heavenward, head shaking from side to side. The one reserved for inattentive store clerks, difficult spouses, and recalcitrant children, which, in her eyes, Alex and I still were. "Why would you want to go there? It's so…" She paused desperately, seeking the right word. "Tacky." It popped out of her mouth, and she smiled as though she'd uncovered the secret codes to an Iranian missile base. "Besides, your father has planned a lovely celebration for you boys at his club tonight." Now she tossed in "the other look," head tilted down, eyes half closed with sadness, and a shrug of her shoulders. "He'd never say it himself, but he'll be very disappointed if you don't go. He's so looking forward to it."

This was the first I'd heard of it. Dad hadn't said a word, and he'd had plenty of opportunity to mention it. I was wondering just whose plan it was exactly. Now that Mom had us all back in the nest, she wasn't going to let us fly away so easily, even for just a few days.

I may not have mentioned my dad before. His presence tends to be a bit overshadowed by you-know-who. He's a great guy. Tall and handsome with dark gray eyes and streaks of silver in his dark brown hair that gave him a distinguished air. Alex and I both favored him. He's very patient, as you can imagine. Tough in business—he's an investment banker—but warm and giving in everything else.

What could we do? We gave in, of course. Well, Alex did and poked me in the ribs until I agreed. Sure, it was easy for him to do. I'm the one who'd have to cancel the limo and call his friends to inform them the booze and bad behavior were off the table. We'd all be convening for a rollicking evening at the New York Founders Club instead. Big whoop.

"Good. Now that's all settled." I could see Mom mentally ticking off one more thing from her "to-do" list. "I'm sure you'll have fun, boys," she tossed over her shoulder as she breezed out of the room. "Your father said to meet him at the club at seven."

I wouldn't put it past her to have arranged the whole evening on her own. Now she'd call Dad and tell him we'd suggested getting together at the Founders if it was okay with him.

I gave Alex a look of my own. The one that said, "We've been played by a master."

Mom, Simone, and Marina went off to be pampered, pummeled, and patted while I made my calls and my excuses for switching venues. I couldn't very well tell these men my mom made me do it. I'd never live it down.

Since Alex and I now had the whole day to kill before meeting Dad, we decided to do some pre-wedding shopping. He and Simone were planning to honeymoon on a private island off the coast of Spain. A friend of Dad's and a partner at the bank, Bart Phillips, had offered his villa to them as a wedding present. Believe me, he didn't have to ask twice.

I, on the other hand, still hadn't figured out what to get them, and time was running out. The wedding was on Saturday, only three days away. Marina told me it would come to me, and I'd find the perfect gift. I think that crystal ball she gazed into must have been a little cloudy since I couldn't think of a thing Alex and Simone needed or wanted other than each other.

I put it out of my mind as we hit Gordon's Department Store. It was one of New York's most upscale emporiums, with crystal chandeliers lighting the burnished wood and glass showcases and the polished Italian marble floors. We'd been shopping here since we were kids. Alex and I used to hide under the racks filled with boys' pants and jackets while Mom picked out our school clothes. She'd be calling our names, and of course, we didn't answer. We just started cracking up instead until one of the salesmen separated the clothes that concealed us, gave us a wink, and motioned us out.

"Here they are, Mrs. Donahue." He smiled as he handed us over. He had to be nice to her. We didn't. But we were big boys now, at least chronologically, and should try to behave that way.

Alex pretty much needed a whole new wardrobe and a suit for the wedding. He'd left London with only the clothes he had on when we high-tailed it out of Switzerland. He couldn't just call SuisseBank and ask them to forward his things from the Zurich villa he'd been living in. Not that they'd oblige even if we hadn't ruined their business and made sure their Chairman was rotting away in prison. The Swiss are funny about things like that.

All the old salesmen I remembered from Gordon's were gone, probably retired years ago. The new guys looked more like customers than help in their Armani and Tom Ford suits. These duds carried a hefty price tag, and I wondered how they could afford to dress so well, even with an employee discount. Maybe I should give up gambling and go into retail instead. I was suave, and I dressed well. I could charm the pants off—or in this case on—customers, couldn't I?

In the men's department, Alex explained he needed everything from underwear on out. His salesman's eyes lit up like a slot machine pouring out a jackpot with a win on the max line. Today was going to be a good day for him.

I left Alex in his hands and sat down in the men's lounge with a steaming Cappuccino—a freebie thrown in with the many thousands of dollars we were spending—and thought about how lucky we all were to have made it home alive.

If I never saw Mr. Tomasso—"Tommy B" Bonnannaio—and his henchmen again, it would be too soon. The ten million I handed over to them in Monte Carlo marked that adventure as paid and done. At least as far as I was concerned. Another chill. Could Tommy B somehow know I was in New York and come calling?

Then there was Florian Emminger, the former head of SuisseBank, emphasis on former, now ruined banker, who was serving a good long sentence for murder, fraud, money laundering, and other offenses too numerous to mention. I wondered if the Swiss were as meticulous about locking up their prisoners as they were about locking away their money. Either way, I was going to be gone from Switzerland for a long time.

C'mon, Nick. That's all behind you now, I thought. *No one's going to come looking for you. Those days are over.*

I sighed and licked a bit of foam from my upper lip. I had Marina now. We were happy and safe. What could be bad about that? I was staring out the window at the crowds on Fifth Avenue, pondering life and sizing up any man who resembled Tommy B, when Alex came in to show me the suit he'd selected for the wedding, an Ermenegildo Zegna black wool with a fine gray pinstripe.

"What do you think?"

"It looks good." I nodded my head. "I think Simone will like it."

His face lit up as he went off with Arturo, the store's tailor, to have it altered.

A snip here. A stitch or two there. If only everything was that simple. I wished it were as easy to put thoughts of Tommy B and Emminger out of my mind. I finished my coffee and decided to check out the gift department for a wedding present.

I was hoping to find something unique. Hoping but not too hopeful.

Chapter Three

The Founders Club was an old and venerable New York institution on Park Avenue and Sixty-Seventh Street. It looks exactly like you'd imagine a private wealthy members-only club: paneled walls with wainscoting, a giant library with floor-to-ceiling book-filled shelves, and roomy leather club chairs atop the worn Persian rugs scattered throughout. And quiet. Very. Quiet. Men—so far, only a few women had stormed the barriers demanding to become members; they had more sense than that—with lots of money, preferred it that way. Mycroft Holmes would have loved it here.

The butler—yes, the butler—greeted us inside the ornately carved wooden doors and ushered us into the library.

Dad was waiting, ensconced in a huge armchair, holding a snifter of brandy, and speaking with a man I'd never seen before. They turned toward us as we approached and stood to greet us.

My father was beaming. He couldn't hide his pleasure at having both his sons by his side. He gave Alex and me a big slap-on-the-back man hug, smiling all the while. I hate to admit it, but my mother was right. Dad would have been disappointed if we'd gone to Atlantic City instead.

After the greetings were over. He introduced us to the man with him. "Nick, Alex, this is Adnan bin Haddad, a client of mine from Dubai. Adnan. My sons Nick and Alex."

Adnan was tall, dark, and, yes, handsome. I instinctively looked for his "tell," but his big, deep brown eyes didn't give away a thing, and his generous, bushy mustache hid his mouth. He looked more like a young Omar Sharif than a big-deal billionaire. I could almost see him pursuing Julie Christie through the snow in *Doctor Zhivago*. My mom had seen the movie when she was a young woman. She loved it and Omar and brought out her VHS tape of it every once in a while, and insisted I watch it with her. Then she talked about it for days. She was very sad when Mr. Sharif died.

Bin Haddad shook Alex's hand, then leaned in closer as he grasped mine with both of his. "Ah, the blackjack player." His grip was almost crushing. "I have heard all about your recent exploits. Well done."

I managed to hide my surprise and shot a glance at Dad, who shook his head slightly as if to say, "It wasn't me." My recent exploits weren't something I bandied about.

Before I could respond, Adnan spoke again. "And how is your lovely friend, Ms. DiPietro? I would very much like to meet her." He knew about Marina, too. Where was this going? "Perhaps we can speak another time." His eyebrows lifted slightly as he slid a business card into my hand. "I hope you enjoy your evening." He nodded at me, then at Dad and Alex as he made his way from the library.

Just then, Alex's pals piled into the club, preventing me from asking Dad what that was all about. Usually a boisterous bunch, they seemed to have been stunned into silence at the subdued tone of the hallowed halls, not to mention being greeted by a butler. It was definitely not your usual bachelor party digs.

I slipped bin Haddad's card into my pocket and turned toward the group, staring into their blank faces. "Well, guys, let's get this party started."

Chapter Four

We had a great time. Dinner was delicious. Chilled jumbo shrimp and crab claws to start, man-sized sirloin steaks, potatoes loaded with sour cream and butter, and creamed spinach for our main course, plus cheesecake for dessert—all presented with impeccable service. Dad had asked the owner of Peter Luger's, another of his clients, for the loan of one of his chefs for the evening. He cleared it with the club, and their on-staff chef didn't object. I'm sure a nice bonus made a night off from the stove even more palatable.

Of course, our father chose the best wines from the club's cellar: a crisp Sancerre to go with the shrimp, a full-bodied Brunello di Montalcino to sip with dinner, and a tawny, twenty-year-old port along with dessert.

At about eleven, we moved into the library for after-dinner brandy and cigars, most likely the youngest group that had ever occupied the space.

A half-hour later, Alex looked my way and gave me our boyhood sign—a finger on the right side of the nose—that it was time to get going. Something we'd stolen from Redford and Newman in *The Sting*. We'd done our best for Dad, and he was grinning from ear to ear, whether from happiness or the brandy, I couldn't tell.

It was time for me to leave the table. "Dad, thanks for a great evening. Everyone really enjoyed it." I lifted my arm to encompass our crowd and then looked at my watch. "I'm beat. Think I'll head back to the hotel and Marina."

"Sure, sure." He patted my arm and gave me a wry smile. "I know you boys did this to please me, and it means a lot." He glanced over at Alex and his friends. "I'm sure those guys have someplace they'd rather be. Let's not disappoint them." He called Alex over. "Why don't you and your buddies hit the road?" His eyes strayed toward Alex's friends again. They'd started making toast after toast to the portraits of the club's founders hanging on the walls. "Those guys look like they're ready for something a bit livelier."

Alex started to invite Dad to come along. But he demurred. "Got a busy day tomorrow." Dad was no fool. He knew the neighborhood bars were calling to the bachelor party like a blackjack dealer fanning out his decks of cards. He tossed us a goodnight over his shoulder as he slipped into his jacket and left the club.

"What about you?" Alex was ready to leave, as well.

I shook my head. "Going back to the Carlyle. Marina must be pining away for me by now. Especially after a day with Mom."

He grabbed a wadded-up napkin from the table and tossed it at me. "Dream on. I can't understand what she sees in you anyway."

Marina and I were staying in a suite at the hotel. Hey, if it was good enough for Prince William and Princess Katherine, it was good enough for us.However, that was not the way my mother viewed it. She'd made her displeasure known as forcefully as a casino manager denying a player credit. But practicality won out. The apartment only had two working bedrooms, and there wasn't enough space for all of us. The third one, my former digs, had been converted into an office. I suspected Mom had changed it the moment I told her I was going to travel the world playing blackjack. Renovation by spite was how I thought of it. I, of course, deferred to the soon-to-be wed couple. Not much of a sacrifice on my part.

I stepped out into a star-lit night and turned up the collar of my jacket against the cool breeze coming off the avenue, dreams of Marina crowding my thoughts. I was so involved with her image that I never noticed the man in the chauffeur's cap approaching me.

"Mister Donahue?"

The sound of my name startled me. It was a déjà vu moment from London when Tommy B's thug had invited me into his car. The man ignored my response and continued as though I'd been expecting him.

"Mister bin Haddad would like to have a word with you."

He pointed to a sleek black Mercedes sedan idling at the curb. The car sat so low on its oversized tires, it had to be armor-plated.

I nodded and followed him. Adnan bin Haddad was inside and gestured for me to get in next to him. I guess this was his idea of speaking at another time. The chauffeur shut the door and walked around the front to the driver's side.

"Let me give you a lift to the Carlyle."

I hadn't mentioned where we were staying, but that hadn't deterred him from finding out.

He rapped on the glass partition, and the Merc glided away from the curb.

"Perhaps you could call Ms. DiPietro and see if she would care to join us in the bar for a drink."

I sat back and gazed at him surreptitiously. He stared straight ahead, unblinking, and immobile. After a few moments, I pulled out my cell, sure Marina would be as happy about meeting bin Haddad as a pit boss having to smile at a high roller.

Marina answered on the first ring, "How was the bachelor party?" Her voice held a playful tone. "Did you boys have fun?" I gave her a quick answer and then relayed bin Haddad's request to meet for a drink. Surprisingly, she acquiesced immediately. "I'll meet you in the bar in fifteen minutes."

I nodded yes to Adnan and waited for him to speak. He told his driver we were ready to depart and remained silent after that. He knew entirely too much about my business and me, and I'd bet the bank it wasn't accidental.

Chapter Five

The "bar" was Bemelmans's, the Carlyle's Art Deco homage to Ludwig Bemelman, the creator of the Madeline children's books. Bemelman and his family lived there for a year and a half while he painted the fabulous murals that decorated the walls. Marina was waiting for us at the long black granite bar, a Champagne flute in hand, totally at ease as if she owned the place and dressed as though she'd known she'd be going out. I knew from experience how long it took her to get ready. And this was a first. I couldn't hide the frown that crossed my face as I kissed her hello. She raised her eyes in a questioning look as we moved to a small table in the corner under the twenty-four-karat gold leaf ceiling. As you can see, I'd read the brochure the hotel management left in our room.

As I made the introductions, Adnan took both Marina's hands in his. "Ms. DiPietro, it is delightful to meet you. I am so glad you could join us on such short notice." He bowed slightly as he spoke.

"My pleasure. And it's Marina."

"Then, you must call me Adnan,"

They were beaming at each other, her green eyes shining brightly, and he was responding in kind. They were still holding hands when I cleared my throat.

Hello, remember me?

Marina shot me a look that said don't be a schmuck. Apparently, she had a plan that I knew nothing about.

Adnan continued to be his charming self, to Marina, that is. He complimented her on her hair, more tousled than usual; her dress, a lovely form-fitting black sheath; and her choice of Champagne, a bottle of Cristal. It was getting a little boring. I was about ready to chug the rest of the Cristal and tell Marina it was time to call it a night. Marina kicked me under the table—I swear the woman can read my mind—and tossed Adnan a fetching look, and then finally got to the point.

"Adnan, this has been delightful, but it's time to tell me why you wanted to meet me—and Nick," she added, dipping her head in my direction, "and what it is you really want."

At least she'd included me.

He seemed a bit taken aback by her forthrightness and sat back against the banquette. A deep sigh escaped as he nodded at her. "You are right. I should explain." His tone was matter of fact, but his dark eyes were clouded over, and his expression intense. He spoke to us in the here and now, but it felt as though his thoughts were miles away.

"I need your help. Someone has threatened me, and I am unsure of how to respond."

It was a puzzling statement. I'd been in the fortified Merc with the chauffeur, who was undoubtedly a bodyguard, as well. He was sitting at a table across from us, his eyes scanning the room like laser beams crisscrossing a museum to protect it from theft. If Adnan needed more protection, he certainly had the resources to obtain it.

Marina raised her hand, questioning the statement. "Threatened you, how?" She took a breath before she continued, her expression puzzled. "In what way?"

"They are threatening to maim all my horses, one by one—and they have already begun."

Chapter Six

Adnan had gotten our attention. One glance at Marina told me we weren't going anywhere just yet. Her former puzzlement morphed into a frown, and her eyes zeroed in on Adnan, waiting for him to explain.

"I have a stable of Arabians and Thoroughbred horses, all of whom race here and at home."

"Yes, I know." Marina nodded, urging him to continue.

She knows? This is all news to me. What else does she know about the guy?

"The pride of my stable, my colt, Devil Wind, is scheduled to run in the Kentucky Derby in a bid for the Triple Crown." He paused for a moment as he reached inside the front of his jacket and removed a business-size envelope, which he placed on the table between us. It had no address written on it, just Adnan's name typed in the center. "I received this a few days ago." He nodded toward the envelope. "The sender threatened to blind Devil Wind unless I paid a ransom of a hundred million dollars."

He opened the envelope and removed its contents: a white sheet of paper folded in thirds and a photo. He handed the paper to Marina. "To prove that they were serious, they sent this, as well." He turned the photo to face us. Marina stopped examining the paper, and both of us bent closer to get a better look. It showed a chestnut-colored horse lying on its side. In the space where his eye should be, was a huge hole. It was obvious that the animal was dead, its tongue hanging out the side of its mouth. "That was Devil Spirit, one of the colts that share Devil Wind's bloodline. He was blinded at the Meydan Racecourse in Dubai. I learned of this at the same time I received the photo and letter." He glanced down at the photo before handing it and the letter to Marina. "Of course, he had to be put down," he continued, and I could see the pain it had cost him as he lowered his eyes.

I wasn't much of a racing fan, and I didn't know anything about Adnan's horse, Devil Wind, much less that he was running in the Derby. I'd always enjoyed watching the Derby, the Preakness Stakes, and the Belmont Stakes when I lived in the States. These three races, the most prestigious in the world, take over the sporting stage from the first Saturday in May to the first week of June.

In twenty-fifteen, the horse American Pharaoh had won the Triple Crown, finally breaking the thirty-seven-year record held by Affirmed since 1978. Then, a few years later, a horse who'd never been defeated did it again. Justify, a three-year-old, crossed the finish lines of all three races far ahead of the competition.

Even though racing wasn't my game, it wasn't too hard to figure out that the worth of a Triple Crown winner can be mind-altering. I remembered reading that when Affirmed won, his owners took in nearly two and a half million dollars just for racing. With my gambler's mind for math, I figured that probably didn't include stud fees, which must have brought the total to a staggering amount for that time. I could hardly imagine what Devil Wind would be worth if he duplicated this feat just a couple of years after Justify's victory. Maybe the extortionists thought they had an inside track with Devil Wind. No wonder they were asking for such a huge amount of money.

All this ran through my head as Adnan watched for Marina's reaction to his story. So intent was his gaze, I thought he might have stopped breathing. For a moment, I felt like the gigolo who escorts a rich matron on her arm just to smile and look handsome. I brought myself back to reality quickly enough. Adnan had a serious problem, and Marina had the deductive skills and resources to solve it.

"As you can see, I need to act quickly. Devil Wind is already in Kentucky with my trainers, and the race is in less than three weeks. I do not know when these people might contact me again." He paused as if to let his words sink in. "Would you be willing to help me find those who are behind this?"

He gestured to the photo of Devil Spirit with his missing eyes.

Marina reached over and shook his hand. "You can count on it."

"We're supposed to be on vacation," I reminded her once we were back upstairs in our suite, trying not to whine but not succeeding very well. "No work or gambling until after the wedding, and we're back to London. Your words, not mine."

She rolled her beautiful eyes at me. "And what do you call your plan to have the bachelor party in Atlantic City with all those casinos there to entice you? Good thing your father intervened and took you all to his club instead."

Hmmm. Was that actually Mother's idea, or Marina's?

"Oh, and what about your meeting with Adnan tomorrow? What category does that fall under?"

Marina had agreed to see Adnan in the morning at his apartment to review his case further and sift through any information he had that might help find the people responsible. I was invited to this meeting but declined. I planned to stay at the hotel and sulk.

Marina ignored me and looked at her watch. "I'm going to call Nikki and Ana and get them started looking into Adnan's stables in Dubai and his personnel." It was one a.m. here and eight in London. She knew her staff would be in the office. Her voice softened as she sidled up close to me and put her arms around my neck. "I'll be right here with you, darling. I won't do a thing until after Simone and Alex are off on their honeymoon. I promise." She used her most sultry tone and pecked me on the cheek, then turned and reached for her phone.

Nikki and Ana were Marina's two employees in her newly founded investigative firm, DiPietro & Associates. Nikki St. John, a tall, willowy blue-eyed blonde, and Ana Dios, a beautiful, brown-eyed brunette, worked alongside the redheaded Marina. I secretly called the three of them Nick's Angels. A guy can hope, right? Although Marina would probably shoot me if she ever heard me say that aloud.

I knew Marina had been in touch with them several times since we arrived in New York. They were minding the office and keeping track of a few ongoing cases. Both were excellent undercover operatives trained by Marina for fieldwork. As she had done with me when we first met, they've used their charms to entice and finagle their way in and out of some serious situations.

"Absolutely." She beamed at me from across the room. "I'll tell him." She clicked off and sat down on the king-sized bed that dominated the space. "Nikki and Ana say hello. They miss you." She waited a beat. "They can't wait for you to get back with the booty you promised them from the duty-free shops."

Sure, messenger boy and gofer. That's what I'd become in the short space of a week. I didn't like it. Not one bit. Well, not until Marina patted the bed and smiled seductively.

Chapter Seven

Marina was already up and having breakfast when I joined her in the suite's sitting room. We'd chosen a premier suite on a high floor, facing east toward the morning sun, a splurge for our first real vacation together. Marina had picked it out from the hotel's website. With its French provincial period furniture, it was a little girlie for me, and I was afraid I might bump into one of the Louis, whatever number replicas scattered throughout, and knock it over. But Marina was delighted with our choice.

Sunlight poured through the large bay windows that faced Madison Avenue and backlit her with an aura that added a fiery glow to her red hair. I bent over to kiss her, then sat down and poured a coffee for myself as I eyeballed the heaping pastry and fruit tray room service had delivered along with the coffee and today's paper. We picked up and discussed Adnan and where we left off before bed.

"Your father certainly has some interesting clients," Marina spoke around a mouthful of chocolate croissant. "And rich ones, to boot." She nodded toward her laptop, which had a story about bin Haddad on its screen.

"Dad's been an investment banker for years, and his bank is up there with the best of them." I reached for a croissant myself, only to have my hand slapped away. "The wedding?" She reminded me, "And your tux that's a tad too tight?" I sucked in my stomach and sat up straighter as she continued. "Hamilton Capital must be the best then."

Marina was referring to Dad's bank. "Adnan is one of the richest men in the United Arab Emirates. In the world, actually." She popped the last bit of pastry into her mouth and licked her fingers.

"I wondered why you were so agreeable when I suggested meeting with him on such short notice." I paused. "You already knew who he was."

"Yes," she shook her head at me in wonder. "Most of the people on the planet have heard his name at one time or another." She ran her fingers over the keypad and brought up several images of bin Haddad: shaking hands with the president, meeting with the queen, posing with several celebrities at Cannes, and his stables with Devil Wind.

The man certainly got around. "Should I be jealous?" I was only half kidding. I remembered the flirting that had gone on last night from both sides of the cocktail table.

"Don't be silly. Do you think a few billion dollars could ever come between us?" She patted me on the head as she rose from the table. "Time to get dressed for my meeting. Sure you don't want to come along?" she teased over her shoulder as she sashayed from the room.

While Marina was busy primping, I sat sipping my coffee and took small bites of the croissant I'd put onto my plate the minute she was out of sight. I tilted my head and glanced down toward my stomach. It wasn't getting flabby, was it? Not that I could see. I took another bite and thought about Adnan bin Haddad. He stage-managed our meeting and, from my father's surprised look when he mentioned getting together, hadn't told Dad he wanted to meet me or Marina.

I slid her laptop over to my side of the table and decided to do some digging of my own. I liked the guy, really, I did, billions and all. It's not that I didn't trust his motives—but I didn't trust them entirely. With his money, he could have hired a whole army of private detectives. So why was he hiring Marina and her small firm, and what did he want from me? The thought was nagging at me like a casino cocktail waitress waiting for a tip.

I heard Marina coming out of the bedroom and quickly clicked over to an online news site. No sense in letting her know I was checking up on Adnan.

She entered the room and was dressed to kill. How could she make a simple black dress look so good? She noticed the appreciation in my eyes and smiled.

"Be good while I'm gone. And I'll bring you a present when I come back."

A present? I already knew what I wanted. And so did she.

I spent another hour searching Adnan bin Haddad online while I enjoyed the rest of my breakfast. I picked an almond croissant to go with the chocolate and slathered on some strawberry jam. My tux fit just fine, I told myself. I probably could have spent a month on the computer reading every entry about the man, billionaire, diplomat, philanthropic donor, socialite, and entrepreneur with holdings as varied as racing stables, food production, and high-tech companies. There were thousands of hits. I had a better idea. I picked up the phone and called Dad. We made plans for lunch. I was sure he could tell me everything I needed to know.

I took a longer look at the copy of Devil Spirit's photo and the note that had accompanied it. Adnan had given Marina the originals last night so she could copy them. She was returning both to him this morning. Reading the note, I shook my head. I was sure bin Haddad had said the extortionists wanted a hundred million, but that wasn't in the message. All it said was *Give us what we want, or Devil Wind will be next.* Had he received another message? One he didn't mention to us? That was strange. Maybe I missed it while I was sulking. I'd have to ask Marina about it when she returned.

In the meantime, I'd get dressed, walk up Madison Avenue and try to find just the right present for the happy couple. I was running out of time. Sunday would be here before I knew it.

Chapter Eight

Dad's bank, Hamilton Capital Group, was tucked away on Seventy-Eighth Street between Madison and Fifth Avenues, just a few blocks from the hotel. There were no ATMs or pictures of smiling tellers in the window advertising the latest interest rates or low-cost mortgages. It wasn't that kind of a bank.

If you didn't know it was there, you might miss the restored colonial building of terracotta-colored bricks with white columns in front of a white wooden door. A small plaque in the middle announced the name of the firm with Private Client Finances engraved underneath. Discreet hardly covered it. Nestled between a high-end fashion designer's retail shop and a very tony jewelry store, it was often mistaken for one of the upscale retailers in the brownstones dotting the street.

Hamilton Capital had been in business since the early eighteen hundreds and had offices around the world, including Dubai. I assumed that was how Dad came to know Adnan bin Haddad. I was sure a client of this magnitude received lots of handholding, and no one was better at it than Dad.

He was ready to leave as soon as I arrived, and we hoofed it around the corner to a small French bistro that was his go-to casual lunch choice. Done up in the bright blues and yellows of Provence, it had a hammered brass bar dominating the front of the restaurant. The small tables opposite were already filled with customers chatting away, mostly the ladies-who-lunch crowd with shopping bags from the pricey boutiques up and down Madison Avenue.

As soon as we were through the door, the hostess greeted Dad by name and whisked us away to a table for two in the back dining room. I'm sure she would have done the same if Dad had arrived with a group of twenty. He slipped a folded bill into her hand and thanked her. He knew how to treat people and always tipped well.

I felt the atmosphere change as soon as we stepped through the archway into the smaller dining area. This is where the big boys ate. Conversations were more subdued, and the ambiance much quieter. I could only imagine the multi-million-dollar deals being made over paté and cornichons.

A few minutes later, two glasses of Bordeaux arrived at the table and were deposited by a beaming waiter with a *"Pour Monsieurs."* I'm sure I'd gotten it right: Dad knew how to grease everyone's palm. We both ordered the steak frites rare and then got down to bin Haddad.

"What can you tell me about Adnan?"

Dad swirled the wine around in his glass before replying. "He's been with us for at least twenty years, now. The firm considers him a highest-priority client."

"What does that mean?"

Dad smiled. "It means, if he says jump, we all ask how high?" He took a sip of wine and murmured, obviously enjoying it.

I laughed at his answer. I could never see Dad jumping for anyone. Well, maybe Mom.

"You know I can't discuss the details of his finances." His tone had grown serious. "Suffice it to say, he's very, very wealthy with investments all over the world. I've found him to be straightforward in all our dealings. He's never asked us to cut corners or do anything that could be considered shady. Not like some billionaires you hear about."

Billionaire, right? At least Marina shouldn't have a problem getting paid.

"I know you can't give me any financial details," I replied.

It would be a breach of ethics to tell me the specifics of bin Haddad's business with Hamilton, at least to my father, who was as straight an arrow as there was. It made me think about Alex, who'd followed Dad into the banking business and had the same sense of integrity. A virtue that had nearly gotten us killed in Switzerland. Thank God I was a gambler. No one expected me to be that upright.

"I was as surprised as you were when bin Haddad showed up at the club." Dad gave me a look that said he'd been thinking about it. "Of course, he's a member, but he rarely stops in. Now, I understand that he was there to meet you. But I still can't figure out why."

I noted the puzzled expression on his face. *Gee, thanks for the vote of confidence,* I almost blurted out but sucked it up before I replied.

"He was there because he wanted to meet Marina."

I hadn't had time to fill him in our late-night conversation with bin Haddad. As I explained what he wanted, Dad's usually happy countenance turned into a frown then back into a smile as our lunch was delivered to our table. The juicy steak and pile of frites the waiter presented smelled great.

I thought of my snug tux and Marina's admonition as my meal was placed in front of me. Thankfully, it was just a momentary blip. I tucked into that steak like a man who's been on a desert island for years with only fish and fruit to eat.

After a few bites, a few frites, and a sip of wine, Dad got back to our conversation.

"I have to admit, it seems a little strange for him to seek out Marina." Dad lifted his hand in a what-if gesture. "It's odd he didn't pursue a recommendation from his security staff."

"Maybe he doesn't trust them," I ventured. "Or has some other reason for going outside his own network."

Dad gave that some thought. "Possibly. But why choose a small, fledgling firm like hers? Nothing against Marina, you understand."

Marina's firm might be fledgling, but her experience was eagle quality. The agency was set up to deal with high-end art and high-level fraud, which she'd mastered as an undercover operative for MI6. I hadn't told Dad about her ties to the British spy agency and her undercover work. To him, she was a smart, entrepreneurial woman who had a small, up-and-coming detective agency that handled cases that weren't very dangerous. What he—and my mother—didn't know would prevent them from worrying about Marina and me. Although, somehow Adnan bin Haddad must have gotten hold of her real history.

Dad finished off his wine and no sooner put the glass on the table, then a waiter appeared to ask if he'd like another. He refused and got that intense look he sometimes had when he was about to speak to Alex or me about something extremely serious.

Uh-oh, here it comes. "Should I be worried about this?" The steak I'd just devoured threatened to come back up.

Dad shook his head. "Not worried, but careful. It's not Adnan that I'd be concerned about. It's more the people who seem to be threatening to maim his horses." He leaned over the table and spoke in a whispery voice that made me nervous. "They're an unknown quantity." He let out a soft sigh and moved back just enough to pin me with his eyes. "Going after a man like bin Haddad isn't like some petty thief breaking into a grocery store. It takes skill and planning, the kind that requires high-level thinking and a well-placed organization to execute the plan. Who knows what they really want? It could be the hundred million—or something else." Dad's voice had gone lower still at the last. Finally, his eyes softened, and he sat back in his chair.

My mouth went dry as I listened. The words on the note flew into my brain: *Give us what we want, or Devil Wind will be next.* Maybe I should be worried.

Dad didn't notice the edginess that crept over me and kept on speaking. "From what you've told me, Marina is very resourceful. I'm sure she'll know if something is dodgy about the investigation and stay safely away."

Yeah, right. Marina wouldn't stay away. Telling her to be careful was like waving a red cape in front of a bull. She'd move in like a matador, tempting the bad guys to come closer and closer before she struck. And, somehow, I knew I'd be her picador, and she'd take me galloping along for the ride.

Chapter Nine

Dad's words were ricocheting around in my head as I walked west on Seventy-Eighth Street, up one block on Fifth Avenue and into Central Park. I chose a bench near the entrance and sat down to think with the high-pitched laughs and squeals of children in the playground behind me as background. His *Who knows what they really want?*' had awakened the memories of Monte Carlo I'd been trying to forget. I was foolish to think I'd beaten Herr Emminger when I won the ten million at Baccarat. Tommy B's face flashed before me with his self-assured smile and underhanded threats. Fortunately, there was an organization behind the win, people pulling strings without my knowledge, thanks to the surreptitious planning by my friend Nigel Phillips and his position at MI6.

I shook myself out of my reverie and texted Marina, who replied she'd be back at the Carlyle at about three. It was a lot of time for her to spend with bin Haddad. I hoped he was only filling her in on his problem and not plying her with his billionaire status. I trusted Marina. She loved me, and the feeling was mutual. She'd managed to save my life and hers. Almost being murdered makes for a close bond. Still, bin Haddad could have anything he wanted. I just hoped it was only Marina's investigative services and not the woman herself.

I rose from my bench and watched the kids in the playground running around and laughing like only carefree children can. Mom had brought Alex and me to the park often when we were kids. We both especially loved the children's zoo, which had changed quite a bit since then. Like many New Yorkers, I felt a bit over-protective of this green space in the middle of the city and was glad I'd stopped in, even if it was just to brood.

I gave the playground one last look, walked onto Fifth Avenue, and headed across Seventy-Ninth Street to Madison. I had about an hour to kill before I met Marina. Enough time to worry about Dad's words and Marina's situation.

I arrived at the Carlyle a few minutes after three, ready to grill her about her meeting with Adnan. She was at the desk in the suite's living room when I walked in, speaking on the phone.

She waved and continued her conversation. "That's right, Sabrina.Uh-huh, at seven? Perfect. We'll be ready. Thanks, you too." She clicked off her cell.

"Ready for what?"

"That was Adnan's executive assistant, Sabrina Ferrer. He's sending his jet to fly us to Kentucky. His driver will pick us up at seven on Monday morning. It will make things much easier, don't you think?"

"I think," I said as I bent down to her for a kiss, "that you could get used to all this private jet and executive assistant stuff."

Marina chose to ignore my dig. "How was lunch with your dad?"

"Fine. How was your five-hour meeting with Adnan?" I knew I sounded like a petulant child or a jealous lover and looked at my watch to prove it. "And why are we going to Kentucky on Monday?" I knew the answer, but I was just being a twit.

"The meeting was…interesting." Marina packed a lot of wiggle room into that one word.

"Interesting, good, or bad?" I couldn't decide which from her expression.

She tilted her head, thinking about it, then laughed. "Honestly, I'm not quite sure. Adnan went into detail about what's been happening to his stable of horses. The blinding of Devil Spirit seems to be the tip of the iceberg. He has letters threatening more of the same—"

"—unless he pays up," I finished. "I wanted to ask you if you found out how he heard about your firm."

Marina nodded. "He mentioned Nigel passed along my name. Don't worry, I texted Nigel and confirmed he recommended me." She smiled. "So, we have a new client, and we are going to Kentucky to watch over Adnan's colt, Devil Wind, while he trains for the Derby. And to see if anyone tries to blind or otherwise hurt him."

"You think Adnan's on the up and up?" I'd gotten caught up in our exchange. My dad's thoughts about the people crafty enough to have it in for him were coming through loud and clear. That, plus the fact that he could have chosen any one of the big investigative firms. Was she being set up for a fall?

Marina's expression grew thoughtful. Her eyes focused inward at my question. "What makes you think he's not?"

I sighed as I thought about how to explain what I was feeling. "Well, the note for one thing. It didn't say anything about a hundred million."

She nodded. "Yeah, I noticed that, and we discussed it. He said he received a text after the note and photo were sent." My expression must have telegraphed that I still had doubts. "Tell me," she added. "What else is bothering you?"

"He's a billionaire."

Marina shrugged. "Nick, I know that."

"You don't get to be a billionaire without making some enemies. Enemies as rich as he is probably have the means and methods to fight him on his own turf, so to speak. Dangerous people. I wouldn't want you to be between them and Adnan if, and when, they make themselves known."

Marina rose from the desk and took my face into her hands, staring into my eyes. "You're really worried about this, aren't you?"

An image of Tommy B grinning at me filled my mind as yet another shudder immobilized me.

She let go and took a step back, assessing my demeanor. "Do you want me to rethink this?"

I knew this could be an important case for her, something to put her small firm on an even playing field with the big guys. If I told her to bow out of the case and explained my reasons why she should do just that, she probably would. And also, then probably resent me for it somewhere along the line. I didn't like anyone telling me what to do, and Marina wouldn't either.

I shook my head. "No. Don't do that. It'll be fine." I tipped her face up until her eyes met mine again. "You know me, I'm just a worrier."

I hoped my smile masked the feeling in my gut that the stakes were higher than we thought and that, just maybe, we might have a losing hand.

Chapter Ten

All thoughts of Adnan bin Haddad and maimed horses were eliminated from my memory bank as we prepared for the rehearsal dinner for Simone and Alex's wedding.

Mother had hired a wedding planner. The young woman, Mary Kay Donnelly, came highly recommended. She was capable, knowledgeable, and knew how to get things done promptly, in a timely manner, and on budget.

But was that good enough for Mother? Not really. When Marina and I arrived at the apartment, Mom and Mary Kay were seated catty-corner from each other at the dining room table, going over the seating plan for tonight's dinner for at least the tenth time. Mary Kay's eyes had a certain glazed look that I recognized only too well. I'd had it often myself when trying to reason with this particular parent. I'm sure I didn't make it any better as I peered over their shoulders and shook my head.

"What?" Mom barked at me, her voice tight and controlled.

"Oh, I'm just surprised you'd seat her next to him." I pointed to two random names on the seating plan. "I heard they were having an affair," I added for good measure.

Mary Kay's eyes jumped from the seating plan to mine. I winked in time to relieve the panic I saw there. It took Mom a few beats longer to get that. I was only kidding.

"Nick—" she started.

I cut her off before she finished, bent down, and kissed the top of her head. "I know. Go to my room."

Marina took me by the arm and led me away. "Let's leave your mom and

Mary Kay alone and see if Simone and Alex need anything."

I got the message and went with her in search of the happy couple. They were on the balcony that ran the length of the living room, sitting, sipping wine, and talking quietly.

"I see Mom's commandeered the wedding." I nodded toward the apartment by way of saying hello.

"Your mother has been incredibly helpful and generous," Simone replied. "We couldn't have done this without her."

Alex threw me a look we shared often. Some might call it helpful, but we both called it something else. Controlling comes to mind.

"Stop teasing, Nick." Marina smiled sweetly, but her voice held a warning tone that I'd come to recognize.

"Got it." I put my hands up in mock surrender. "But seriously, do you two need help with anything before dinner tonight?"

"Can't think of a thing," Alex replied. "Sit down and have some wine."

"Sounds like a plan…" I trailed over my shoulder as I went inside in search of two more wine glasses, carefully avoiding the dining room. Marina might spank me if I butted in again.

The rest of the afternoon passed in a peaceful glow, the wine warming my insides and the view of the city in my mind. I never realized how much I missed New York until I came back for a while. The energy was a force all its own, as though it pulsed upward from the very depths of the streets, scaling the buildings, and bursting into the atmosphere around you. It took hold and made you complicit in wanting to do more and be more. I was in its thrall right now, looking out over the balcony and watching as day turned into evening.

Marina's gentle kiss on my forehead brought me out of my reverie. "Time to go back to the hotel and get ready for dinner."

I sighed and gave the city in front of me one last longing look. "Ready." I put down my wine glass, and we said our goodbyes. It wasn't like me to be this nostalgic. It must be something in the air. I certainly couldn't be homesick.

Chapter Eleven

Il Colosseo had moved from its old address on Fifty-Fifth Street to a new space at the bottom of the prestigious Bloomberg Building on East Fifty-Eighth. One of New York's premier restaurants, it had a classic charm and amazingly good food all watched over by the man who created it, Marco Ventituri. A combination that was just as successful today as it was since the restaurant first opened in the late seventies.

Dad was standing just past the vestibule with Marco, who was also a client at the bank. Both turned to greet us as we entered.

"Marina." Dad took her hand in his. "You look lovely. Let me introduce you to my good friend, Marco. He owns the place," he added with a wink.

Marco poured on the Italian charm he was known for as he took Marina's hand in his and kissed it. "*Signorina, benvenuto.* Welcome to my restaurant." He smiled and, finally noticing I was there as well, nodded at me. This was getting to be a habit I didn't much like.

When he finally got around to releasing Marina's hand, he took the one I was holding out and shook it. "Nick, you look well. It's been a long time. It's good to see you. Please, go inside. Everything is ready for the dinner."

At his words, a young woman appeared at his side, nodded, and led us to the dining room with its modern take on the Roman Coliseum to one of several large round tables in a private area set off by faux columns and greenery that separated us from the rest of the Friday night crowd.

Some of the guests were already seated, drinking Champagne, and chatting amongst themselves. I introduced Marina around; then we took our seats next to Alex, Simone, and Mom, who'd visibly relaxed since this afternoon.

"You did a great job," I whispered in her ear and gave her a peck on the cheek.

Dinner couldn't have been better. From the royal Ossetra caviar to the Bisteca Fiorentina with shredded Pecorino Pienza cheese and arugula to the homemade Napoleon cake created by the restaurant's pastry chef, it was one of the best meals I've ever eaten. And I wasn't alone in my assessment. Multiple oohs and aahs accompanied each course as it was presented.

It wasn't until toast time that everything started turning sideways. I cleared my throat and prepared to rise. I'd practiced my speech on Marina and she patted my arm in encouragement.

"Hello, everyone," I began, lifting my glass of wine toward our guests and starting to make eye contact with each one as I spoke. "Tomorrow, Alex and Si—"

That was as far as I got. Just then, the one person in all of New York I never wanted to see again turned around in his seat a few tables behind the columns and grinned at me. It was Tommy B.

He nodded and lifted a glass in my direction. I stood there with my mouth open until our guests started to fidget. Finally, Marina poked me, and I continued, all the while trying not to look at Tommy B and give him the satisfaction he'd rattled me.

The toasts continued for a while, with Dad, Mom, and Alex offering heartfelt speeches. I stared at them all with rapt attention, although I barely heard any of what they said, so hard was I concentrating on not glancing over at my former nemesis.

It didn't matter. I knew he knew he'd gotten to me and was probably enjoying my discomfort. I was right.

Just before Alex finished his toast to Simone, a waiter appeared at my side with several bottles of the restaurant's most expensive Champagne. "With the compliments of the gentleman at table six." He handed me a note.

> *Nick,*
> *Didn't know you were in town. We should meet.*
> *Tommy*

Meet? As in a sit down with the Capo to discuss the weather? Or for another ride in the country? By the time these thoughts crossed my mind, he was gone. I swallowed my panic and slipped the note into my pocket.

As the waiters were popping corks, Dad leaned toward me. "I didn't know you still had any friends in the city. Especially, such generous ones." He accepted a flute of the bubbly wine and raised his glass to mine.

For a moment, I thought that Tommy had somehow planned this and enlisted Marco's help. That seemed crazy. Marco was a restaurateur, not a mobster. He wouldn't turn anyone away, not even Tommy B. Was I being paranoid? He probably came here all the time. Like mob boss Paul Castellano at Ruth Christ's, a good customer until he was gunned down by John Gotti outside the restaurant's front door. *Jeez, knock it off*, I told myself at this particular memory from many years ago. I looked around for any suspicious characters but saw people like us, affluent New Yorkers, out for a good dinner.

Tommy had sat with his back to us all evening, and Dad had not realized it was he who sent us the Champagne. Even Dad would have recognized the infamous face of the mobster who'd been on the front pages of every newspaper in the city numerous times, including the *Wall Street Journal*. I nodded and made a non-committal "umm."

Marina lifted her eyebrows in a questioning look. "Later," I mouthed softly. She hadn't noticed the mobster either. If she had, dinner would have had an entirely different ending.

Soon after, everyone was ready to call it a night. Alex and Simone thanked my parents for the lovely party and their guests for coming. They walked out with Mom and Dad and Marina and me.

As we were leaving, Mom tilted her head in my direction. "Nick, you look so pale. Is everything all right?"

Instead of the smart mouth quip she probably expected in reply, I hugged her. "I'm just a little tired."

Surprise flicked across her face, then morphed into a smile. "Okay. See you tomorrow. And you and your brother better not be late," she added for good measure.

I might have been off my game, but Mom was square on hers.

35

Chapter Twelve

I t was a perfect day for a wedding. Sunny, warm, and as clear as New York ever got. Marina and I rose early. We were expecting Alex to arrive at any minute. Mom insisted he not see Simone on the "big day." She said she'd made up the pullout couch in the den and told him he had to leave the apartment before Simone awoke. Alex tried to talk her into changing her mind, but she wasn't having any of it.

"It's bad luck for the groom to be with the bride the day of the wedding. You can dress at the hotel with your brother, and Marina can dress here with us." She crossed her arms in front of her midsection for emphasis and put a warning in her voice I knew well.

Is that your final answer, I wanted to say, just like Regis on the old *Who Wants To Be A Millionaire?* But I held my tongue. I promised Marina I'd be nice, and the truth was I didn't want anything to spoil the day.

Alex arrived, and Marina blew us kisses as she left for my parent's apartment shortly after, carrying a garment bag with her maid of honor dress inside. She hadn't shown me her wedding garb either. I wondered if there was some hidden message in that but was afraid to dwell on it for too long.

"Behave, you two," she admonished as she gave both of us a stern look and closed the door behind her.

Alex and I ordered room service for breakfast, which we ate at the table under the window while reading the *New York Times*. The muted sounds of early Saturday morning traffic served as background to our meal. I helped myself to coffee, a muffin, and a croissant. Well, Marina wasn't here to chide me, was she?

Alex hadn't uttered a word in the last ten minutes and had been staring at the same page of the paper for quite a while. He didn't look as happy as I thought he would. It seemed more like he was eating a last meal before going off to be executed, rather than getting married.

"Not having second thoughts, are you? My words broke the silence.

"Not about Simone. I love her. It's just being married, which makes it all seem so final."

Yeah, look at Mom and Dad, I wanted to say. Poor guy's serving a life sentence. For the second time in as many days, I thought before I spoke and held my prison metaphor in check. I knew my parents loved each other and always had.

"It's not the end, Alex, it's the beginning. Simone's an amazing and brave woman. It's obvious how much she loves you. Getting married is just the start of the great times and good experiences you'll have together." Truthfully, their last experience hadn't been all that wonderful. Especially the part that included fleeing Switzerland five minutes ahead of the Swiss police with nothing but the clothes on their backs. If sticking together after that isn't true love, I don't know what is. "You've just got the bridegroom jitters," I added like I knew what I was talking about. Years of having a poker face came in handy every once in a while.

My words seemed to have reached him, and Alex gave me a nod and a sheepish grin. "I know. You're right."

Satisfied I'd done my job as both brother and best man, I reached into the pastry basket for another croissant. Alex slapped my hand away.

"I promised Marina," he said as he filched my intended pastry from the basket and placed it on his own plate.

Saint Patrick's Cathedral on Fifth Avenue was the center of the Catholic Church in New York City. The last time I was in the city, the nearly 150-year-old church was undergoing a massive renovation. It was finally finished, and the cathedral looked brighter and more majestic both inside and out.

Alex and Simone were to be married in The Lady Chapel on the east end of the cathedral behind the main altar. A beautiful space with stained glass windows, it was smaller than the main altar and equally as popular for weddings, with a waiting list that stretched to a few years.

Since Alex and Simone had only been in Manhattan a short time, it took a little finessing to get them to the head of the list. Fortunately, Dad was well acquainted with the cardinal, and somehow things worked out. I began to wonder if there was any big wig in the city he didn't know. Several of those I recognized were among the fifty or so guests seated in the chapel's pews.

At the stroke of three, Alex and I took our places on the right side of the altar. He asked me if I had the rings. For the tenth time, I told him yes. As he was about to ask me again, the organist began playing the wedding march, and all eyes turned to the doorway at the back, waiting for Simone to appear.

First down the aisle was Marina. Her bottle-green dress matched her eyes perfectly. She seemed to float down the center of the chapel rather than walk, and it was hard to take my eyes off her. But avert them, I did as Simone, flanked by my mother and my father, walked through the door. If Alex had any doubts that she loved him, all he had to do was glance at her beaming face. She looked delirious with happiness and as beautiful as a bride ever was in my mom's wedding dress.

I shifted my glance toward Alex and was glad to see that he was beaming, as well. They'd kept the dress a surprise from the men. And it had worked. Nothing could have been more fitting than to see Simone, who was now her daughter, in Mom's dress. I thought back to my parents' wedding photo displayed on their dresser. They may have grown older since the photo was taken, but despite the years, they were still in love. Even I, Mr. Fault Finder, could see that. Maybe I'd given Alex the right advice after all.

As the trio reached the altar, the music ceased. Mom and Dad each kissed Simone, and Dad gave her hand to Alex. Then he and Mom took their seats. Marina and I grinned at each other from opposite sides of the couple as Father Gavin began the ceremony.

Fifteen minutes later, the organist began playing again as the happy couple, now husband and wife, walked back down the aisle, followed by Marina, my parents, and myself. We formed a receiving line near the Fifty-First

Street side entrance to the cathedral and accepted the good wishes of the guests who would reconvene shortly at The Corner Lounge on the lower east side—Alex's old pre-banker, pre-Switzerland hangout—for cocktails and a buffet.

I could only imagine how Mom and Dad's crowd would feel about heading down to Tenth Street. Strangely enough, Mom had thought it was a great spot with delicious food. I bet she had a few cocktails when she and Simone went to check it out. I, on the other hand, was selfishly hoping the party would be at the Carlyle, where Marina and I could wobble to the elevator and our room if we imbibed too much.

I turned to see how many more people were still waiting to offer their congratulations, and the smile I'd been sporting slipped from my face. I caught a glimpse of someone who looked exactly like Tommy B at the edge of the throng. Was it him? If so, what was he doing here in a church? Maybe hell had frozen over.

All the good cheer I'd been feeling drained out of me. Seeing Tommy B once could be chalked up as a coincidence; twice was a disaster. When I looked again, he was gone.

I pulled myself together before Marina noticed the change in my demeanor. She didn't need to know the mobster had crossed our path again. If she caught sight of him, she'd probably jump him and beat him senseless like I'm sure she wanted to do when he held her captive. That would certainly give the wedding guests something to talk about, not to mention ruining her beautiful dress. I was delighted we were leaving for Kentucky on Monday. The contented feeling I had about being home in New York with my friends and relatives was gone. In its place was a knot in my stomach that was getting tighter and tighter. It was time to cash in my chips and hit the road.

Chapter Thirteen

The Corner Lounge was jumping. The wedding guests were enjoying themselves and the special Swiss Miss cocktail the bartender had created in honor of the happy couple. Alex had hired a band he knew, and people were up and dancing. Except for me.

Marina had tried to coax me onto the floor, but I kept refusing. She finally gave up, calling me an old grouch, and joined a group who were gyrating to the band's cover of a Stones song.

While they danced, I watched the door. Every time it opened, I expected to see Tommy B walk in. I know, I know, it was stupid. I felt like a beginner blackjack player, sitting down for the first time and betting a few hundred on my first hand and hoping to win a thousand. It probably wasn't going to happen, and wishing wouldn't make it so. Not that I wished to see Mr. Bonnannaio again. It was exactly the opposite. I was terrified that I would.

Marina interrupted my melancholy musings with a big kiss and a call for more Champagne as she slid onto the banquette beside me, taking a break from dancing.

"Alex picked a great band," she said, fanning her flushed face, which looked more beautiful than ever to me. "I need to rest for a few minutes; then you are getting off your cute booty and onto that dance floor." She dipped her chin to the crowded spot she just left.

"Yes, ma'am, sir." I was smart enough to know when I was defeated. "Maybe they'll play something slow so I can hold you tight." My attempt at levity sounded false even to me.

"What's wrong, Nick? You've been sulking ever since we left the church."

Her big green eyes were filled with concern.

"Nada," I shook my head. "Honestly," I added in my most sincere voice.

"Good. In that case, let's go." She got up and pulled me onto the dance floor.

"They're playing 'Uptown Funk.' I love it."

I had no idea what she was talking about, but I followed her lead like I always do.

You can see where that got me.

The after-party was at a giant warehouse space on the west side. A crumbling facade with an industrial-sized elevator loaded with partygoers that creaked as it moved slowly to the basement. It looked like the kind of place that should have a sliding peephole and a secret password to enter. Inside, dim light bulbs hung from the ceiling, keeping the club in semi-darkness. I smiled to myself. The owners probably had the same idea as the people who ran casinos: always keep it dark with no windows to let patrons see if it was night or day and keep it noisy so it sounds like everyone is having a great time. You can tell I've been in too many casinos.

Alex had invited Marina and me. It was not our usual post-wedding venue, not that we'd been to any other weddings together, but I could hardly plead fatigue at ten p.m. The huge dance floor was packed, and so was the bar. Alex slipped the hostess a folded bill and scored a "reserved" table in the back of the club, away from the band. Reserved for those with deep pockets. It seemed he'd picked up several pointers on New York etiquette from Dad since returning home.

The party lasted until four a.m. By then, we were starving. Dancing the night away can do that to you. And Marina made sure I was on my feet for nearly every dance. Most of Alex and Simone's friends had bailed, leaving the four of us to soldier on. I remembered a twenty-four-hour diner on Canal Street and Greenwich Avenue that served the after-hours club kids. They were famous for their pancakes and omelets. Alex and Simone joined us, and we made quite a sight marching along the streets in our wedding clothes, winding between late-night hipsters and tattooed Goth girls.

This time, I slipped the hostess a folded bill, and she escorted us to a booth in the back, away from the not-quite-sober crowd up front.

The happy couple still looked like they could go for a few more hours, while Marina and I looked like we could fall asleep where we sat.

We ordered coffee all around and the breakfast special with an extra side of bacon. I told Marina I earned it with all the calories I burned off dancing.

While we waited for the food to arrive, we rehashed the wedding dinner. Alex, Simone, and Marina were laughing about Mom's old friend, Belinda, who flirted shamelessly with the bartender at The Corner Lounge, a very handsome guy who politely pretended to ignore her advances. Then there was Dad's banking buddy, who followed Marina like a shark homing in on the scent of blood.

"Every time I turned around, he was there. I was running out of excuses to get away from 'Hi, my name is Don, and who might you be?'" She mimicked the deep voice of her admirer and his lascivious tone and turned to me. "And you weren't any help. Didn't even try to rescue me."

"I knew you could take him if it came down to it," I said around a mouthful of pancakes. I had other things on my mind at the time.

"Hey," Alex said, looking out the window at the street, now coming to life, "isn't this the street where that after-hours gambling club was, the one with the dealer you dated?"

I shook my head slightly, trying to warn him off. It was too late. Marina, who was speaking with Simone, had caught what Alex said.

Her head swiveled in my direction, and her eyebrows rose in a question.

"That was a long time ago." I swiped my hand down in a negative gesture. "Before I moved to England." It was obvious Alex still had a lot to learn about being part of a couple.

I did remember the club and the dealer, a pretty brunette who was only too happy to take my money at the table and a little something extra on the side. It had been a pretty low-key kind of place, unusual for an after-hours establishment, but, as I recalled, the mob owned it and ran it, and they didn't take any crap from anyone, which I knew all too well. Somehow, the mob had lodged itself into my brain, and I couldn't shake it off.

I signaled the waitress for our check. It was time to go home.

43

Chapter Fourteen

Sunday was a day of leisure. Marina and I were exhausted and even getting up seemed like too much of an effort. When we were finally ready to start the day, it was already half over.

We dressed and went down to a coffee shop nearby for lunch, then headed over to my folk's apartment to say goodbye to Simone and Alex. Dad had a car coming to take them to the airport, and they were as excited about their honeymoon as two puppies playing in a pet shop window, laughing, touching, and whispering with wild abandon. For as much as they noticed us, we could have stayed in bed much longer and had a much more interesting time.

When they took off, we did, too. Mom planted a kiss on my forehead. "Alex, you were a great best man."

I looked into her eyes and could see how proud she was of me. Dad just stood behind her, nodding in agreement.

"Goodbye, you two." Marina reached out and hugged them one after the other. "It was so nice to meet you and be here with your family for this amazing wedding. You have to come to London, to us, next time," Now it was my turn to nod my head. What a girl. She knew just what to say.

"When you're done in Kentucky, come back for a few more days." Dad knew why we were going to Louisville and was a little anxious about Marina working for bin Haddad. "You'll have to fill me in." He raised an eyebrow as he patted my shoulder. A man-to-man gesture meant to let me know he'd be available if we needed him.

Once we were outside, I shook off my tiredness. Since we were leaving for

Louisville early tomorrow morning and Marina hadn't been in New York for a while, I decided to show her some of its newer sites.

We headed downtown to the meat-packing district on Manhattan's west side. Many of the city's hot chefs had set up outposts around Little West Twelfth Street. Galleries and trendy hotels sprouted amongst new high-rise construction, including the building housing the relocated Whitney Museum. High-end designer flagship stores butted up against each other, offering luxury goods they couldn't keep on their shelves. The neighborhood was hotter than a craps player on a Vegas winnings streak. I was surprised by how much the area had evolved since my last visit. All these new businesses had reinvigorated this once-derelict district, and New York's newest park rose above them all, The Highline.

I steered Marina up a metal staircase and explained that the park had been a working railroad used to deliver meat from the midlands to the wholesale butchers below Fourteenth Street.

"This is beautiful, she said, "a gorgeous spot in the middle of the city."

"You should have seen it before." I remembered passing by when I was a kid. "It was an abandoned eyesore for many years until a group of enlightened New Yorkers had the vision to turn it into a park filled with greenery and great vistas of the Hudson River."

Several stories above street level, it ran from Twelfth Street to Thirty-Fourth and offered a birds-eye view of all the old buildings around it being renovated for new high-rise condos and rentals.

"This is the newest addition." I pointed to the new, monumental Hudson Yards complex. "It's got something for everyone—apartments, hotels, restaurants, high-end shops, even galleries. You can even hang out on the Edge, a suspended sky deck 100 stories up. I heard it makes you feel like you're floating in the sky."

"Should we give it a try?" she asked teasingly.

"Not today," I replied and steered her along, neglecting to mention my fear of heights in open spaces.

Marina stopped in front of an artist's rendering for one of the new high-rise apartments. "That looks nice." She nodded toward a sketch of a spacious full-floor apartment with river views.

"Don't get any ideas," I replied, noticing the three-point-six million starting price for a one-bedroom in the small type. "We can't afford it."

"Not yet, anyway." Marina grabbed my arm and laughed as we continued our walk. "But wouldn't you like to live in New York again?" she asked, her merriment turning serious. "It is your hometown, after all."

I shrugged and made light of her question. "Not many blackjack games going on around here, at least not the legal kind."

She gave me a look like she knew I was somehow avoiding her question. I couldn't tell her that my nostalgic feelings for home had been cut to the quick by my sighting of our favorite mob boss or that I'd neglected to mention his presence to her.

Talk about paranoia. While we were walking, I was looking over my shoulder every few minutes. I did it again, and for a second, I thought I saw one of Tommy B's bruisers in the crowd. When I glanced back a moment later, the guy was gone.

Hoping Marina hadn't noticed, I bent over and kissed her on the cheek. "You know how much I love London, especially since you're there with me."

She let it be as she took my hand. We continued our walk uptown, with me pointing out the sights along the way as we fed each other the gelato we purchased from one of the vendors. At Thirty-Fourth Street, we descended and took a cab to the hotel. We got back to the Carlyle just as dusk was settling over the city. Both of us were tired after our long walk. Marina thought we should stay in, relax, order room service, and enjoy dinner in bed.

That sounded pretty good to me.

As tired as I'd been all day, I couldn't sleep when we finally got into bed. We'd done all our packing and had a room service dinner, but I was still wired from the wedding celebration.

Tossing and turning, I punched the pillows, pulled at the covers, and stared at the ceiling, random thoughts running through my head. I tried to do all this quietly so as not to wake Marina, who was snoring softly on the other side of our huge king-size bed. I tried to figure out why I was so restless.

Everything had gone perfectly this week, including Dad's bachelor party and Mom's wedding planning. Marina was on a case that could take her small agency to the next level. And I was happy to have a vacation from blackjack. But something was eating at me. I just didn't know what, but I hoped to figure it out soon. Little did I know it would be sooner than I imagined.

Chapter Fifteen

We arose early and were waiting in the lobby when Adnan's car and driver arrived. He took our luggage in hand and escorted us to the Merc, where a different, well-dressed bruiser stood at attention. Once our luggage was stowed in the trunk and we were settled in the back seat with a carafe of coffee, the car headed east, then downtown to the Midtown Tunnel for the ride out of Manhattan to Kennedy Airport.

Marina read over some files she'd taken from Adnan on his personnel in the US, the people we would be looking into at Churchill Downs. I spent the time gazing out the window, taking a long look at the city and the huge changes it had undergone since my last visit home. For once, there was very little traffic on the Long Island Expressway and the Van Wyck, and we arrived at the airport in about forty-five minutes.

Since we were departing on a private jet, we didn't have to go through regular airport security. Instead, the car drove onto the tarmac and around to a small building. As we pulled up, a steward greeted us and took us through the metal detectors inside. He explained that the jet was late in departing from Louisville and would be arriving in about a half hour. Once through the private checkpoint, he asked us to follow him to the member's lounge, where we could make ourselves comfortable.

We settled in, and he reappeared with menus for breakfast. He was a handsome young man in yet another Armani suit, his dark blue eyes brightening with a special glow when he glanced Marina's way.

Marina rewarded his attention with a big smile. "Thank you." She looked up at him. "We'll have coffee first. Then give us a few minutes to decide."

The embossed menus he'd handed over would have made the finest restaurant in the city proud. "Certainly, miss. I'll be right back with your coffee."

"What a nice young man," Marina cooed.

Nice, my butt, it was the "miss" that got her.

A few minutes later, he returned with a silver tray and a steaming coffee carafe, his attention focused on Marina as he poured. I counted myself lucky I wasn't scalded when he poured the hot liquid into my cup.

"What else can I get for you?" He directed his question to Marina, who ordered the fruit plate. I was next and officially last on his list. "How can I help you, sir?"

I chose the scrambled eggs and bacon. Well done.

As soon as he moved away, Marina took one look at me and started laughing. Pretty soon, I joined in. It was kind of funny. We had to try hard to keep from breaking into gales of laughter when he returned with our breakfast.

"What does preparing food in the *sous-vide* method mean?" It was how my eggs were listed on the menu. I questioned Marina as I poked at them. They looked like any regular scrambled eggs you'd get from a diner.

"I think it has something to do with sealing the food in a plastic bag and steaming it at a certain temperature for a long time." She popped a strawberry into her mouth as she told me.

"Now that sounds really appetizing." I scrambled my eggs some more and picked up a piece of bacon. It was nice and crisp, probably not *sous-vided* to death.

After breakfast, Marina looked over some papers relating to bin Haddad's horses while I busied myself with my laptop googling Churchill Downs.

Chapter Sixteen

Louisville:

The approach to Louisville's Blue Grass Airport was exactly as the online photos portrayed it. Our plane glided over lush rolling hills dotted with mile after mile of white fences and herds of horses that looked like miniature toys from the air. Not surprising really, since the state was billed as the horse capital of the world.

The fasten-seat-belt sign came on and the jet nosed down gently and then taxied to a stop in front of a building set apart from the main terminal.

When Marina and I walked down the gangway, we were met by yet another of bin Haddad's drivers-slash-bodyguards and escorted to a waiting limousine. My dad's words came back to me. *'Why choose a small, fledgling firm like Marina's?'* Now, I wondered again, why bin Haddad had hired Marina with all the burly talent he had around him. Of course, valuing my life, I kept that idea to myself and tossed a smile her way instead.

"What?" she asked me, a suspicious look bringing her features together in a scowl.

"Nothing," I replied. "Just happy to be here with you."

"Hmm." Her eyebrows went up as she slid into the back of the car.

I followed her and settled in for the drive to bin Haddad's farm.

Twenty minutes later, the car coasted up the long and winding driveway of the Winged Valor Farm. In a few moments, we found ourselves in front of a huge, sparkling white ranch house with a wide front porch surrounded by bushes of red roses.

Adnan stepped through the massive front doorway and greeted us like long-lost pals with an effusiveness I didn't expect. "Marina. Nick." He pumped my hand. "It is so good to see you. Please, come inside and rest a bit after your journey."

Maybe it was a show for anyone who might be watching, like a casino greeter at the front of the house smiling at the thought of how much you'd be depositing in the vault.

The inside was as grand as the outside. If this was his farm, his home in Dubai must be a palace. The great room was enormous, with a fireplace anchoring one end and double doors that led to a patio at the other. Through it were lush fields and gardens as far as the eye could see.

The room held several contemporary couches flanked by antique end tables piled with books and photos. And the artwork on the walls was a who's who of Impressionist painters. Two Monets and a Degas. The real deal, not copies, I'd bet. I wondered if Adnan had watched reruns of the '80s TV show, *Dallas*, when he was younger and decided he'd like a ranch just like J.R. Ewing's South Fork, only grander.

He turned just as a young man came in through the patio doors. "Ah, Rashid, you are right on time." He nodded toward him and then explained to us, "Rashid is the head trainer here in Kentucky." He put his hand on Rashid's shoulder and continued. "I have told Rashid about everything that has happened, and you may count on him to assist you with anything you require."

Several inches taller than Adnan with coal-black hair and deep brown eyes, Rashid was larger and stockier than most Arab men. He dipped his head shyly to Marina and me as he shook each of our hands in turn. "I am totally at your disposal. When you are ready, I will take you to meet the beautiful Devil Wind." He looked up at us now, and his voice took on a prideful tone, almost as though the thoroughbred belonged to him.

Now it was my turn for an "Hmmm." A little too obsequious, I thought. Was he angling for the job of worldwide head trainer instead of just here in Kentucky? Maybe I was just being suspicious but, given the circumstances, it wasn't totally out of the question. I wasn't so sure Adnan should have been so open with him about the situation, at least until Marina had a chance to start the investigation. I'd have to ask her about her impression of Rashid later when we were alone. She also needed to find out if he was in Dubai when Devil Spirit was maimed. If Adnan had taken others on his staff into his confidence, it would make Marina's job much more difficult. Forewarned is forearmed, as they say.

I blocked out what the others were discussing while I considered the possibilities. When I tuned back in, I caught the end of the conversation as Adnan and Marina discussed the next steps.

"I hope you will be comfortable staying here at the farm." He raised his hand to encompass the room. "Josef—" He nodded toward another man who had entered quietly while he was speaking. "—will bring your suitcases to the guest wing."

Marina replied that we were delighted to be his guests. "I'd like to change clothes and then go meet Devil Wind," she added. "The reason we're all here."

Chapter Seventeen

"Guest wing?" I whispered in her ear as we followed Josef to our room. When he opened the door, I almost whistled. It wasn't exactly a room. It was more like a small house, with two bedrooms, two baths, a living room, kitchen, dining room, and a private enclosed patio. "We could move in here," I told Marina as I took in our well-appointed surroundings.

"And be waited on hand and foot?" she replied as she rolled a suitcase in my direction. "Please try to curb your fantasies and unpack your bag. Devil Wind awaits."

Ten minutes later, we were back in the great room, ready to head to the stables. We'd both changed into work shirts, jeans, and boots, which fit in with the rest of the staff at a working horse farm. I thought I looked pretty good as a cowpoke, even if there were no cows around.

Adnan was waiting for us and ushered us out the front door and onto a golf cart for the trip to Devil Wind's stable. I noticed a stable and paddock just off to the side of the house, one we could have easily walked to. "Isn't Devil Wind in there?" I asked, nodding my head in that direction.

Adnan shook his head. "No. He is in a stable by himself. I feel it is safer to keep him separate from my other horses."

He maneuvered the golf cart onto a narrow paved road that skirted the property and finally turned off at the entrance to a small stable set next to a private paddock. "This is where I usually keep the horses that are standing at stud. But Devil Wind is alone here at the moment."

The stable was a smaller version of the one we had passed on our way. Its paddock was off to the right, about fifty feet, with a training track behind that. Inside the enclosure, we could see a gleaming black horse tossing its mane and whinnying at a man in jeans and a Stetson. His posture was as casual as his clothes, both arms resting on the top rail of a white wooden fence. He was standing next to Rashid, who looked almost formal next to the cowboy.

"That is Devil Wind." You couldn't mistake the pride in Adnan's voice. "Shall we go and introduce him to you?" He gestured toward the paddock.

The colt must have caught our scent right away and pranced over to the rail. He cocked his head to the side as if assessing these humans who were approaching him. When Adnan moved closer and patted his forelock, which fell over a small white star, Devil Wind nudged him back in greeting. Adnan held out a carrot he'd stashed in his back pocket and fed it to the horse, who gobbled it up in two bites.

"Y'all know you're going to spoil him, don't you?" the man at the fence drawled and shook his head ruefully at the gesture.

"Perhaps you are right." Adnan smiled and patted Devil Wind again. "But he deserves it. Tim, I would like you to meet my friends from New York, Ms. DiPietro, and Mr. Donahue. They are here for the races and will be staying at the farm."

That answered my question about who else he might have told about hiring a private detective firm.

"It's Marina and Nick," she replied as she held out her hand to the trainer.

"Pleased to meet y'all. Welcome. I'm the stud master here." He tipped his hat and drew out the last words.

I'll just bet you are. I could see by his grin he expected a reaction. He probably got a lot of mileage out of that one.

"Tim is in charge of the breeding for the farm, Adnan noted by way of explanation. "Right now, looking after Devil Wind is his sole responsibility, as there are no brood mares on the premises." He gazed at the colt again. "And, of course, this is Devil Wind."

Marina stepped forward to pat him, and he did the same thing to her as he'd done to Adnan, nudging her hand affectionately. When I tried to touch him, he backed up a step and showed me his teeth. They were large, very large like a pit boss who showed his through a pasted-on pretend smile when you were winning. Rashid grinned at the horse's behavior. I took the hint and turned away, shaking my head. Even horses liked Marina better than me. A guy just couldn't win.

Marina asked Tim if he could show us around later that afternoon. He agreed—too readily, if you ask me. Rashid took over and invited her to watch Devil Wind's workout. As usual, I'd just be along for the ride.

The workouts were usually in the mornings, but Adnan had instructed Rashid to wait until we arrived. We said our goodbyes, and Adnan led us into the stable, where he introduced us to Devil Wind's groom, a very young man called Namal, and the assistant trainer, Rehan. Marina had made notes about these two from Adnan's files. They were both from the UAE and had been with his stable for a few years. There was also an exercise rider, Mike, who was off the farm now.

Adnan escorted us back to the main house, and we regrouped in his study, which was a surprisingly small space cluttered with racing forms, thoroughbred breeding books, and the paperwork involved with running a working horse farm. On the walls were photos of his horses, among them several from Devil Wind's lineage: Devil Volcano and Devil Star.

He settled in behind his desk and motioned to the seats in front of it. Leaning forward, he rested his elbows on its surface and placed his chin atop clasped hands. "As you can see, the only other person who knows what you are here for is Rashid. I trust him implicitly."

Marina held up a hand to stop him. "I'm not doubting how you feel, or his loyalty for that matter. But—" She paused. "—there is quite a bit at stake here, not just your horses, but extorting a hundred million dollars from you, as well."

For a moment, Adnan seemed disconcerted, his eyes blinking rapidly as a series of emotions played across his face. "Yes, of course. The money. You are right," he agreed, seemingly calm again. "Please understand, Rashid, is like a son to me. It is a long story, and it is best left for some other time, perhaps. However, he is the one those extortionists have contacted, the one who brought their ransom demand to me."

Marina started to speak, then thought better of it. Her body language was sending out warning signs. She held back whatever it was she was going to say.

Adnan didn't seem to notice and took up the thread of his conversation. "I have told the other people who work for me that Nick is a professional gambler here for the races and that the both of you will be staying at the farm as my guests. I intimated that you—" He nodded at Marina. "—were fond of riding and might like to go out on one of the stable mounts. I hope that was acceptable."

"That's fine, Adnan." Marina's voice had turned just a touch cooler. "I would enjoy a ride, and I will take you up on your offer. Now—" She looked at her watch. "—I think it's time for Nick and me to watch Devil Wind's practice.

Adnan excused himself from joining us, and we set off for Devil Wind's stable on foot, following the path we'd driven earlier.

"Okay, ante up," I told her once we were clear of the main house. "What were you going to say to Adnan before he sidetracked you with riding? And by the way, I didn't know you did," I added in a slightly wounded voice, "ride that is." We gamblers had lots of practice at sounding offended.

"You didn't know I rode because I never talk about it." She shook her head. "It's been years. I had a bad fall from a skittish horse and broke my collarbone. I rode some more after that but eventually lost interest." She stopped walking and turned to me. "How did *he* know I rode? It's so long ago; he must have had to dig deep to find out I ever did." Shrugging her shoulders, she got back to my question. "It was about the ransom. When I mentioned it, he seemed to have forgotten all about it. It ties back to what you remembered about the hundred million not being alluded to in the note."

As we walked along, it crossed my mind once again that Adnan knew entirely too much about us. Not to mention the resources he'd employed to vet us, it also begged the question of why he'd chosen Marina's firm.

Somehow, that thought just kept popping up.

Marina, shaking her head from side to side, brought me back to the present. "Hey, you'll figure out what's going on, and you don't have to get up on a horse if you don't want to do it." I put my hands on her arms and held her.

"I know that." A cunning look came into her eyes. "But it is a good way for me to check out Mike, the exercise rider."

I'd bet the farm that Mike would like that idea.

Chapter Eighteen

Mike was saddling Devil Wind when we arrived at the stable. Slim and short with a shock of sandy blond hair that dipped over his forehead like the forelocks of the horses he rode, Mike nodded shyly as Rashid made the introductions.

Rashid explained what was going to happen as Mike mounted Devil Wind. "He will let him jog for a bit, then do a two-minute lick." Rashid noticed Marina's puzzled expression at his words. He smiled. "By that, I mean Mike will take him into an open gallop, which takes about two minutes for a mile."

We watched as Mike steered the horse onto the dirt track, and we took our places along its fence. Rehan and Tim came out of the barn and joined us. Tim tipped his Stetson to Marina and nodded at me. As we waited, another horse and rider jogged up the path and entered the ring.

"That is Devil Dancer, or Rakkas, as we call him. He and his rider, Taleb, will race against Devil Wind just as they would in a regular horserace."

Tim smiled at me. "It's always good to have a little competition, isn't it?"

I wasn't sure if he meant that as a warning. But I let it go for now as the horses stood head- to-head, pawing the ground, anxious to gallop away.

Mike nodded to Rehan, saying that he was ready. As he tapped Devil Wind gently with his whip, Rehan clicked the stopwatch he was holding as the horse flew forward as though he'd been shot out of a cannon. Watching from this close was mesmerizing. A ton of agility, speed, and spirit thundered down the track. That Devil Wind had been born to run was evident in every stride he took, quickly creating a wide chasm between himself and Devil Dancer. After two minutes, Mike began to slow him down and finally brought him to a stop in front of us. Rehan clicked the stopwatch and nodded approvingly at Rashid as the rider dismounted and slid the reins over the thoroughbred's head. He started to walk him around the track.

The horse was whinnying softly in what sounded like a self-satisfied sigh. I looked at this horse with fresh eyes. He knew he was a champion. I don't know how, but it was true. His stance and his stare dared anyone to try and beat him. Kind of like a blackjack player on a hot streak breaking the bank. He was all in.

I say walk, but as we watched, it seemed more like the horse was prancing, turning his head in our direction to make sure we knew he'd had a winning performance.

Marina looked my way, her green eyes wide with excitement, her smile sunny. When she turned back toward Devil Wind, I could see her demeanor change by degrees. Her eyes became focused pinpricks, and her mouth closed in a firm line. No one was going to hurt this animal; she seemed to be saying, not on my watch.

We followed Rashid, Tim, and Rehan back to Devil Wind's stable. "Mike will cool him down for about half an hour," Rehan told us. "Then they will return here, and he will have a bath.

"What did y'all think of our boy?" Tim asked.

"He's amazing." Marina was smiling again but I wondered if the two men had noticed that look of determination on her face just a few minutes ago.

"Will Adnan race him at the Blue Grass before the Derby?" I asked. I'd bet on him to win. The men didn't seem surprised that I knew about the race. After all, they thought I was a racehorse aficionado. I'd noticed a poster on the way from the airport billing the race as part of the lead-up to the Derby.

"No, he won't be racing. He doesn't need to. Devil Wind has more than enough points to run in the Derby. We will let him rest instead," Rashid offered.

"This is one horse that doesn't like to rest." Tim smiled at the thought. "What would you do?" he asked. "Adnan mentioned that you follow the ponies."

Great. I felt like he was testing me. What I knew about racing could fit on the back of a postage stamp. What were the points Rashid mentioned? I had no idea what they were talking about. Had Adnan overplayed my cover story and was Tim calling me out on it?

So far, this case had more twists and turns than I bargained for. I was saved from answering by Marina.

"Mike, I understand that you and I are going riding this afternoon. That is if you're not exhausted by your ride on Devil Wind." Her voice had gone all feminine and flirty, and the young exercise rider was tripping all over his tongue to answer. Was she batting her eyelashes at him?

"Ohh. Ahh. Of course, ma'am." His words came out in a squeak. "I'll just go up to the main stables and saddle up a horse for you."

"Why don't I come with you and make sure you pick a nice, easy ride for me." She gave the words *easy ride* a new meaning. One that flustered the young man even more. Marina slid her arm through his, and I could see him blushing. "See you later, Nick, gentlemen." She waved over her shoulder as they walked away.

I smiled like an idiot, hoping no one would ask me anything else about horses or I'd sure as shit be in deep manure.

Chapter Nineteen

"Think I'll head back and do a little handicapping for tomorrow's races." I was trying to sound self-assured but was probably coming off like an ass as I tilted my head toward the main house.

"Let me know if you have any good tips." Tim smiled, barely masking the snarkiness in his voice. He, Rashid, and Rehan walked away laughing.

Yup. Ass, I thought.

I made my way through the main house, scooping up some racing magazines from the great room on my way to the guest quarters. I fully intended to bone up on which mounts had the best pedigree and the best trainers and all that points stuff, but the minute I sat down on the nice soft couch in the living room, magazines in hand, my eyes began to close, and I was out for the count.

Marina woke me up gently when she arrived back from her ride. Her hair was all tousled, and her cheeks flushed. I hoped it was from the ride and not her riding partner.

"Looks like you had a good time." I sat up and kissed her.

"Looks like you did a little reading." She gestured to the magazines that were strewn around me on the couch. "Learn anything new about horses?"

I shook my head. "Not a thing. I read for a while, then packed it in." I didn't want to admit to falling asleep in a New York minute. "How about you?" I pulled her down next to me, and she rested her head on my shoulder.

"Well…" She stared at the ceiling as she spoke. "My ride was very interesting. Or, I should say my riding partner was." She sat up, turned to face me, and rested her arm on the back of the couch. "Mike Burnett is twenty-two years old and worked as a stable hand at Blackburn Farms outside of Louisville before coming here. He got the job through Tim Eggers, who was dating Mike's sister Julie, but she broke up with him a few months ago."

"Did he tell you why?"

"It's not what you might think, given that he seems to enjoy referring to himself as the 'stud master.'" She made air quotes in front of me and continued. "At some point, Mike realized he might be telling me too much." She shrugged. "But I pushed a little, and eventually, it all came out." She sat up straighter and crossed her arms around her middle. "It seems Tim has a little bit of a gambling problem." A self-satisfied grin appeared on her face. "What do you make of that?"

"It depends. If he plays high-stakes poker or loses at the casino, it's certainly not good. But if he plays the ponies—" I lifted my hands skyward. "—it could be even worse."

"So, whatever his habit, it's bad?

"Right, if he owes anyone big money and they know he works with racehorses, they could be leaning on him—"

"—to fix a race." Marina completed my thought, and I nodded in agreement.

"Did Mike give you any more details?"

"No, but I could tell he was shaken up about his sister and Tim." Marina shook her head. "Do you think he knows about the threat to Devil Wind or what happened to Devil Spirit?" Her eyes clouded over. "If he does and puts it together with Tim's gambling—"

"—and calls him on it, he could be in danger." Now, I was the one finishing her thoughts. "That's if Tim is the guy we're looking for. Betting on races where his farm's horses are running might not be illegal, but I'm sure it's frowned upon. If Adnan found out, it could cost him his job and probably his career."

We both sat quietly for a few moments. I remembered something else my dad had said, *'Going after a man like bin Haddad isn't like some petty thief breaking into a grocery store. It takes skill and planning, the kind that requires high-level thinking and a well-placed organization to execute the plan.'* Somehow, I didn't think Tim had what it takes to play on that level. But you never know. Owing money to the wrong people can drive a man to do desperate things. I'm living proof of that.

Marina jumped up from the couch and grabbed her laptop from the low coffee table in front. "I'm emailing Ana and Nikki and asking them to do an in-depth background check on Tim Eggers. I'd rather have them do it from the office than use my sources here." She flipped open her computer. "As I understand it, the racing world is pretty tight, and I don't want anyone to spill the news that we're checking up on him."

"What about the files Adnan gave you? There was a stack piled on the table, as well.

She shook her head. "There's very little information on Mike or Tim other than their full names and addresses. I was going to speak to Adnan about that. It's almost as if he were excluding them on purpose or because he knows the threat is coming from somewhere else."

She bit her lower lip and started typing her message to her staff. I knew Ana and Nikki would get on it right away. And I had a pretty good idea what was nagging at Marina. Adnan might be playing his cards a little too close to the vest, and my girl wasn't going to take that sitting down.

Chapter Twenty

Dinner was a quiet affair. It was just the three of us and Josef who served the meal. Marina looked thoughtful, and Adnan seemed distracted. I tried to keep the conversation going with urbane banter and smart wit, but all I got in return was head nodding and several "uums" and "oohs." After a while, I stopped trying. I was wasting my talent on my dinner companions. I'd probably have better luck doing card tricks in the kitchen for Josef.

After we finished the main course of barbecued ribs with the trimmings—a first-time-in-Kentucky tradition, I was told—Adnan stood to excuse himself. Marina was having none of that. She stood as well and said she needed to speak with him. His face showed his reluctance, but he dipped his head, yes, and they headed off to his study.

I was relieved that they'd left. I retired to the guest wing—I still liked the sound of that—where I planned to immerse myself in the game of horse racing with the magazines and books I picked up earlier in the day.

Adnan had invited us to spend tomorrow at the races as guests in the Triple Crown Room at Churchill Downs. The plan was for Marina to nose around and sniff out the other owners, jockeys, grooms, and stable staff that would come into contact with Devil Wind during the Derby.

My job was to act like a seasoned horseman who knew his way around the track.

After half an hour with my training materials, I was no further along than when I started. I didn't have much time, and I wanted to at least figure out what a real handicapper would know. There was only one thing to do. I picked up my cell and punched in Melvin Cowl's number.

Mad Mel, as he was known in New York, never missed a day at the track if he could help it. He was probably studying tomorrow's sheets for Belmont right now and figuring the odds. Of course, he wasn't betting his own money—what bookie is dumb enough to do that? He was merely trying to protect his business interests by taking in more than he had to pay out.

"It's Mel. Speak." He answered before the first ring finished ringing. "I'm waitin'," he added before I could utter a single syllable.

"It's me, Nick.

"Well, well, well. Nicky, Nicky, Nicky. To what do I owe the pleasure? I thought you was in London livin' near the king, stoppin' by the palace for tea and teaching him how to play hearts." He kind of snorted-slash-laughed at what he thought was his hilarious repartee. "Nicky? Ya still there?"

Mel had a big, rough longshoreman-from-Brooklyn kind of accent but was short and slight like those Hollywood leading men who look more imposing on the big screen than they are in real life. Time had done nothing to improve it.

"Don't call me—" I started to reply, then stopped. He knew I hated being called Nicky. I sucked it up and cut straight to the chase. "I need a quick lesson in pari-mutuel betting, handicapping, and jockey stats, plus anything else you can throw in. And I need it right away."

I could hear his sigh over the phone and imagined him shaking his head in disgust. But he owed me. A few years ago, I helped his son out of a jam with an illegal after-hours casino and its owners. Ironic, right? Since his business wasn't exactly kosher.

"All right, Donahue, here's what you gotta know." He proceeded to spend the next twenty minutes talking a mile a minute as I took notes. When we said goodbye, I felt a slight glimmer of hope that I might be able to read a racing form and not make a fool of myself.

Well, we'll see about that tomorrow.

I awoke to birds singing and the sun streaming in through the bedroom windows. I reached over for Marina, but she was gone. For a moment, I panicked at her absence, totally thrown, like a newbie blackjack player who can't decide if he wants another card or not and knows the other players are licking their chops waiting for him to make a mistake. Then I heard the shower running and knew she was safe.

I couldn't remember what I'd dreamt, but it must have been something that felt dangerous. Oh wait, it was all coming back to me—a day at the track. Today. My own *bête noir* going viral.

I lay back down and thought about the day to come. I'd reviewed Mad Mel's info and was pretty sure I could fake my way through the day if it came to that, including discussing the point system used to rate horses for their worthiness to be entered in the Derby—the more races they won, the more points they accrued. I heard the shower go off, and soon Marina emerged wrapped in a white terrycloth robe, looking gorgeous. It brought back memories of the night we met, she in a different terrycloth robe and me with my tongue hanging out. I patted the bed, and she strolled over, mischief twinkling in her eyes. I'd been a goner that first time. And, as you can see, nothing had changed.

Chapter Twenty-One

"And they're off." The track announcer was calling the fourth race of the day, a claiming stakes for two-year-olds.

When we arrived, Adnan shepherded us into the private Triple Crown Room in the Jockey Club Suite Clubhouse. It was decorated to impress the owners and their guests with earthen pots filled with colorful flowers brightening the space, white linen tablecloths, elegant china, and gleaming silverware. The *piece de resistance* was the large balcony overlooking the track.

He introduced Marina and me to a half dozen men whose horses were running today. The two of us went off to get drinks, leaving Marina amidst them.

At the bar, Adnan looked back over his shoulder and whispered, "She will not have any trouble inducing those gentlemen to speak with her. They all are what you might call full of themselves." He tapped the rim of my flute with his. "Enjoy your Champagne." With that, he was off to place a bet. I thought it wise to stay put while Marina did her sleuthing.

Adnan was right. It didn't take much to get them talking. Or fawning. From my spot at the bar, I couldn't hear what was being said, but I could read the body language pretty well. Several of the men had moved to stand in front of a wide-screen TV to watch the next race. But two, who'd been introduced as Donald O'Rourke, a grizzled Irishman with a buzz cut and sharp blue eyes—all that was missing was the newsboy cap and knickers— and Neil Petrocelli, a lanky, good-looking guy with blond hair and a baby face, was still by her side.

Marina appeared to be asking them a lot of questions, and Petrocelli looked like he was tripping all over himself to answer. After a few minutes, O'Rourke shook his head and excused himself. Marina waved goodbye, and Petrocelli jumped right in, patting her on the arm, talking up a storm, and gesturing toward the exit to the stands. She shook her head, smiled, and started walking toward me.

"So, how'd that go?" I jutted my chin toward the Petrocelli's back as I handed her a glass of Champagne.

"Nothing so far, except an invitation to see his horses later today, then dinner afterward." She grinned up at me. "I told him I'd think it over."

I ignored the jibe. "What were you grilling them about? O'Rourke seemed a bit agitated."

"He was. Didn't seem to like Adnan or his horses very much. He called him 'a rich upstart who thought he could come here and take over like he owned the place.' Swore his colt was never going to win the Derby, that his horse Fire Walker was going to take the Triple Crown this year." She put a lot of swagger into her voice, as I imagined O'Rourke had.

"Jealousy?" I asked.

"Maybe a bit more than that. I'm sure he bears looking into."

"You were talking to that Petrocelli guy for a long time." I jutted my chin toward the lounge's exit.

"Oh, I asked both of them about how the horses were trained and if they exercised with other horses entered in the race before the big day. Petrocelli was explaining that owners kept their horses separate from those of other stables until they were slated to race against each other. His thoroughbred, Night Music, will be running in the Derby, and he hoped I'd be here to see it."

Of course, he did.

Marina and I left the Triple Crown Room and took the elevator down to the grandstand to watch the horses parade for the next race. Adnan joined us, and he and Marina began discussing O'Rourke and the enmity he'd shown. He was on Marina's radar and there he'd stay until she checked him out thoroughly.

Adnan had gotten us special passes that allowed us entry to any area of the track. I excused myself and told them I was going to wander around on my own for a bit. I suspected O'Rourke's *Sturm und Drang* could have a little more behind it than just words. He was well placed to know Adnan's horses and businesses, and how to get at both, especially if he had an inside man.

I didn't know what I hoped to find, but I thought I'd start with the barn area. I passed an information booth and snagged a map of Churchill Downs. The track was huge, and the barn was on its far side, behind the infield. It housed the horses running in the current meet. I took off in that direction to get a glimpse of O'Rourke's Thoroughbred, Fire Walker, for myself.

For a busy track, the barn area was awfully quiet. A few horse vans were queued up near the horsemen's entrance, waiting for their charges. I assumed some had already left and were headed for their home farms. Several grooms were standing off to the side that faced the track, talking amongst themselves and watching the horses being led out for the next race. I don't think they noticed me as I walked behind them toward the barns in the rear. These were arranged in two long rows with stalls back-to-back, each with a horse's name tacked over the doorway. Many of the stalls were empty, and I figured those horses were already gone. There were a couple of stalls with horses poking their heads out of the open, top half, but no trainers or grooms to be seen.

This was where the grunt work got done. Feeding, brushing, saddling. All the tasks that went into caring for a Thoroughbred racehorse. Out of the public's view, the grounds were not as well maintained. Not a flowering plant or clipped shrub in sight. It was downright barren and plain. A dirt pathway edged around the barns and became muddier the farther out I walked. By the time I found Fire Walker's stall, my shoes were splatted with muck.

His stall was along the backside, the last one down at the end. And as far away from the infield as you could get. I wondered if he didn't get along with other horses and they kept him separate for that reason. His name was tacked over the doorway but the stall was empty, guarded by an orange and white cat that opened one eye at a time and rose from a nap at my approach.

I'd heard that horses often had their pets of their own, which helped keep them calm. Maybe O'Rourke should get one for himself, as well, I thought. "So, where's your buddy, Fire Walker?" I asked as I bent down to pat him on his head and was rewarded with a soft purring. A tag on his collar identified him as Merlin.

"Let's go take a look, why don't we, Merlin?" I opened the bottom half-door and stepped inside, the cat following behind, tail standing up like a weather vane moving from side to side to check which way the wind was blowing. The stall appeared as I imagined, with hay and a water trough on one side, a harness hanging from a peg near the entrance, and a saddle tossed over the side wood planking.

"What's that?" I said to my new pal as I noticed something shiny poking through the hay in one corner and moved closer to get a better look.

As I bent down to retrieve it, Merlin let out a screeching howl. Startled, I began to turn around and glimpsed the end of a baseball bat, aiming for my head. I raised my arm to try and ward off the blow and was stopped by a meaty hand with tattooed knuckles twisting it around and nearly ripping it out of the socket just as the other hand cracked the bat against my skull.

That's the last thing I remember until I woke up on the couch in Adnan's living room. Marina and Adnan had found me knocked out on the stall floor. Someone had coshed me good on the back of the head, and I had a lump the size of an apple to prove it.

Chapter Twenty-Two

We were worried when you didn't come back for the last race." Marina paced back and forth as she spoke. "Adnan sent Rashid and Rehan to look for you. I thought you might have gone back to the Triple Crown Room, so he and I went there to check. Finally, it occurred to me you might be over by the barns. While you were out Adnan stayed with you until the track doctor arrived. When I knew you'd live—" She smiled weakly. "—I started looking for witnesses. I questioned the grooms, stable hands, and trainers. No one saw anything. I also asked the track steward for the security DVDs for the barn area." She sighed. "He hemmed and hawed, but I mentioned Adnan and how we'd like to avoid calling in the police, and he relented. He's averse to any bad publicity for the track, especially not this close to the Derby. He'll have the video ready by tomorrow afternoon."

She sat down, her face ashen with worry. "I'm so sorry about this, Nick." Her downcast green eyes looked as sad as I'd ever seen. "I put you in danger again." She grasped my hands with both of hers and held them tight.

"This is not your fault. I'm here to help you, remember?" I released my hands and tipped her face up to mine. "I'll be fine. Honestly. Okay? But what about Merlin?"

"Who?" she asked, a worried look coming over her face as if she thought I was hallucinating.

"The cat. Fire Walker's pet."

"Pet? We didn't see any cat around."

Her expression was puzzled. I'd somehow confused things even more.

"Never mind. It's not important." I smiled, all the while thinking, I hope whoever did this to me didn't kill the cat. He was probably hiding somewhere. I'd look for him when I went back tomorrow.

"Okay." She took a deep breath, and her shoulders eased back as she went into investigator mode. "Do you remember anything about your attacker? See anyone? Hear anything?"

I shook my head. Big mistake. The room started spinning around. "No." I finally croaked out through waves of dizziness. "Nothing."

There was one thing I did remember. That big hand that gripped my arm like iron. It was decorated with tattooed knuckles with smudged blue ink that spelled out f-u-c-k-u. I didn't want to tell her, or Adnan, about it. Not yet, anyway. Not until I had a chance to check it out. Maybe the guy would show up on the security tape. But somehow, I doubted it. His decoration had looked to me like a prison tat, which opened up a whole new can of nasty. Something about it was familiar. Although, I didn't have any former inmates as intimate acquaintances. None in Kentucky, anyway.

Adnan and the doctor he called in once we were home were standing on the opposite side of the room, talking quietly. After a few more minutes, they shook hands, and the doctor departed.

"Doctor Blair says you will be fine." Adnan nodded his head up and down as he spoke.

"See, I told you so." I turned to Marina, trying to put a positive spin on things.

Adnan continued. "The doctor suggests we keep you awake for several hours to make sure you do not have a concussion. And he suggests a sling for your arm, as well."

Yes. The arm I'd raised to protect myself. It hadn't worked. Or, maybe it had, splitting my attacker's attention so the blow he delivered wasn't fatal.

Adnan paused and looked at me with such a pained expression I was afraid; contrary to what the doctor had told him, he thought I was going to die.

"I am so sorry this has happened to you while you were here as my guest. We will find out who did this. I promise. This will not go unpunished." His face reddened, and his raised hand shook with fury as he spoke.

All I could do was nod slowly, trying to keep the spinning from starting again.

"I will leave you and Marina now. Please call Josef if you require anything."

As he closed the door softly behind him, Marina made a face. "That was a little intense, don't you think?"

I was about to nod when I realized maybe I shouldn't. "Maybe just a bit over-solicitous if you ask me."

"What were you doing back there anyway?" Marina stood up and resumed her pacing.

"While you two were discussing O'Rourke, I thought I'd get a closer look at Fire Walker. He won his race earlier today. I thought the horse would still be in his stall, but he was already gone. I was just looking around with my new pal, Merlin—the cat that's Fire Walker's pet—and something twinkling under the hay in the corner caught my eye. I stepped over and bent down to take a better look and heard Merlin howl like someone stepped on his tail. I was just turning around to look when whoever it was hit me from the side." I inched my spine back against the pillows propped behind me and sat up slowly. "It was strange, though. There wasn't anyone around back there. It seemed deserted."

"Maybe someone made sure it would be." Marina ventured, her suspicion rising with her words.

"What did Adnan tell you about O'Rourke?

"He and Adnan have bad blood between them. It seems Adnan outbid him on a few horses O'Rourke had his eye on, and he felt cheated." She shrugged. "You know, Adnan confirmed what O'Rourke said this afternoon that O'Rourke thought of him as a rich Arab stepping on the working-class Irishman who pulled himself up by his bootstraps to make a name in horseracing. Not exactly a new theme."

"You think there's more to it than that?" I sat up a little bit more, trying to keep the room in focus.

"There usually is."

Something else was odd and nagging at me. Mad Mel told me that good owners didn't race their horses more than twice a month. It made me wonder why O'Rourke was racing Fire Walker so close to the Derby. Did the horse need the points to qualify? Or did O'Rourke have another, more sinister reason? I'd mull it over before I mentioned it to Marina.

"So, what's next?" I asked instead.

"Next, I'm going back to that stable and having another look around. We don't know how long you were there before we found you. Whoever did this to you might have left when he heard us coming. He might not have had time to pick up whatever it was that attracted your attention. So, it may still be there."

"I don't like the idea of you going back to the track by yourself." I looked at my watch. "It's late. It'll be deserted. We'll go together tom—"

Marina sat next to me and put her finger to my lips to stop my diatribe. "I won't be going alone. I'll ask the Stud Master to go with me. I don't think he'll refuse. Do you?"

Great. That's all I needed. Marina, alone with Eggers at a deserted racetrack. Could this day get any worse?

Chapter Twenty-Three

You know what lawyers say about only asking the questions to which you know the answers?

The day, or the night, I should say, did get worse. While Marina was out gallivanting around with Stud Master Tim, Ana called from London with an update on both Mike and him.

"Hi, Nicky," she purred into the phone. As much as I hated being called Nicky, I didn't mind it when one of my "angels" said it. "How are things in Kentucky?"

"Let's just say there's a lot going on." I touched the lump on the back of my head, which was still pounding. "I'm sure Marina will fill you in when you speak." I didn't want to tell her about being waylaid. I had my position as the male head of the office to think of, even if I didn't officially work there, and they all out-ranked me. "Why are you still at work?" I asked. It was two in the morning in London.

"I'm teaching Nicolo a lesson," she said, the purr gone from her voice. "One he greatly deserves for taking me for granted. I'm letting him wonder where I am this evening."

"Okay." Revenge by working late. I didn't want to touch that one, even from America. "So." I tried to get her back on track. "What have you found out?"

"Our man, Tim Eggers, has been a very naughty boy." Her English accent made the word "naughty" sound like something fun and exciting. I was pretty sure it wasn't. "He's been arrested twice for aggravated assault and spent some time in prison for the last one. Something he neglected to mention on his employment application for Winged Valor Farms." It sounded like Ana had tucked her cell under her chin. I could hear her rifling through papers. "His previous employment was with a High View Farm owned by a Donald O'Rourke."

Bells started going off in my head like a slot machine paying out big time. I interrupted Ana to ask a question. "What did he do for them there?"

"It appears he was an assistant trainer before he was let go for assaulting a stable hand. It looks as though the assault was quite serious. The other lad sustained several broken bones. He was in hospital for weeks."

"Listen, Ana, I have to go. I need to find Marina. She'll call you back in the morning."

"But, Nick, I'm not done. There's more I need to tell you about this wanker." Ana sounded flustered. "Nick, wait. Don't hang up. Nick?"

I could hear her calling my name as I disconnected. I stood up quickly, and a wave of nausea and wooziness overpowered me. Damn, I laid my hand on the back of a chair to steady myself, then made my way to the hall that separated the main house and guest wing. My head was pounding, but it didn't matter. Concussion or not, I had to get to Marina. She was at a deserted racetrack with a convicted felon, and she had no idea what he was capable of doing. I had to find her.

"Josef!" I called, then called louder, "Josef, I need you."

The butler came running into the hallway. "Mr. Donahue, what is it? What has happened?"

I'm sure I scared the poor man half to death. I was sweating and panting as I tried to get the words out. "Please, get Mr. bin Haddad. We need to go to the racetrack right now. Immediately"

Josef took my arm and led me into the great room. He tried to help me into a chair. I shook him off. "But Mr. bin Haddad is not here, sir. He is out—at a meeting."

Even through the fog that was enveloping my brain, I could see that he was reluctant to ante up bin Haddad's whereabouts. "Then give me the keys to a car. I need to find Ms. DiPietro. Now, Josef."

"Mr. Donahue, I do not think you should be driving. Please sit down." He indicated the chair next to me.

"No." I was adamant. "The keys." I held out my hand. I'd seen several jeeps and SUVs in the farm's garage. Any one would do.

"Very well. I will be right back."

He returned moments later with a set of keys in his hand. I reached for them, and he shook his head. "I will take you where you need to go."

I was in no condition to argue. I'd had more of a bang on the head than we'd thought. Strictly speaking, a concussion wasn't out of the question.

"Fine. We're going back to the racetrack. And, Josef, we need to hurry."

Chapter Twenty-Four

The track was as dark and deserted as I'd imagined. Lights mounted on posts around the perimeter cast deep shadows over the paths and buildings. Josef had barely pulled into the owners' lot when I slipped off my seat belt and attempted to book it out of the car.

Attempted is the operative word. I'd barely lifted a foot toward the ground when I had to stop. Whoever had knocked me out knew how to make the blow count. I remembered that hand grabbing onto my arm with its charming tattooed message. My throat closed, and I gulped at the thought. I sat back as Josef came around to my side. He admonished me in rapid-fire Arabic. Even though I couldn't understand a word, I got the message loud and clear.

Yes, I was a stupid American, even though technically I lived in London. And yes, I must have wanted to get myself killed. Finally, with much head shaking and arm waving accompanying his words, he calmed down enough to help me from the car.

I stood up as straight as I could, trying to look as though I had control of my body. I tried Marina from my cell. No response. She must have silenced it, or someone did it for her. My imagination was working overtime, even if my brain wasn't.

I told Josef to wait here while I went to look for Marina. He didn't like it but stayed put as I moved off to the stables on shaky legs.

Back there, it was even darker and more foreboding. Only a few dim lights illuminated the pathways, which gave the track a ghostly feel. And the flashlight from my phone didn't penetrate the shadows. Walking as quickly and as quietly as my weakened state allowed, I kept close to the buildings, hoping to arrive at Fire Walker's stall unobserved.

My imagination went wild. Would I find Eggers standing behind Marina, ready to bang her on the head? What then? I'd rush in and save the day. Thankfully, my imagination was disappointed. Fire Walker's stall was still empty and as far as I could tell, there was no shiny metal object poking up from the straw. Of course, that begged the question: Where was Marina if she wasn't here with Tim?

I hobbled back to Josef and the car, poking my nose into each stall I passed on the way. A few had horses inside, bedded down for the night. Off to the left of the barns, a low building showed lights coming through several of its windows. Adnan had mentioned it earlier. It was housing for the grooms and stable hands who remained at the track. Didn't look like much of anything was going on there.

Josef saw me coming and walked over to assist me. Once I was settled in the passenger seat, he fired up the engine and headed for home. When we arrived, Marina and a very worried-looking Adnan met us at the front door.

"What did you think you were doing?" Marina snapped, her frustration showing in her words and flushed red cheeks.

"Well—"

"Never mind. I don't need to know. I'm sure you had your reasons for wandering around with a concussion." She shook her head, her auburn hair swaying from side to side.

"Technically, I don't have—"

She cut me off again. "Be quiet, Nick. Just…just go to your room." She crossed her arms in front of her middle, signaling anger, and watched as I turned toward the guest suite.

"Yes, ma'am," I tossed over my shoulder as she turned toward Adnan.

Marina joined me a few minutes later after saying goodnight. I could see she was still angry with me for going after her. It didn't take much to figure out why I'd gone back to the track. I tried to explain that Ana had called with information on Tim Eggers. That I thought he might try to harm her, and I was worried. She listened then and sat down next to me on the couch. "Ana said there was more information about him."

"He was a perfect gentleman. Held the flashlight for me and talked about horses and racing, like he hadn't a care in the world. I wonder what Adnan will make of his having worked for O'Rourke?"

"Are you going to rat him out?"

"Not just yet. What worries me more is that Adnan didn't uncover Eggers's felony record or his previous employment when his people ran a background check. Someone on his security staff should have caught that."

"Maybe they did," I added.

"Yeah, and for whatever reason, didn't want to share it."

I could almost see the wheels spinning round and round in her head.

"Let's see what else Ana has dug up. Then I'll decide what to tell Adnan." She looked at her watch and noted the time. "I'll call her in the morning, our time. She's probably gone home by now. She can fill me in then. I don't think the Stud Master will take a hike between now and then. Do you?"

"Probably not," is what I said, but was thinking he just might if he were feeling pressured by Marina's presence. Time to change the subject. "So, did you find anything in Fire Walker's stall?" I asked.

"Not a thing, especially no shiny bauble sticking up from the straw." She shrugged. "Eggers said it looked as though the stall had been mucked out and made ready for his next appearance. Fire Walker's running again the day after tomorrow."

One of the things Mad Mel had told me was that owners often left their horses at the track if they were racing on multiple days. Usually, a groom stayed with the animal and slept in the bunkhouse. But O'Rourke had taken the horse back to his farm. Maybe he felt safer on his home turf. And, just maybe, he had a good reason for that.

Again, I wondered why he was racing his Thoroughbred so often before the big race. Was he pushing him hard to set him up to lose? If so, what was his motive?

I lifted my hand to my mouth to stifle a yawn and saw Marina doing the same.

She smiled. "C'mon, Nick," she said, "let's hit the hay. No pun intended."

Chapter Twenty-Five

I woke to the smell of coffee wafting through the air and tickling my nose. The bedroom door was open part way. I could hear Marina speaking softly on the phone as the aroma of freshly brewed java enticed me from my bed. I looked at the clock on the bedside table. It had just turned nine a.m., which would make it about three p.m. in London. Marina was most likely speaking with Ana and getting the rest of the information on Eggers.

I was down for the count the minute my head had touched the soft down-filled pillow and slept for much longer than usual. I sat up slowly, happy to be dizzy-free. My head still hurt, especially where I'd been hit. But the lump was going down. My arm was better, as well. I lifted it and stretched. It ached, but at least it moved. I didn't need a sling after all. My attacker had had an iron grip. I could still feel his hand squeezing my forearm, where I now had finger-shaped black and blue marks. Thankfully, it wasn't broken. It was nothing a few more aspirin couldn't cure. After a few minutes of contemplating my mortality, I rose, walked into the living room, and gave Marina a good morning kiss.

She'd just closed her phone and was typing away on her laptop.

I jutted my chin toward her computer. "What gives?"

"It seems our Mr. Eggers has had a considerable amount of trouble he's managed to keep secret." She tapped the keypad with a finger. "Several years back, he was working the circuit in Ireland and landed a job at one of their big racing stables. Their star, a gelding named Leapin' Leprechaun, was racing at Limerick Racecourse in the track's biggest event, The Munster

Grand National. Serious money was riding on him. Somehow, he managed to come in last. The owner suspected foul play, and tests revealed that the horse had been given a sedative. Eggers was suspected of tampering with Leapin' Leprechaun, but no one could prove he'd done it—there were too many people around the horse to be sure. He was let go and soon after began working for O'Rourke, who also races his mounts in Ireland.

Coupled with his gambling problems, this added up to a strong case for him being the bad guy.

I listened quietly while Marina related this information. My mind jumped ahead to questions she probably already thought of. "Were any of O'Rourke's horses in that race?" Marina nodded. "Did one of them win?" Another nod. I could see where this was leading. It wasn't anywhere good. Not for Eggers, at least.

She closed her notebook and looked at me. "It's time to tell Adnan what we've discovered. Eggers could be the key to finding the extortionists." Even as she said the words, I heard the doubt in her voice.

"What," I asked. "You're not convinced yet, are you?"

"No." She shook her head. I wasn't either. Although it would have been very convenient to think we'd found our man—or one of them, at least.

"I'm not sure Eggers is an extortionist. I do think he's a real opportunist. One who found his way to O'Rourke and made the most of the bad blood between the two men as well as a way to indulge his gambling habit. He probably had O'Rourke help him fake a reference so he could get the job here."

Marina was listening intently. She was processing all the facts. "And do his bidding."

I nodded. "Adnan's problem is bigger than petty revenge," I recalled again what Dad had said about being a well-planned operation. "I don't believe Eggers and O'Rourke conceived it on their own."

"You might be right. So, we keep digging. But first, we have to let Adnan know his Stud Master is in horse manure up to his eyebrows."

"Mr. bin Haddad has left for the morning," Josef informed us when we went to the main house.

Marina frowned. "Do you know where we can find him?" Josef's slight shake of his head indicated not. "Or, when he'll be back?"

"I am sorry, Ms. DiPietro, I cannot say." His steady gaze and upright posture gave away nothing. Except to me. I liked—and believed—the Josef from last night much more than the one this morning. All fired up and having at it in Arabic like a player on a streak at the craps table. Those were his true colors. Not this nearly perfect portrait of a manservant.

I tipped my head toward Marina, indicating we should leave. "Thanks, Josef. We'll try Mr. bin Haddad on his cell. But if you see him first, please tell him it's important that we speak with him."

I caught the look of relief on Josef's face as I steered Marina toward the front door. "Let's take a walk," I whispered in her ear.

She nodded okay, and a moment later, we were outside.

"What gives, Nick?"

"Josef's lying. Bin Haddad is avoiding us. And I wonder why."

Marina gave me her full attention as we began walking around the house to the path toward Devil Wind's stable. "Last night, Josef wouldn't call him when I wanted to look for you." I hated bringing up my paranoia-fueled behavior, but Marina seemed to be over my trying to butt in. "And he wouldn't tell me where I could reach him."

She stopped and turned to me, her back to the house. "I don't like it either. I need my clients to be honest with me. We'll settle this as soon as we see him."

As she was speaking, a movement in a second-story window caught my eye. A curtain twitched, then went still as I looked up. It was bin Haddad up there. I was sure of it.

Chapter Twenty-Six

We walked over to Devil Wind's stable, expecting to find Eggers. Only Mike was there, brushing the horse's beautiful black coat into a glistening shine. Marina patted his nose, and he returned her affection by nuzzling her hand. The moment I got a little closer, he showed me his teeth again. Mike and Marina looked at me and shrugged. Then they started laughing. Nice, I thought. Rejected by a horse. Must have the same bloodlines as a casino owner.

Marina restrained her laughter and got back to business. "Have you seen Tim?" she asked.

Mike shook his head. "He called in sick this morning. Just a little while ago. Said he thought he was coming down with something and better fight it off before the Derby."

I gave Marina a look that said we might have blown it. Tim might have made a run for it already.

"Thanks, Mike. We'll catch up with him tomorrow." Her tone was casual. You'd never know she was upset about what we just heard. "Goodbye, cute boy," she added as she patted Devil Wind again. The look on Mike's face said it all: He wished she'd been talking to him.

We set off for the main house at a leisurely pace. As soon as we were out of sight of the stable, Marina grabbed my arm and we put on some speed. "We need to pay Mr. Eggers a visit. I've got his address on my laptop notes." She was practically running. "I'll get them while you ask Josef for the car keys." She looked me up and down like a buyer eyeballing a plucked chicken. "Tell him I'm driving."

Josef complied and handed me the keys to a jeep while Marina gathered what she needed. We were on the road in a matter of minutes. Marina drove like an Italian in Rome. She expected everyone to get out of the way. If they didn't, there'd be no telling what might happen.

I plugged Eggers's address into the GPS—120 Royer Court in North Louisville, about twenty minutes away. I held on to the dash as she wove in and out of traffic. We'd probably get there in ten.

"Adnan was home."

She gave me a quick glance out of the corner of her eye as she cut off a big delivery truck. The driver stuck his middle finger out the window to let her know just how he felt about that. "How do you know?"

"I saw him at the window in his bedroom when we were in front of the house."

"Why is he avoiding us—and lying?"

"Once we talk to Eggers, we can tackle Adnan." I glanced at the GPS and jutted my chin toward the road. "It's the next left. His apartment is on the right."

Marina made the turn and pulled to the curb in front of number 120. It was a two-story, white shingle, semi-attached dwelling with doorways on either side of its middle.

Marina composed herself as she exited the car and waited for me to join her. We walked casually up the front path, and Marina rang the bell on the bottom left with the name Eggers taped over it. We could hear it pealing inside.

After about thirty seconds, she rang again. Still no answer.

"Nick, you go around the back and see if there's a backdoor that's unlocked." She turned her body at an angle and pulled out a set of lock picks. "I'll get in from here."

I surveyed the street. It was very quiet. There were a few cars parked down the street, but no one was out gardening or walking. That didn't mean there weren't people looking out their windows. Breaking in was risky. "You sure?"

"Uh-huh. Get going."

She gave me a little shove. Marina angled her body to conceal what she was doing and started to slip in the lock picks just as I turned the corner. I reached the backdoor and rattled the doorknob, but it was locked. I tried to peek through the curtain that covered the glass on the upper half but all I could see was a little bit of the kitchen sink and cabinets. I moved my face closer to the glass, angling my cheek to the right to try and get a better view. I nearly fell into the room as Marina opened the door from inside.

Her skill with her lock picks was alive and kicking. Unfortunately, Tim Eggers was just the opposite. He was as dead and done as a horse coming in last.

This case was becoming more complicated by the minute. It had started with the maiming of a horse and had moved on to the killing of a man. And we'd barely begun figuring out who was responsible.

Chapter Twenty-Seven

Tim Eggers had bled out on his living room floor. Part of the back of his head was missing. In its place was a gaping red hole that showed part of his brain. The part still left was as gruesome as it gets. His stark white face against all that red was something I'd remember for a long time.

The wall on the side next to the body looked like someone painted Rorschach cards on it. A crimson pool surrounded the body on the floor and was just starting to turn dark. Nothing else had been disturbed. No broken lamps. No tables overturned. Just a dead body lying in the middle of all that blood.

I knew I was staring with my mouth hanging open. I'd never seen a murder victim before. And, "See dead body of murder victim" wasn't something I planned on adding to my bucket list. Although I reminded myself, I'd almost been a victim myself a few times in the last year. The thought brought me up cold.

Marina was speaking to me, but I wasn't focusing on what she was saying. "Huh?" I asked as she touched me on the arm.

"Put your cell phone away."

I looked down at my hand with the phone in its palm, the other on auto-pilot ready to hit 9-1-1. I had no idea how it had gotten there.

"Let's think about this for a minute." She put her hand on my arm and moved it away from the phone.

"We should—" I started to reply, but Marina held up her hand.

"I think we should leave. If we call the police, they'll ask too many questions we can't answer." She stared down at the body and then looked up at me. "We should just go. No one knows we're here. Let's keep it that way."

"Just leave him like that?" I glanced over at Eggers's inert form.

"Yes."

I could see Marina's point but it made me uneasy. I thought about it for a minute, then nodded in acquiescence. What good would it do for us to get caught up in this murder? We'd be alerting the killer or killers that we had a vested interest in Eggers and whatever he was doing. "Okay, let's go."

Marina had wiped off the front doorknob when she entered. We retraced our steps to the back door, checking to ensure we hadn't touched anything in the house. She wiped off the back doorknob and the pane of glass I'd touched as we slipped out the door. The street was as quiet as when we arrived. No one would know we had ever been there. Or so I prayed.

Once back in the car, we didn't get going right away. Marina sat behind the wheel, thinking. At least that's what it looked like. Her eyes focused on something beyond the window, and her mouth was in a tight line.

"We know he was alive this morning." She looked at her watch and turned toward me. "He phoned Mike to call out sick about an hour or so ago. So, this just happened. We may have just missed the killer."

All the more reason to leave, I thought. *What if whoever did this is still lurking around?* "We should go. Now," I said to Marina as I swept the street for any signs of a homicidal maniac.

Marina touched the starter. "He knew his killer. He had to." She pulled out of the spot, and we were finally moving. "There were no signs of forced entry, or anything disturbed. Whoever it was, Tim let them in. Think about where the body was and how it was positioned."

I didn't have to. It was something I doubt I'd forget.

"He fell facing toward the couch. He was probably moving into the living room with whoever it was following. I bet the killer walked right behind him and shot up close." She took a breath and sighed. "He wasn't expecting it. If he was, he wouldn't have turned his back on them."

"So, it was someone he knew or had business with." I mentally ran through the list of the people we'd met so far. Rashid, Namal, Rehan, and even Mike.

Or, O'Rourke. With the right incentive, any one of them could have killed him. Or, it could have been someone from his checkered past looking to pay him back. "Are we going to tell Adnan?"

"I think it's time for Adnan to tell us what's going on, don't you?" There was no mistaking the steely resolve in her voice.

Chapter Twenty-Eight

arina slid the car into an open space in the garage, flung the door open, flew out, and stormed toward the house at a military jog. I had trouble keeping up with her. She burst into the house, and Josef appeared. She must have looked like a Valkyrie, hair flying, eyes blazing, ready to escort a soon-to-be-dead Josef to Valhalla because he turned as white as a ghost.

"Ms. DiPietro." He was tripping over himself, trying to compose himself, but it wasn't working. His words sounded like a squeaky wheel. "What is wrong?"

She ignored his question and fired off her own. "Where is Mr. bin Haddad?" She poked Josef in the chest. "And don't lie to me."

"H—He is not here," Josef stammered, backing away from her.

Marina followed. "Do. Not. Lie. To. Me." She emphasized every word with another poke.

"I am not. Please. Here." He retrieved an envelope from the table Marina had backed him into and handed it to her with shaking fingers. "Mr. bin Haddad was called back to Dubai."

Marina was stunned, and so was I. Josef took the momentary pause the envelope had caused to slide crablike along the wall and out of Marina's reach. "Mr. bin Haddad said you were to read his letter and you would understand. Now, please excuse me." He began edging his way out of the room, his back still to the wall.

Marina turned and marched through the living room to the guest suite with me following. She flung herself on the couch and tapped the letter in her hand, shaking her head all the while.

"Aren't you going to open it?" I asked in what I hoped was a quiet, reasonable tone. She just glared at me. "Okay. What then?"

The morning had already been bad enough. Finding a dead body tends to do that to you. And this letter was not a welcome diversion.

Marina slid her finger under the sealed flap and pulled out bin Haddad's letter.

She stared at the folded page for a moment before opening it and then began to read. When she was through, she handed it to me.

Dear Marina and Nick,

I am sorry to leave you like this, but I have received word of urgent business in Dubai that I must attend to immediately. I understand you will think it is strange for me to depart so suddenly. I cannot explain my reasons at this moment, but you must believe it is for the best. I trust you will look after Devil Wind in my absence. Rashid is accompanying me, but please be assured that Rehan will be entirely at your service for anything that you might need until I return. Please, I ask you to keep my departure confidential and not speak of it with anyone.

Sincerely,

Adnan

"What do you make of that?" Marina asked as I handed the letter back to her.

"What could be more urgent than finding the extortionists and protecting Devil Wind?" I asked, shaking my head. "It's odd." I flapped the letter in my hand. "There was no mention of Tim as someone to count on if we need help with minding Devil Wind. It's almost as if Adnan knows he's been murdered."

I could see Marina was weighing my words carefully. "Almost, but if Tim was killed at the time, we think, Adnan was here." She gestured to the house. "You saw him yourself, standing by the window."

"That doesn't mean he isn't responsible. He has minions working for him."

I shrugged my shoulders to emphasize my point. "It probably wouldn't be too hard for someone in his employ to find and hire a killer."

"Is that what you think happened? Why would Adnan want to kill Tim after entrusting Devil Wind to his care? It doesn't make any sense."

"Murder doesn't always. Especially since I'm not convinced, Tim Eggers was one of the extortionists."

Marina booted up her laptop and opened her file. "I know what Ana found was damning, brawls and scams, gambling and prison. But it all seemed penny ante, nothing big enough to lead to his murder." She tapped furiously on the keyboard. "What are we missing?"

"It could be, though. Serious enough, I mean. Maybe he finally scammed the wrong person and pissed them off enough to do him in. A guy like that, you never know."

I remembered a blackjack player I knew who talked a disgruntled dealer into fixing the game. It didn't last long. One of the pit bosses noticed it after a few nights. The dealer was fired, and the gambler was lucky to walk away with just a broken hand. He didn't play blackjack for a long time.

"The police will find out he worked here with Adnan." An idea had taken root, and I was going with it. "If they discover his references were faked and that Adnan learned about this, it's enough to make him a suspect."

"But we know it wasn't Adnan, at least not physically." Marina closed the laptop. I nodded in agreement. "And if they figure out we were at Tim's house and found the body, it's going to be hard to explain why, especially with Adnan gone. It'll look like he took a bunk."

"Let's not worry about the police right now." Marina held up the letter. "I need to speak with Adnan to—"

A sudden knock at the door interrupted Marina. Josef poked his head into the room and hemmed and hawed, hesitant to enter. "What is it now, Josef?"

He shrank back a little at Marina's hard tone, probably afraid she was going to poke him again. "Excuse me, Ms. DiPietro." He was almost whispering. "The police are here. Since Mr. bin Haddad is not...available—" He was letting us know he hadn't spilled the beans on Adnan's departure from the country. "—they want to speak with you and Mr. Donahue."

"Me?" Marina's eyes pinned Josef's, and he took a step back. "Why should I speak with them on Mr. bin Haddad's behalf?"

"I am not sure, but they seem to know who you are and asked to see you."

Great. Speak of the devil, and he knocks at your door.

I took the letter from Marina's hand and slipped it into one of Adnan's horse breeding magazines as Josef was showing the police in. He departed quickly—I didn't blame him—and left it to us to make introductions.

I held out my hand. "Nick Donahue," I said, "and Marina DiPietro." I nodded toward Marina, who was now by my side.

"Detective Ben Harris." He took my hand in a firm grip, then turned toward Marina with a nod. "Ms. DiPietro." Harris was short and stocky with a pasty complexion that made him look like he lived at his desk. His yellowing shirt and stained tie added to this impression. "And this is Sergeant Braeton."

The sergeant, younger and taller, aimed piercing blue eyes at us and nodded.

"What can we do for you, Detective?" Marina's voice was calm and reassuring, a total one-eighty in tone and attitude from a few minutes ago.

"I'm sorry to be the bearer of bad news, but one of Mr. bin Haddad's employees was found dead in his home this morning."

I noticed he hadn't said murdered or killed. My paranoia was in full-on crazy mode, sure this was an opening gambit to trip us up and see if we knew anything. I'd watched *Law and Order*. I knew how this worked.

"Who might that be?" Marina came right to the point, tilting her head to the side and looking him in the eye.

"A Mr. Tim Eggers."

He waited for a reaction. When none was forthcoming from Marina, he turned his attention to me.

As far as I was concerned, he could wait for a reaction until we sent a man to Mars. I had perfected my poker face over many years of gambling. I knew how to hide my tells.

"I'm very sorry to hear that," Marina finally said, not giving anything away. "How did he die?"

"I'm afraid I'm not at liberty to say."

CHAPTER TWENTY-EIGHT

I bet you're not.

Harris tried pulling a poker face of his own, staring at Marina.

Sorry, buddy, she won't crack, either.

"I see," she replied. "I don't know how we can help you. We only met Mr. Eggers a few days ago when we arrived here as Mr. bin Haddad's guests." She emphasized the last word.

"It was my understanding that you're working for Mr. bin Haddad."

If Marina was surprised he knew this, again, she hid it well. "That's a private matter. Nothing to do with your investigation." She smiled sweetly. "If there's nothing else, Mr. Donahue and I have a previous engagement."

"Of course, ma'am." He was as polite as Marina had been. "When you see Mr. bin Haddad, please tell him to get in touch." He handed Marina his card and then walked to the door. Right before he left, he turned back to us. "Just one more thing."

Jeez, he must have been watching those old *Columbo* TV programs with Peter Falk while I'd tuned into *Law & Order*. With his wrinkled suit and disheveled appearance, he certainly looked the part. I almost expected him to put his hand to his head in a "my memory is faulty" gesture.

"Please don't leave Louisville without letting us know." Then he was gone.

A minute later, I had a brandy in my hand and held up the bottle, offering to pour one for Marina. She shook her head no. She was as angry as I'd ever seen her, lips in a tight, straight line.

"Damn bin Haddad for leaving us in this position. How did that detective know I was working for him? Who told him? The only other person who knew was Rashid, and Adnan spirited him off to Dubai. More importantly, why was he trying to connect us to Egger's death?"

I was wondering the same thing, although I didn't have much of a chance to get a word in while she was in rant mode. I waited until she paused for a breath, then slipped right in. While the detectives were interviewing us, I remembered something that could change everything.

"Marina. There's something else."

"What?" she barked, then whipped her head my way. I must have been frowning because she apologized. Sort of. "Okay. What is it?"

"When we got to Eggers's place, I was checking out the street." She nodded, and I continued. "There were only a few parked cars and a panel truck down at one end of the block." I paused to visualize what I'd seen. "When we left, I looked over the street again. The panel truck pulled out and made a U-turn."

"It might have belonged to someone in one of the other houses. Or it could have been delivering something."

"You're probably right, but…it had some sort of logo on front—grapes on a wine barrel. I know I've seen it somewhere before. I just can't recall where." The image was clear in my mind, yet the harder I tried to remember where I'd first seen it, the more elusive it became.

Marina's anger had dissipated and been replaced by concern. Her tone softened, as well. "You think this is important, don't you?" I nodded. "Take it slow, and it will come to you."

"There's something else." I closed my eyes, trying to conjure up what my brain had stored away. "When we were turning onto the road to the villa, it passed by. I noticed a guy in the passenger seat looking at us. He turned away when he saw me staring back. That can't be a coincidence, can it?"

Marina seemed to take my words in stride, her face calm. She rose and reached for the bottle of brandy I'd placed on the table. She poured herself a good amount. That's when I noticed her hands were shaking. For all her measured calmness, she was scared. She raised the glass to her lips and took a large gulp before speaking. "I think we just missed Tim's killers by a few minutes." She gazed down at the brandy, then up at me. "This time, we were lucky."

For how long, I wondered, now that they knew where we were.

Chapter Twenty-Nine

E ven the thought of what our fate would have been if we'd gotten to Eggers's apartment a few minutes earlier didn't stop Marina from wanting to wrap her hands around Adnan's neck and squeeze until he begged for mercy.

She tried reaching him on his cell. He was traveling on his private jet and she knew he could take calls if he was so inclined. Instead, he let her messages go to voice mail. Frustrated as well as angry, she summoned Josef once again and demanded the number for Adnan's home in Dubai—the private one she assumed to which only very few people were privy. He stammered it out from the doorway, still too shaken up to venture into Marina's poking range. Once the number was hers, she decided to wait to call him until the plane landed and he was comfortably ensconced at home.

With all that had gone on this morning, it was nearly lunchtime before Marina called the track and set up a time to view the security footage from the day before.

"I told them we'd be there by three. In the meantime, I'm going go through these employee records again." She clicked on a file from Winged Valor Farm and tapped her fingers on the table impatiently until it opened. "There's got to be something I'm missing, and I'm going to find it."

Discounting Tim Eggers, everyone else working at the farm had checked out, as did Adnan's employees at his stable in Dubai. Of course, there were his many other businesses, mostly in the Middle East and Europe. Anyone from one of those could be the extortionist. Marina was planning to tackle them next with help from Ana and Nikki. She believed inquiries into these employees would get a better response if they came via several dummy companies in Britain rather than the United States. Or at least she hoped so.

"What am I missing?" she said again, stretching back into the couch and rolling her head from side to side. I sat next to her and swung her around so her back was facing me. I began to rub her neck and shoulders.

She relaxed for a moment and let out a satisfied hum. "The last thing I want to do today is go back to the track. I hope looking at the security footage will jog your memory."

"I didn't see much. The guy came at me so fast, I barely had time to react." I rubbed my sore arm, which had started to ache the minute I thought about my attacker. Talk about mind over matter. "Did anyone find Merlin?" Marina turned her head to look at me and bit back a smile.

"You mean Fire Walker's pet, the cat?" Her smile got wider, and her green eyes twinkled.

"Don't scoff. If he hadn't howled, I'd never known anyone was there. He saved my life."

Marina rolled her eyes.

"Okay, think what you will. I can see that you need some alone time." I took my hands from her shoulders and swiped them together in an "I'm finished" gesture. "I'm skipping lunch and going out for a walk instead." I left her shaking her head at the computer, but I knew the disapproval was meant for me.

It was a beautiful day, and I was determined to enjoy at least part of it, this morning's brush with death and the phantom panel truck notwithstanding. Or maybe despite it. The air felt good. Cleaner than in London or New York. The lush and plentiful foliage and trees probably had a lot to do with that, and I breathed it in as I walked along the path to Devil Wind's barn.

As I approached, Mike was saddling up Devil Wind. "Hey," I called from the path, not wanting to get too close and spook the horse—since we know how much he liked me. "Taking him for a ride?"

"More like he's taking me," Mike replied as he mounted and tugged on the reins to turn the horse toward the track.

He waved as they took off in a nice, easy jog. I watched for a minute, then let my gaze roam over the barn and fields. It was well-kept and clean. Even the myriad of trees and shrubbery was perfectly manicured. The deep, green-leafed mulberry trees were full of those dark red berries that people always warned you not to eat. They made you vomit or—

I jumped back in shock as adrenaline pumped through my body. My brain caught up a moment later. Standing there with my mouth hanging open, I realized where I'd seen the logo on the van. *This can't be happening,* I thought as I raced back to the main house. *Not again.*

Chapter Thirty

I slowed down once the villa was in sight. I couldn't go running in there half-crazed with worry and rile up Marina any more than she already was. Could this be possible? I thought, as one of my blackjack player buddies used to say when he was sure he had a winning hand, but still got bested by the dealer.

I shook my head and then closed my eyes, trying to trick my mind into making the truck and its logo a figment of my imagination. No luck. No conjuring trick would change the picture. It still came up the same, like three cherries on the payout line of a slot machine instead of three pots of gold.

The grapes on a barrel were the logo of Mulberry Street Wine Distributors, a business owned by my favorite mob boss, Tomasso "Tommy B" Bonnannaio. I only found out he owned the distributorship by happenstance after our escapade in Monte Carlo was over. He'd sent me a case of wine as a "thank you" for getting his ten million back. Oh yeah, he also returned Marina, who he was holding as a hostage. I dropped the wine off at the docks. I figured the price of the wine came to roughly eight hundred forty thousand a bottle. I hoped one of the French sailors from the yachts found it and had an all-night party with his pals.

You can only imagine how Marina would react when I told her what I was beginning to believe—Tommy B was involved in Tim Eggers's death. I knew I had to come clean, but now wasn't the right moment. If she'd been angry earlier, she'd go ballistic over this. She'd sworn to shoot Tommy B on sight if he ever crossed her path again. And she wasn't kidding.

Eggers's murder was beginning to make sense. Sort of. If he was into Tommy B for a bundle and couldn't pay up, one way or another, he had to go. Tommy didn't like leaving loose ends lying around. Getting rid of Eggers would also serve as an example, in the great mob tradition, to anyone who thought they could screw him over. If that's what happened, it made sense for Tommy's boys to be here in Louisville with their wine delivery truck. Nobody would even notice another panel van driving around. Except lucky me.

I gulped back my anxiety, remembering how close Marina and I had been to becoming loose ends. But that was in the past. I didn't think Tommy B had what you might call introspective tendencies. He was more of a "take care of one problem and on to the next" kind of guy. No looking back.

Tommy B must have had a piece of the action here at the track or a way to rig the races. I wondered if Eggers was more than a deadbeat gambler. Maybe he worked for Tommy fixing races then got greedy and started skimming too much? Was there a connection between Adnan and the mob? These and about a hundred other questions were flying around in my poor, concussed head.

"For Christ's sake," as Tommy B would say.

I calmed myself down, took a deep breath, and ambled into the villa. "Hi." I greeted Marina brightly with a big smile. "Did you find anything new?" You're right; I was too chicken to tell her what I just discovered.

Marina gave me her own "What's going on here?" look before she replied. "I might be onto something, but it seems odd." She shook her head and then glanced at her watch. "I'm famished. Didn't stop to eat once I got started." She gestured to the notes she'd made, now surrounding her and her laptop. "How about grabbing lunch at the track before we review the security footage?"

"Fine, whenever you're ready." I was relieved she didn't follow up on quizzing me about my walk.

Marina shut down her laptop and placed it in her tote bag. "I'll just freshen up a bit before we leave. Won't be a minute."

"Take all the time you need," I tossed back at her and let out a long breath the minute she was out of the room. I was tempted to open the laptop and peek at what she found. She'd packed up her notes as well. Not much chance for snooping. So far, the clues in this case were few and far between. If Marina had a new lead, we might finally make some progress.

I had to fill her in on my thoughts about Tommy B at some point soon. I knew I'd made a connection. I just didn't know what it connected to yet.

Marina came back a few minutes later and grabbed her bag and the car keys, which she'd held onto from this morning. I put my hand out to take them from her, and she shook her head.

"No way, Nicky boy, not until I'm convinced you don't have a concussion."

I shrugged my shoulders and followed her to the car. It was going to be a bumpy ride, no matter how I looked at it.

Chapter Thirty-One

It was another busy day at Churchill Downs with a full card of afternoon races. The spring meet was galloping along, all leading up to its premier race, the Derby.

The track was in the process of being spiffed up for the big race. It had been open for almost one-hundred-and-fifty years and was undergoing a needed renovation. Workmen were scrambling all over, working on the new construction, an updated paddock that offered a better view of the twin spires, new seating, and video boards. Its architecture reminded me of an antebellum plantation, all white with lots of columns, balconies, and turrets. We still had our all-access Winged Valor Farm passes and headed for the Millionaires Row on the fourth floor of the clubhouse. Adnan's name had pull and we were escorted to a prime table next to the window looking out over the track. Marina toyed with her menu, her focus on something far away while I studied mine intently, as though it were a treasure map I had yet to decipher.

Our waiter returned, and we placed our orders, and sipped ice water silently, each lost in our thoughts.

"Nick."

"Marina."

We'd both started speaking at the same time. I'd finally gotten up my courage to tell her about Tommy B. I hesitated for a moment. "You go first." I lifted my hand in a magnanimous gesture and hoped she couldn't sense I was stalling.

"You know, I mentioned I might be on to something. Well, it's been nagging at me. I put aside the files I was looking through on Adnan's employees here in Kentucky and moved on to his international businesses. There was something I'd seen in one of the files that I stored away. At the time, it didn't have any significance. But when Adnan left with Rashid, it popped back into my mind. I finally found the file again today." I waited patiently for her to continue. "Rashid's father, Latif Khaleel, also works for Adnan. He's the chief of scientific research at ABH Technologies in Ajman, UAE."

"So that's how Rashid got the job." It was the same everywhere. Connections got you in.

"Probably," she replied, "but Adnan never mentioned it, or ABH Technologies. It was buried in one of the documents I'd looked through. Just a memo about a meeting with an executive from one of his other companies with Mr. Khaleel. This morning, when I went back over the files, I found it again and dug a little deeper. There was Latif's CV and a bio, probably for prospective clients, that mentioned his family: his wife, Janiki, his daughter, Samira, and his son, Rashid. All living in Ajman."

Marina slipped her laptop out of her bag and fired it up. "Look at this." She turned her screen toward me so that I could see the map she'd clicked on, and then zoomed in for a close-up of the area. "There's a lot of industry in Ajman. It's right on the sea, an easy run down the coast to Dubai. But ABH's complex is way out of town, in the suburb of Manama, all by itself, smack in the middle of an agricultural region. Odd, don't you think?"

"Maybe they're researching new farming techniques," I ventured.

Marina shook her head as she used Google Earth to zoom in for a close-up look. "I don't think so."

As she zoomed in, the picture on her computer became sharp and focused. There was no missing the barbed wire fence around the perimeter and the tower that was manned by an armed guard. The building itself was huge, several stories high, and built in a quad with an open space in the middle. The section that faced the driveway sported a glass front spanning three stories from ground to roof, giving the building an open, modern public face. The rest of the building was enclosed in light tiles with small windows at the top of each floor.

"The 'official' description of the company is very vague. 'Developing strategic solutions for high technology industries.' And the website is just a home page. If you want more information, you have to email the company. I'd bet there's spyware embedded on the site to capture the internet address of anyone who clicks on it."

"So, we're busted?" I asked Marina.

"Not as busted as Adnan." She picked up her cell and punched in the number Josef had given her. I could hear it ring and recognized Adnan's voice when he answered.

I left Marina quietly lambasting Adnan and wandered out to the deck attached to the restaurant. It was a good thing he couldn't see her. She'd turned her body away from the other tables, or she'd frighten away their diners. Her eyes were mere slits, her mouth tense, and her body language combative. Watching her lay into him was not a pretty sight. I knew if he didn't come clean about the extortionists and his real reason for hiring her firm, Marina would quit on the spot, and we'd be heading back to London.

Leaning on the railing facing the track, I reviewed my own situation. I sighed so loud, that one of the people standing a few feet away turned and stared. Probably thought I was a loser who contemplated jumping. He was half right.

Of course, I still needed to tell Marina about Mulberry Street Wine Distributors and its connection to Tommy B and, most likely, Tim Eggers's death. *Man up*, I told myself. *Don't be a wuss. Just do it.* I would, the moment she finished with Adnan. *Right. Sure.* None of these platitudes worked.

Something was bothering me about the whole situation. Something? That was a joke. More like everything. It's not that I couldn't see Tommy B maiming or killing a horse—I'm sure he'd seen *The Godfather* at least a thousand times, taking notes on the good parts. But I doubted that it would benefit him. He was into making money, as I learned all too well when I recouped his ten million from Herr Emminger and his Swiss bank. Adnan's horses—all of them—were potential money-makers. Tommy B wouldn't bite the hooves that fed him, so to speak. He'd most likely want to keep them alive and racing.

The more I thought about it, the more certain I was he'd made a deal with Eggers to ensure his chosen mounts won, or lost, their races. I wouldn't have put it past Eggers to renege on the deal and Tommy B to send his boys to take care of it.

I was sure there was a way I could find out without involving Marina at this point. Although, it hadn't come to me yet.

Marina was finished speaking with Adnan when I arrived back at our table. She'd kept her voice low, so I doubted anyone in the restaurant had heard the conversation. She was just about to tell me what had transpired when the waiter arrived with our lunch. He set our dishes in front of us, then lifted a hand toward the bar. "Compliments of the gentleman over there."

We both turned in the direction he was pointing and were rewarded with a big smile and wave from Neil Petrocelli, who was sauntering toward us. Just what I needed. All questions would have to wait until we could get rid of the pushy owner as fast as possible. At least that's what I thought.

Marina had other ideas. "Neil, how nice to see you. Please join us."

I know what you're thinking. But you're wrong. I wasn't jealous, not this time. Just anxious to hear Adnan's replies to Marina's questions, and Petrocelli was cramping my style.

I tucked into my BLT with gusto and kept throwing looks at Marina to do the same with her salad Nicoise. Finally, Petrocelli left after much fawning over Marina and a curt goodbye for me.

"So, what—"

Marina shook her head and cut me off. She looked at her watch and said, "I'll tell you later. We'd better get going, or we'll be late. We can't afford to waste any more time."

I know I must have looked puzzled, but she ignored it and just got up and got moving.

Chapter Thirty-Two

We hoofed it over to Churchill Downs security, which was housed in an inconspicuous building next to the grandstand entrance. Utilitarian and devoid of any decoration, the large room seemed out of place in the otherwise colorful setting. Two men with the word *Security* printed on their blue uniform shirts in big block letters were waiting for us. They led us to a bank of TV monitors that were recording the activity in various areas of the track.

They'd cued up the footage from yesterday afternoon. I spent the next hour and a half fast-forwarding through the footage, stopping it now and then for a closer look. I didn't recognize anyone coming or going from the stable area. It was a waste of time. But it did give me an idea about starting an investigation of my own regarding Tommy B.

Marina had been quiet the whole time, feigning interest in the video and nodding at me every once in a while. Whatever Adnan had told her must have been a whopper. I'd never seen her this intense, her beautiful face like a stone mask, her posture rigid.

We left the security office, and she made straight for the exit. Our ride was on a fast trot. Once outside the building, I took Marina's arm and tried to slow her down. "What the hell is going on?"

She shook her head, then leaned against me and whispered in my ear. "I promise I'll tell you everything once we're home." She glanced around the parking lot before she spoke again, even though there was no one nearby to overhear us. "We're leaving for Dubai the day after tomorrow. It's serious, Nick. More serious than you can believe. Adnan needs us." Again, I wondered what was happening. And I was tired of waiting to find out.

Marina got us home in record time; the lush fields and manicured landscape of Louisville whizzed by in a blur. Once we were settled on the couch in our guest quarters, Marina composed herself and began to relay her conversation with Adnan. As she filled me in, I became increasingly horrified. The upshot of it was worse than I could have ever imagined. Rashid's sister Samira was being held hostage by ISIS, the most prominent Islamic State terrorists, and the hundred million dollars was just the beginning of their demands.

"You will give us everything we ask for, or she will be executed. But not until she is raped, beaten, and paraded about as an infidel," was how they phrased it. "If you do not meet our demands, then we will come for the rest of you."

My stomach rolled over at the thought of any young woman being a captive of these monsters. History had proven that their demands were non-negotiable and often just a subterfuge. Ruthless and brutal, they would kill Samira as easily as I might flick away a fly.

"What exactly is it that they want?" I asked Marina.

"I don't know. Neither does Adnan. He says he begged them to tell him what else besides the money they expected from him, but they refused. They said he would receive their orders when they were ready."

"Jesus. Who are they? Did he have any idea where the extortionists were holding Samira? What did he think? Why involve Rashid's family?"

Marina had few answers to my questions. "All I know at the moment is that Rashid was the person who received their demands the first time."

"They must have found the family connection and learned Rashid was like a son to Adnan." The words left a bitter taste in my mouth. Of course, they'd use this knowledge to terrorize everyone involved. I thought back to the original extortion note and its lack of specifics.

Marina continued with her story. "Rashid was told to convey the information to Adnan, but he had no idea they had taken his sister."

"Did they really ask for a hundred million?"

Marina nodded. "It was their way of getting Adnan's attention." Her voice was strained, as if every word was an effort to articulate. "When he hired my firm, he believed it was about protecting his horses. Now he knows blinding Devil Spirit was meant to make sure he understands they're serious and are planning to do much more damage. We'll have to wrap things up here by tomorrow." Marina rose and started pacing. "I'll contact some people I know in New York to come out and watch over Devil Wind." She gazed off toward the stable. "He's the least of our worries now."

I wasn't so sure about that. Marina was so wrapped up in these new developments that she'd almost forgotten about Eggers's murder. But I hadn't. Tomorrow, I'd put my plan into effect. If I was wrong, I didn't have the faintest idea what I'd do next.

Chapter Thirty-Three

Marina spent most of the evening on the phone with her contact in New York, a private detective she worked with a few years ago on an international art theft case. The woman who ran McCorkendale Investigations could be in Louisville by tomorrow afternoon. She would be bringing several of her top operatives with her and would call in more if they were needed.

Marina planned to meet her at the airport and go over the pertinent details regarding Devil Wind. She'd start by taking the team to the track and then bring them here to the farm. The investigators would be staying in town but would split up to divide their time between the track and the farm.

Marina and McCorkendale decided it was best to position the team as extra security before the big race. It sounded plausible to me, and I figured Josef, Mike, Namal, and Rehan would accept it as a security measure Adnan had put in place to protect Devil Wind. What they would not learn is that the team was also going to keep an eye on each of them.

"All under control?" I asked Marina as she put down her cell.

"It better be." She rolled her neck from side to side, trying to ease the tension. "It's the best I could do under the circumstances, and McCorkendale and her people are top-notch." She rose from her chair and walked over to me. "Honestly, I think Devil Wind is going to be safe."

"You do?" I know I must have sounded a little incredulous.

Marina nodded. "Now that we know about Rashid's dad and his sister, I think they'll forget about Adnan's horses and concentrate on what they're really after." She sifted and made herself more comfortable. "Horrible as that is, now that he knows he's dealing with terrorists and the threat to Samira, he needs to prepare himself and decide if he'll meet their demands." She paused and looked around the room as if a solution to the problem would appear. "I don't think he'll let any harm come to Samira if he can prevent it. He and the Khaleel family are very close. He'll give them what they want." Her words rang with certainty.

"And he has no idea what that is?" I found that hard to believe. Adnan was a businessman through and through, and he must have some inkling of what these people were after besides the money.

"So he says. For now, I'm not going to push it. Once we're face to face, it will be a different story." Marina yawned, then pecked me on the cheek. "I'm going to bed. I have to be up early to prepare everything for McCorkendale's team." She rose and offered a hand for me to join her.

"I'll be with you in a little while."

After she left, I sat there thinking about everything that happened over this very, very long day. From finding Eggers's body to recognizing the van to my plan to find his killer, to Adnan's phone call, it felt like I was stranded in the middle of a grand casino with all the bells and whistles going off in a deafening roar and no way to shut them down or get out.

And speaking of my plan, such as it was, I still hadn't mentioned Tommy B and my suspicions to Marina. There was always tomorrow for that, although she'd be extremely busy, which, for me, was working out to be a good thing. I'd have a chance to get away and set things in motion. If anything went wrong, I'd be able to get out of Dodge and take off for Dubai. Let Tommy B try to reach me there.

With all these thoughts floating around in my head, I finally got up and turned off the light. It was time for sleep and hopefully good dreams instead of the usual nightmares.

Chapter Thirty-Four

Marina was gone when I woke up. For once, I'd slept soundly. The lorazepam I swallowed before I fell into bed probably helped. There was a note for me on the dresser. Marina would be out most of the day, probably for dinner, as well. She ended it with her usual, *Stay out of trouble, Nick.*

Why did she assume I'd get into trouble if she wasn't around? I hadn't mentioned one word of my plan to her, or anyone. I was on my own. A lone wolf prowling around and marking his territory. You get the idea.

After showering, I felt more human and picked up the house phone to order breakfast. Josef appeared with my eggs, bacon, and toast ten minutes later. He must have known Marina was not in the house as he wished me a good morning and set my plate down with a smile on his face, instead of grimacing and shaking with fear.

"Thank you, Josef," I said. "Have you seen Ms. DiPietro this morning?"

That was enough to get him stammering and leaving as quickly as possible. I couldn't help pulling his chain. I planned to make it up to him with a very generous tip when we departed tomorrow.

I hated to admit it, but Marina was right. I was going to miss being waited on hand and foot. *So, I told myself, better get back to the here and now,* and picked up the towel I dropped in my wake on the way to the living room.

I surfed the net while I ate and found what I was looking for. Then I called Adnan's assistant, Sabrina, in New York and asked for the address I needed. I was good to go.

I arrived at Julie Burnett's home a little after ten a.m. I'd learned from Marina's conversation with Mike that Julie worked at the Royal Palms Casino in Louisville as a poker dealer. A quick call to the casino gave me the information that she had the late shift, so I anticipated her being at home when I showed up on her doorstep.

A pretty blonde with a round face, blue eyes, rosebud lips, and a mug of coffee in her hand answered the door. "Can I help you?"

I smiled brightly and replied, "I sure hope so. I'm Nick Donahue, a friend of Adnan bin Haddad, your brother Mike's employer."

Adnan's name brought her up short, and she gave me a wary look, squinting at me with those big baby blues. I thought she might be ready to close the door in my face.

"Mike isn't in any trouble," I added quickly. "Really. Please, can I come in?"

She hesitated a moment, then stood back to let me in. We were in a narrow hallway with doors on either side. I could see straight back to the kitchen, where Julie led me. It was a bright, sunny room, filled with light from a wide window over the sink. She gestured to a chair at a round oak table and motioned that I should sit.

"How can I help you, Mr. Donahue?"

"It's Nick, please."

She nodded, and her blonde ponytail bobbed up and down with the movement. "Okay, Nick."

"It's about Tim Eggers," I said in a gentle voice, watching for her reaction.

She wrapped both hands around her mug as if trying to absorb its warmth before speaking. "I heard about his death." She gazed up at me with eyes filled with sadness. "Do you know what happened? My brother won't speak about it, and the police won't tell me anything."

I hadn't figured on the police questioning her. Of course, it made sense, given her relationship with Eggers, but I couldn't imagine them looking at her as a suspect, not after how he was killed. I might be wrong, but she didn't look like a woman who sneaked up behind a man and shot him in the back of the head.

Confusion mixed with frustration colored her voice. I took my time answering, considering how much to tell her about my suspicions. "I know this must be hard for you to lose someone you were close to."

She gave me a rueful smile, then glanced down at the table. "That was a while ago. We haven't been close for some time."

"I understand that you and Tim broke up because of his gambling."

She shook her head at me. "I can see you've been talking to my brother."

I hated to rat him out, but it was the best way to get to where I was going. I nodded, then continued. "Did any of his gambling buddies come here to see him?"

"If by buddies, you mean the loan sharks and lowlifes he owed money to, the answer is yes." She paused and lifted her cup toward me, "Would you like some?"

I nodded yes, and she picked up the pot next to the stove and filled a mug for me.

"Milk, sugar?" I shook my head, no, and she placed it on the table in front of me. "Tim nearly always met those people when I wasn't at home." She shrugged. "But once or twice, I came back before they were gone. Some 'buddies.'" She snickered. "They looked like a pair of brutes for hire." I knew she was right. They were. "After a while, the money he owed to them got to be too much, and his promises to me too empty." She lifted her hand to the sky. "He started doing other jobs for them to pay off his debt." She paused and took a sip of her coffee.

I imagined fixing races fell under this category. I waited for Julie to continue.

"He didn't understand he'd never be free of them. We fought about it, and I told him we were over, that he had to leave." She turned toward the window, and shadows from the sun played along the angles of her face.

"Do you think you'd recognize these men if you saw them again?" I tried to keep my tone light, but she started with fear nonetheless.

"Saw them again? Oh god, did they kill Tim?" She shot up from the table in a panic. Are they coming back?"

"No. No. Calm down, no one's coming here." At least, I hoped so. "I promise. Please sit down."

It took a few moments for me to get through. Finally, she nodded and slipped back into her chair, her eyes darting around like a cornered animal.

I didn't want to spook her more by telling her that I'd seen Eggers's body and most likely his killers. I decided to fudge the truth just a little. "I'm here with a friend, an investigator Mr. bin Haddad hired on another matter." She was listening intently, so I continued. "She was going through several files and came across these two men." I opened my cell and called up the pictures I'd gotten from the internet. I angled the phone so she could see each of them. "Did you ever see either of them here with Tim?"

Julie slid her finger over the images going back and forth between the two. Finally, she pointed to the photo of the second man and nodded. "Him. I've seen him. He's been here a few times."

That's exactly what I was afraid she'd say.

Chapter Thirty-Five

I left Julie, assuring her she wouldn't be getting any visits from the man in the photo. I believed I was telling the truth because by now, Biggie, born Johnny Malatesta, Tommy B's top henchman, was probably back in New York, playing cards and sipping espresso in the Mulberry Street social club where the crew hung out. After all, what else do you do after you knock off someone for the boss?

Biggie was a hard ass, a stone-cold assassin who'd just as soon shoot you as look at you. I met him when Tommy B and I had our first encounter in London regarding his missing ten million dollars and then again in Monte Carlo. I'd looked him up after they grabbed Marina, which made getting her back even more harrowing.

Julie didn't recognize the photo of the other man. I found it when I Googled Louisville, Kentucky, and Mafia hit men. The search returned several names and photos of "alleged" local mobsters. Good old Google, even they hedged their bets. After looking them over, I recognized Vince Cambiato, the owner of a private trash collection company, as the passenger in the van. These guys should learn to diversify, I thought. Being in the trash business was such a cliché.

Vince also allegedly ran the mob's Louisville operation. Yesterday he was a chauffeur, murder assistant, as well as head of the branch office. Who knew what else the future might hold for him?

As I drove back to the Winged Valor Farm, I digested the information I just acquired. I knew I was making light of these guys to stave off my fear. I hoped Biggie hadn't recognized me, but I wouldn't bet on it. He and Vince had followed us, so he must have been suspicious or just cautious. If they couldn't see who was in our car, we should be safe until we left for Dubai tomorrow. That was a big "If."

Putting all that aside, I still had a decision to make. If I went to the police now and relayed my suspicions, they'd want to know how I knew about the murder, why I was accusing Biggie and Vince, and what were Marina and I doing in Louisville in the first place. Unless we lied and used the cover story that we were here for the races, it would involve discussing Adnan's private and confidential affairs, which Marina would never do.

If I told Marina what I uncovered, she'd be angry with me, not only for keeping her in the dark about my chance encounters with Tommy B, but also, most likely, want to head back to New York to rip his heart out.

It was easy to see none of this was going to work. I needed to come up with a solution. And I needed it by tomorrow morning.

Chapter Thirty-Six

I packed my belongings as soon as I returned home from seeing Julie Burnett and spent the rest of the evening before Marina's return deciding what to do about my now-confirmed circumstances surrounding Eggers's death. It was a dammed if you do, dammed if you don't, choice.

If I contacted the police, I had no doubt Tommy B would hear about it—if he was operating in Louisville, you could be sure he had some of the police on his payroll. If I didn't, Eggers's murder might go unsolved. Much as I disliked him, he hadn't deserved to die, and I felt he should have some justice.

If I'd been in England, I would have called Nigel Phillips and dropped the matter into his capable hands. His ties to MI6 ensured it would be handled quickly and discretely. But Louisville was a far cry from London, and so were its criminals. I needed a different solution.

There was one person who might be able to help, that's if she didn't hang up the phone the minute she heard my voice. *Suck it up, Nick. Be a big boy and make the call.*

I took a deep breath and punched in the number I still knew by heart. She answered on the first ring, her voice crisp and down to business even at this hour.

"Ramos." She waited a beat, then spoke again. "Who's there?"

"Lydia," I said her name softly as if she might not realize it was me. No such luck.

"Nick."

Mine came back at me over the airwaves. A digitized version that rose at the end in a "well, well tone" and then silence. I could almost see her staring at the phone, weighing the benefits of clicking off without another word being spoken.

"Please don't hang up. This is important."

"As important as leaving New York without even a goodbye? Give me one good reason why I should talk to you after all this time."

"Tomasso 'Tommy B' Bonnannaio. Is that good enough?" I waited.

Finally, she spoke matter-of-factly. "Go ahead, I'm listening," she said, her voice giving away nothing.

Lydia Ramos was the SAC, the Special Agent in Charge, of the FBI's New York Field Office Criminal Investigative Division. We'd known each other long ago before I left the city to pursue a career in gambling. We had a little thing. Well, maybe more than a little. And Lydia was right. I skipped out without a backward glance.

Since then, Lydia worked her way up through the ranks to the position of SAC. She'd been after Tommy B even then, and I prayed that hadn't changed.

"What's he done to put him on your radar?" she asked.

I almost started with London, where I first met him and our subsequent dealings, but then I'd have to tell her about Marina. Instead, I told her as much of the present story as I could—that I was a guest of bin Haddad, a friend of my dad's, in Louisville for the races. I heard from people at the track that Tommy B was after one of bin Haddad's employees, Tim Eggers. Later, I learned that he had been murdered and how, and I put two and two together, which in my mind added up to a mob hit. I filled in a few more details, but nothing that put me at the scene. My words were deserting me, and it was time to get off the phone.

"That's it? You call me out of the blue for this? Forgot that I work in New York, not Louisville, Kentucky?" Her suspicion and disdain came through loud and clear. "Nothing else? Just hearsay?"

Time had not changed Lydia's attitude toward me. I thought my story was solid, but she obviously didn't share my feelings.

"What do you expect me to do? Run to Kentucky on your say so? Is there anyone who can verify your story, someone who's an actual witness?"

No one I could tell her about. "It seemed like something you'd be interested in knowing, especially if you were still chasing him down." I tried to sound humble and believable.

"Yeah, right." She paused for a moment, and I heard her clicking her pen open and closed, which was a nervous habit she had when I first knew her. "This better be on the up and up. I'm going to have to call the Louisville office and get them on board. That's if I decide to pursue this."

The pen had stopped clicking, and I heard only silence. I knew Lydia would go forward. How could she give up the chance to stick it to New York's *Capo di Tutti Capi*, the man she'd been chasing for ten years? The silence dragged on. She was making me wait for it.

"Where can I find you, Nick, if I need to get in touch?"

The way she said my name made me cringe, but the rest of her statement encouraged me; she had decided to investigate the murder. "I, um, I'm leaving Kentucky for Europe tomorrow. I'll call you in a day or so and see how it's going."

"Yeah, I'll be waiting," was her last remark before she clicked off.

True to her word, Marina didn't arrive back at the farm until the wee hours. She looked beat, which wasn't surprising. She and McCorkendale had been meeting with the team all day, preparing them for their duties. I knew they were going to reconnoiter every inch of the farm, noting vulnerable spots and working out their plan to protect Devil Wind. She kissed me on the top of my head and made straight for the bedroom.

"How'd it go?" I called after her.

"Fine. Good. I'll tell you all about it in the morning. 'Night."

I let out the breath I'd been holding since she returned. I was afraid she'd want to sit down and talk about the day. I didn't know if I could do it and not give anything away.

Now, I had two secrets I was keeping from her—my investigative work with Julie Burnett and my call to the FBI and Lydia Ramos. This was not a good idea on so many levels. Most of all, because she would no longer trust me, and rightly so.

I swore to myself I would come clean the minute the jet left the tarmac. At least about Tommy B and my visit to Julie. Marina believed we were leaving the murder to the local police to sort out. Discussing my conversation with Lydia was a whole other problem. She'd want to know how we knew each other and from where, what I'd told her, and why she believed me. Marina would figure it out as fast as a poker dealer shuffling the deck. Not only would she no longer trust me, but she'd probably leave me, as well.

Chapter Thirty-Seven

Dubai:

With seventeen hours of flight time ahead of us until we landed in Dubai, I was worried that Marina would grill me about what I'd done to keep busy and out of trouble yesterday. I shouldn't have bothered. As soon as the pilot turned off the seat belt sign, Marina was up and moving to bin Haddad's office area in the mid-section of the jet.

"I've got a lot to cover before we get there. Hope you don't mind, Nick." She gave me a sweet smile and fired up her laptop.

Mind? I hoped my internal hand pump and shouted Yes! didn't show on my face. Too much glee, and she'd be sure to notice.

"Sure. No worries." I kept my voice neutral. "I've got some reading to keep me entertained."

I held up a mystery novel I'd brought along from New York and hoped she didn't realize it was upside down. I quickly turned it right side up and opened to a random page. My eyes were glued to the text, but my mind was far away.

I figured I'd better check in with Lydia by the end of the day. I didn't want her calling me. Especially since I still hadn't figured out how to explain it all just yet.

I looked around. The jet seemed huge with just the two of us aboard. Huge but open, except for the bedroom and bath. I could always retreat to the bathroom with my cell. Since this was a private jet, there were no rules about using cells or the internet. I thought about Tommy B and instantly felt an enormous lump form in my stomach. Even at a distance, he was proving to be bad for my health.

I tried to banish visions of the punishment the mob doled out for being a rat—genitals cut off and stuffed down a throat came to mind—and focused instead on our task in Dubai. Now that it had become more than money that the extortionists-cum-terrorists wanted and a young woman's life hung in the balance, we had to get it right.

I looked up at Marina, who was shaking her head at the computer. I got up and walked over to her. "Can I help?" I hated to see her so troubled and uncertain, the total opposite of her normal positive, take-charge personality.

"Adnan has quite a few companies in the UAE." She pointed to a list she'd printed out. "I've been searching each one to see what, if any, interest they could be to ISIS. I keep coming back to ABH Technologies."

She held up her hand and started counting off the points on her fingers. "Rashid's father works there." She lifted her index finger in the air. "They took his sister Samira." She held up a second finger. "Now they want something in addition to the hundred million." Three fingers were in front of her face, and she shook her head. "We've got to find out what they're working on at ABH." To say she was frustrated would be putting it mildly.

"No luck reaching Adnan?" I asked. I'd seen her on the phone a few times.

"No. He's avoiding speaking to me." She checked her watch. "He sent me a text instead. He'll meet us at the airport, and we can talk on the way to the hotel." She slammed her hand on the polished teak wood desk, and I could see she was trying to rein in her emotions. "This is a waste of time. If we knew what those disgusting people wanted, we could work out how to catch them."

Catching them was an ambitious idea. It usually took unprecedented planning, the military, and a good dose of luck to catch an Islamic State terrorist. I bent down and kissed her on the top of her head. "You need to get some rest. Why don't you take a short break?" I pointed to the bedroom cabin behind us. "While I see if I can find out anything more about ABH Technologies." It could help, I thought, or at least it couldn't hurt. Was I ever wrong about that!

Marina went to lie down, and I promised to wake her in an hour. I plunked myself in front of her computer and cracked my knuckles like a concert pianist getting ready to play a difficult concerto. With hands hovering over the keyboard, I typed in ABH Technologies, Ajman, UAE, in the search bar. Just as it had before, a page came up with very little information. A generic message about developing technologies for industry. I could see trying to get into the site was not going to get me anywhere. I had to find another way in if I wanted information.

I spent the next five minutes staring out the window at the fluffy clouds below, and finally, a thought hit me.

I brought up Facebook and joined up with an alias I'd put together from a list of common Arabic names. Laiq Moghadam, a new member, lived in Dubai and worked in the technology sector. I typed Rashid Khaleel's name into the search bar. Once I found him, I clicked on Contact and Basic info and noted the list of his friends that were displayed. I checked each of their profiles, which told me where they lived and where they worked. Two men listed ABH as their place of employment. I "friended" these two and messaged them that I was thinking about accepting a position at ABH. I'd heard from Rashid that it was a great place to work. I told them I'd appreciate their input. Then I waited.

It didn't take long. The number 1 popped up next to the message icon, which meant I had one new message. One of the men, Hassan Qureshi, a production technician at the company, had accepted my friend request and messaged me about five minutes later.

> *Hi, Laiq.*
>
> *Welcome. You are going to enjoy working at ABH. There are many interesting projects going on. Our newest project would make the Klingons proud, but it is very secret, and I cannot say more. Perhaps you will be on that team. Make sure you introduce yourself when you start.*

Sure, I will. That's if you're not sacked for discussing proprietary information. I shook my head. That was the trouble with social media. Everyone wanted to shout about what they were doing, where they were going, and who they were screwing without realizing what the consequences could be. I couldn't believe how easy it had been. I found this guy within minutes and here he was telling all.

He assumed I had a job offer and had already accepted it. Not too smart on his part.

But Klingons? He was probably a twenty-five-year-old who must have watched *Star Trek* reruns. How did it relate to the project he mentioned? I thought about the *Starship Enterprise* and its battles with the Klingons.

Suddenly, I got it. I ran to the rear cabin and woke up Marina. "I know what they want, and it's worse than we imagined."

Chapter Thirty-Eight

As I sat on the bed to explain my theory, all the elation at my discovery drained from my body. It was a disaster. This was science fantasy come to life in the most brutal way. It was an Islamic State group that was after something far more important to them than money. A weapon that would give them an advantage in every attack and suicide mission they planned.

They were terrorists of the worst kind who would do anything to bring the world to its knees. ISIS, brought up on al-Qaeda's side, had developed into a lethal militant force of its own. Unbending in their beliefs and as brutal with their enemies as humanly possible. Although the word human hardly applied to these fanatics who listed crucifixion along with beheadings, torture, and mass murder among its ways of dealing with those whom they deemed heretics.

Killing was nothing to them. They wanted to own the world and set civilization back a few hundred years or so.

Unwittingly, Adnan had conjured up exactly what they needed. He'd created the perfect secret weapon for a twenty-first-century terrorist army, a weapon that would allow them to murder at will without being seen.

ABH Technologies had designed a cloaking device that turned science fiction into a mind-boggling reality.

"Cloaking device?" Marina was wide awake and shaking her head at me. "You mean like in *Star Trek*? How is that possible?"

Even Marina, who grew up in Italy, knew all about the iconic program, including the cloaking device of the Klingons, the Federation's worst enemy.

"I read somewhere scientists were working on developing one." I shrugged at the mere idea of it. "I think one of the universities succeeded on a small scale. Something to do with bending light rays to cover an object so you can't see what it is." I raised my eyebrows. "That's about all I know. Adnan will have to explain it more fully."

"Cloaking a small object is one thing, but a group of people? This device would have to be incredibly powerful." Marina was processing what I just told her. "Do you think it will work?"

"I don't know. The best we can hope for is that we never find out."

Chapter Thirty-Nine

The mood on the plane had become somber. Marina berated herself for not being able to figure out the Latif connection sooner, which might have stopped IS from kidnapping Samira.

While she didn't come out and say it, I knew she believed that the terrorists would show no mercy and kill the young woman, even if Adnan gave them what they wanted. That was their MO, and I couldn't imagine they'd change it. They never had before. Led by Abu Bakr al-BaghDadi, caliph of the extremist group ISIS or the Islamic State of Iraq and Syria, claimed religious, political, and military rule over all Muslims worldwide. Their mandate was unflinching: death to all non-conformists to the strictest interpretation of Muslim law. Anyone who's picked up a newspaper, booted up a computer, or turned on a TV knows how they operated. No one was safe, and nothing was sacred from their Jihad and extremist ideology. And there were even worse splinter groups.

All this was going through my mind as I tried to think of some way to stop them from getting their hands on the cloaking device.

Determined to make use of the time before we landed in Dubai, we decided to start with internet searches of both active ISIS groups in and around the UAE and the science behind cloaking devices.

Marina took ISIS and surfed the net for the latest information while I called up scientific sites on my phone. I can't say that I understood all that I read about cloaking. It had to do with cadmium telluride, bending visible light, and negative reflection, none of which penetrated my gambler's brain.

I was tempted to log on to Facebook again and message my new pal,

Hassan. I thought it over and decided it was too risky. If I asked too many questions, he might become suspicious and backpedal on what he'd already mentioned. Or worse, have a crisis of conscience and report it to one of his superiors. I'd rather leave that part to Adnan once we spoke with him about how unmindful of security procedures some of his employees seemed to be.

Engrossed as we both were in our information searches, I was mildly surprised when our stewardess told us we were landing in half an hour.

"Any progress?" I asked Marina, reaching up and stretching the kinks out of my back.

She looked up and nodded. "There's quite a bit of information on ISIS splinter groups. Much of it is put out by them and is just propaganda used to glorify themselves and recruit new members. I've gone through the jihadist mandates of each. Based on what they 'believe—'" She made air quotes with her hands. "—it appears to be the radical splinter group Salafi we're after. They have quite a history as the bloodiest and deadliest of all the ISIS groups. They think the Syrian and Iraqi factions are too lenient, that anyone who doesn't agree with them is a heretic deserving death. They've raided and decimated other splinter groups for not adhering to Allah's commands." A dark shadow passed over her eyes as she paused for a moment. "Their strict, unbending approach to Islam is their excuse for jihad against their enemies. And there's not one case where they released their captives." She was thinking about Samira and the fate that awaited her unless we intervened. "How about you?" She gestured toward the notes I was making.

"All I can tell you is that cloaking is a real scientific breakthrough, and so far, I haven't come across any information on anyone using it on a large scale or found any data on how to disable it."

Marina picked up her phone and started punching in numbers.

"Who are you calling?"

"Ana and Nikki. I want Ana on the next plane here to work with me on gathering everything and anything that can help us."

"Really?" I was surprised that Marina wanted either woman in Dubai. "Can't they do that from London?"

Marina shook her head slowly. "Nikki can be the point person at home. I need Ana here," her eyes regained some of their sparkle, "for what I have in mind."

I didn't like the sound of that, and a chill ran down my spine. Marina had come up with a plan, but she wasn't sharing. I looked at her face but couldn't read her expression. Great, I thought. Another gorgeous female marching around in a place where women, who were covered head to toe, would be shooting her daggers, and men who forgot they were Muslim, eyeing her up and down. I could hardly wait to see how that turned out.

Chapter Forty

True to his word, Adnan met us at the private plane area of Dubai International Airport. He was standing on the tarmac waiting for us along with what looked like a small caravan of men wearing traditional Arab headdresses and black robes. Except, they were all standing in front of armor-plated Mercedes instead of camels. No doubt, they had guns hidden under their robes. I wondered if they would be able to get to them fast enough if the occasion arose.

I put these thoughts aside as Adnan greeted Marina and me tersely and nodded toward the Merc in the middle of the pack where a chauffeur was stationed by the open door. The robed men, whom I assumed were bodyguards, slid into the other vehicles and waited for the signal to leave.

After we took our seats, two more men slipped out of the small terminal and entered the car. One of them caught my attention right away.

Remember the villain in those old Saturday afternoon damsels in distress black and white movies? The one spurned by the heroine who, when she can't pay the rent for the farm, ties her to the railroad track? That was him. Dark hair, expressionless coal-black eyes, and a mustache. Minus the top hat and the rope. Somehow, I thought his means of getting what he wanted involved torture of a different nature. I disliked and distrusted him immediately.

The other gentleman didn't strike me as much of anything. Younger than his cohort, he seemed shy and somehow self-effacing with downcast eyes. He also had dark, traditional Arab looks but a baby face set off by a mouth that was softer and almost feminine with full lips that he licked several times.

He waited for the first man to take the lead and stood there waiting patiently. He knew he was being overshadowed and seemed smart enough not to push things.

Of course, I kept all this to myself as Adnan made the introductions. My new nemesis was Mansur El-Hashem, Director of Security for all of Adnan's holdings in the UAE. So where had he been, I wondered, when Devil Spirit was maimed and tortured?

The other man, Malik Alfarsi, was introduced as the Manager of the Production Technicians and, as I learned later, my pal Hassan Qureshi's direct supervisor.

"Pleased to meet you," I said and offered my hand to both in turn. Marina merely smiled at them and offered our host a stinging look.

"Adnan, we need to talk." She directed her words to him. "In private."

Adnan caught her drift. He couldn't miss it. He looked at his watch. "We will be at the hotel in just a few minutes then we will sit down and discuss all that has happened." He made sure Marina saw his glance toward the chauffeur.

"Fine."

Any man who's heard that one-word response uttered by a woman knows it's anything but. Marina sat back and glared at Adnan. No one spoke until we pulled in front of the Burj Al Nomad, a hotel situated on its own island in the Arabian Gulf. One glimpse of this hotel, built like a soaring sail afloat on crystal blue waters, and even Marina forgot to be angry as her eyes grew wide in appreciation.

Adnan noticed and took full advantage of the moment. He explained the Burj Al Nomad was the most luxurious and elegant hotel in the world. And, of course, he was one of the principal investors. "We will be staying here rather than at my home. Rashid and his family are here already. I believe it will be safer for everyone." He looked over toward El-Hashem, who nodded in agreement.

Marina shrugged. I knew she was anxious to relay our latest information and find out what, if anything, he'd heard from the terrorists. I couldn't understand why Adnan was stalling. I hoped he'd open up as soon as we met with Rashid and his father.

Once we were in the hotel, it was hard to know what to look at first. The lobby was more spectacular than any I'd ever seen, filled with colorful orange and azure marble panels surrounding a raised glass and wood reception area. "It's good to be king," as the saying goes, and this hotel proved it. I'd double down on the bet that some royal money was behind it, as well as Adnan's.

I started wandering off toward the lounge that offered a view of the sea from twenty-foot floor-to-ceiling windows. Marina gave me a nasty look as she tugged on my sleeve and steered me in the direction of the elevator.

We were all staying on the top floor in two-bedroom duplex suites that were fit for a king. I'd stayed in luxury hotels all around the world, but not one came close. Of course, there was one thing missing from this one as far as I was concerned: a casino. There was no gambling at all in the UAE. *Guess you can't have everything.* I'd just have to keep my focus on thwarting the terrorists.

While the staff was bringing in our luggage, I tried not to stare too hard at the surroundings. The suite was decorated in deep reds and golds with a sunken living room, oversized furnishings, and a marble bathroom the size of our London apartment, with a round Jacuzzi tub at its center. It made the twenty-three-hundred-dollar-a-night price tag posted on the back of the door seem almost reasonable. I smiled to myself.

I could hear my mother whispering in Dad's ear: "Who would ever pay that much money for a hotel room?"

When I got back to New York, I'd describe his client's investment property to Dad while Mom was out of earshot.

Marina's voice brought me back to reality. "Let's go, Nick. We're meeting with Adnan and Rashid in two minutes."

I had no doubt Mansur El-Hashem and Malik Alfarsi would be joining us.

Chapter Forty-One

Rashid, his father Latif, Mansur, Malik, and Adnan were seated in the living room of his suite when Marina and I arrived. The bodyguards, who had just minutes ago, escorted us to our suite, stopped us and patted us down before allowing us to enter. The phrase "locking the barn door after the horse has escaped" came to mind.

I won't bore you with the details, but this suite was even more opulent than the one Marina and I were sharing. It was unfortunate to come together in such a beautiful place to discuss a terrible tragedy.

We all took our seats around a low coffee table, and Adnan introduced us to Latif, who, I could see immediately, was barely holding it together. His sunken eyes and ashen complexion were a testament to how little sleep and how much worry he must have endured over the last few days. A bright man who'd seen first-hand the Jihadist attacks of terrorist organizations, he must realize the chances of getting Samira back alive were slim. And how easy it would be for the terrorists to find and kill the rest of his family if they decided to come after them.

The wait staff had brought in food for us: a lunch of hot and cold traditional Arab mezze—hummus, babaganouj, spinach fatayer, lamb kebbah, cheese rakakat, olives, pita bread, and grape leaves. It was set on a buffet at one end of the room, but no one made a move toward it. There was also a bar with open bottles of wine and Champagne chilling in silver buckets. Most Muslims don't drink, but I've heard those who choose to imbibe while in this city are fond of the saying, "Allah doesn't see Dubai," excusing any bad behavior. I figured they had appropriated that idea from "What Happens in

Vegas, Stays in Vegas." Or maybe it was the other way around.

While I stared at the food longingly, Marina got right down to business. "We already know ISIS is responsible for kidnapping Samira and for threatening your horses. All the information I found points to the Salafi splinter group, which is responsible for this. They preach global Jihad. The holiest of holy wars. With them, there's no room for compromise. One either must commit entirely to their tenets or die as a heretic." She waited for a response from Adnan.

He nodded before answering. "When they took Samira, they left this behind in her room." It was a piece of paper folded into a small square. Adnan handed it to Marina, who opened it and read it aloud: *'If you want her back, you will give us what we ask for.'*

It was written in English. A message for us, as well as Adnan, I suspected. But why?

Adnan locked eyes with Marina. "I know this group. They are truly vicious and won't stop—" He was going to say more but thought better of it as he cast his eyes toward Latif with an expression of sympathy and sorrow. The strong, confident businessman I'd met in New York and had gotten to know in Kentucky looked ravished and diminished by these circumstances. He wasn't a young man, and it seemed he'd aged at least another twenty years overnight.

"They're assuming you know what they want. And it isn't the hundred million dollars." I wondered about that, too. It was pocket change for Adnan, given his vast fortune.

"What is it, Adnan? Marina asked with a steeliness in her voice I hadn't heard before. "Isn't it about time you tell us?" She gestured to everyone present.

Adnan nodded and spoke slowly. "Project Blackout, the cloaking device we have developed at ABH, an enormous scientific breakthrough."

Now, it was Latif's turn to look confused. "The cloaking device?" He looked at Adnan with horror. "That's what they want?" His face turned red, and I was afraid he was having a stroke. "It is our most top-secret project. Very few people even know of its existence, and no one outside of this room or my team has even heard of it." His panic was rising as he turned to El-Hashem and raised his hands in a 'how could this be' gesture.

That wasn't true since we were all here discussing it.

Marina was testing Adnan's honesty to see if he'd come clean and make sure he wasn't somehow connected to this heinous plot. A softening in her eyes told me she was satisfied.

Adnan rose and went to Latif. "Please, remain calm, my friend. All is not lost. Not yet." He'd turned and caught Marina's eye as he reassured his friend. "You knew about the cloaking device. Explain how you came to find out this information."

Marina began again. "I don't know how the Salafi extremists found out about Project Blackout, but it wasn't too difficult for Nick to get close to one of your employees and figure out their objective."

That got everyone's attention, especially the chief of security, who snapped his head around, startled at Marina's revelation.

She proceeded to explain how I'd gone onto Facebook and "friended" two of Rashid's pals who worked at ABH. From there, she told them about the "clue" Hassan Qureshi had let slip. With reference to the Klingons, it hadn't been hard to work out. It was a cloaking device they were building. Combined with the maiming of Devil Spirit and the kidnapping of Samira, it made sense that ISIS was involved. Our research led to the Salafi splinter group, who were extremely active in the area, and their hardline militant practices. What a coup it would be for them to acquire the cloaking device. Every other Islamic State group would be at their mercy, of which they showed no signs.

While Marina had explained our thinking, I was watching Mansur. I had distrusted him at first sight and was curious to see how he'd react. He was unable to mask his anger when Marina first mentioned the cloaking device. He was startled, surprised even, then turned and stared at Malik with murderous venom. I knew how it felt to face someone looking at you like they wanted to kill you from my first encounter with Tommy B. Mansur's skin turned red under his deep tan, and I could almost hear the blood pounding in his ears. He was truly pissed.

Malik's face morphed into a mask of pure panic. It was gone nearly as quickly as it had come. But Mansur had caught the look, and so had I. What was that all about? I wondered and turned away before either man could notice my all-out scrutiny.

Mansur regained his control as he quickly rose from his seat. He pivoted and moved close to Malik, his mouth just inches from the other man's ear. "Qureshi is your responsibility. Now, I—we—" He realized where he was and swept his arm around to encompass the room. "—are left to deal with your incompetence." His words seem to flash over Malik like an out-of-control firestorm. Then he stared straight at Rashid. "And you." He pointed his finger at the young man. "You are equally responsible."

Adnan snapped at him. "Mansur, enough. I'm sure they understand."

Mansur seemed to struggle into compliance and backed off at Adnan's implied command. He straightened up, started pacing, and pulled out his cell. His words were a harsh and gruff jumble of Arabic. And while I couldn't understand them, there was no doubt of their meaning. He kept cutting his eyes from Malik to Rashid, both of whom were quaking in their seats.

I wondered if his anger was real or merely put on to impress Adnan. I was positive he was calling ABH to have Qureshi brought to the security office and kept there until he arrived to question him. Qureshi was not on the cloaking device development team, and now we all had a good idea where he'd heard about it. One look at Rashid's face told me we were correct.

Adnan said something else in Arabic to his chief of security, and he finally calmed down. He nodded to all of us, summoned Malik with a crook of his finger, and nodded goodbye, his eyes boring into Rashid's as he left.

After Mansur's accusations, Rashid sank lower into his seat and bent over, holding his head in his trembling hands. When he looked up, his face was a mask of horror. "It is my fault that Samira was taken." He shook his head from side to side. "If it wasn't for me, they would never have found out about what was going on at ABH."

Marina rose, went over to the young man, and leaned down in front of him. "No, it's not your fault. I'm almost certain they found out about the device a while ago before you joked about it with your friend. I don't think he meant to give away any company secrets. He was just…" She paused, searching for the right phrase. "…being a wise guy. He probably didn't think Nick's alter ego would understand."

I had to agree with her and said so. "It was just a lame remark by a twenty-something-year-old who wanted to seem in the know." Now, he would, unfortunately, suffer the consequences of his actions.

Marina continued. "These people knew of your father's position at the plant and that you were also working with Adnan and his horses. That's why they sent the ransom note and photo of Devil Spirit to you in the first place."

She took a deep breath and continued. "They targeted you because of your family's relationship with Adnan. And they had help figuring it out."

"Help?" Adnan asked. "Not the young man on Facebook?"

"No, not him. I'm sure that he's bright and extremely capable. But this kind of operation seems well above his abilities. Someone else brought the cloaking device information to the Salafi extremists." Marina seemed certain. "Someone they would listen to."

"A spy in my lab?"

She just nodded her head. It was all the answer he needed.

As Marina and Adnan spoke, I once again thought of my father's words about this being a high-level operation with meticulous planning. Someone was pulling the strings at the Salafi camp and setting it all into motion. If we could find out who and how he fit in, we just might be able to save Samira.

I left Marina with the three men. Based on what she believed, it had to be someone well-placed at ABH. She was questioning Latif about Malik and the other employees at the plant on his team. I made an excuse about needing something from our suite, and she was too involved in her conversation to object to my leaving.

I walked past the security team outside Adnan's door and smiled at them, trying for a casual insouciance. All I got in return was a stony glare.

I was starving and decided to eat outside at one of the terrace restaurants. The hotel, which stood alone on its own island, had several quiet outdoor spots. It was just what I needed for my call to Lydia.

I had turned my cell off once I'd finished with Facebook. I didn't want to take the chance of getting a call Marina would wonder about.

I sat down, ordered a beer and a falafel sandwich, then punched in Lydia's number. She immediately picked up her caller ID, giving up my identity.

"Nick." There it was again. That snide-sounding pronunciation of my name. "I was wondering if you'd call. Thought I might have to track you down."

I gulped and hoped she hadn't heard it. Her hearing was exceptional, and she could pick up a whisper from a mile away. If she wanted to find me, all she had to do was get one of her tech people to home in on my cell's GPS.

"Well, here I am," I replied evenly. "Any news on the murder?"

"You may be onto something. The SAC in Louisville has been looking into Vince Cambiato, who we know is Tommy B's bag man in Louisville. The SAC confirmed that Johnny 'Biggie' Malatesta was in town the day of the murder." She paused. "It's sketchy, but I convinced the Louisville office to pursue it, and we'll coordinate and add what we can from here." Her voice softened as she continued. "You know, Nick, if you could give us a little more to go on that ties into Tommy B, we finally might be able to get the bastard off the street."

She waited for me to respond. "I told you everything I know. There's nothing else. Honest, Lyd." I spoke over the dryness in my mouth that suddenly made it hard to articulate. ISIS and Tommy B. All at the same time. Somewhere, my life had taken a wrong turn.

"You're lying to me, Nick." A little bit of the sweetness slipped from her voice. "And I'm going to find out why."

"Lydia, I—" She was gone before I finished my sentence.

I stared out at the gulf, feeling sorry for myself. *Screw me.* I somehow never learned to leave well enough alone. Then I thought about Samira in the hands of those monsters. Would we be able to get her back? It was doubtful. And it made my problems seem like a day at the races.

Chapter Forty-Two

Marina's meeting with Adnan and the Khaleels lasted the rest of the afternoon. She came into the suite just as I was pouring a large shot of Johnny Walker Black into a cut crystal highball glass. At the Burj al Nomad, they made sure guests wanted for nothing, from spectacular views to top-shelf liquor.

I held the glass up toward Marina. "Want one?"

She nodded yes, and I handed it to her, then poured another for myself. I sat down on one of the couches facing the view of the gulf and patted my hand on the seat for her to come to sit next to me.

When she did, I slipped my arm around her shoulders and drew her closer. Over the last few days, I'd missed the intimacy we had before the case. It was nice to have a quiet moment, but it was only a moment.

Marina sighed, sat up, and turned toward me. "Where did you disappear to this afternoon?"

I stiffened for a moment, sure that she'd found out about my call to Lydia, then realized it was just an idle question.

"Nowhere special. I went out to the terrace and had some lunch, then walked around the property." I took a sip of my Scotch and savored its smoky taste as it slid down my throat. "You wouldn't notice it if you weren't looking, but the hotel is like an armed fortress."

"I hadn't noticed." That was unlike Marina, who noticed everything. But she hadn't been outside at all today and hadn't seen all the big bruiser types watching and wandering around whispering into their collars.

"They're walking around in pairs." I nodded. "It's not surprising. One of the waiters told me that some of the Saudi royal family stay here on occasion. They like to bring their personal cook with them." I smiled. "Afraid of someone poisoning the hummus, I guess."

"I guess." Marina tried a smile, but it didn't reach her eyes.

"Did you make any progress on working out who the spy could be?"

"Very little. Adnan was reluctant to even entertain the idea that someone he trusted could betray him in this way." She rolled her eyes. "And Rashid kept blaming himself while Latif just paced up and down." She took a last sip of her drink and handed the glass to me.

I got up and went to the sideboard to pour us both another. "Any word from the charming Mansur El-Hashem?"

Marina turned her body and looked at me over the back of the couch. "You didn't like him from the first, did you?"

"Was it that obvious?" I walked back with our drinks.

"To me." She tilted her head and studied my face. "Tell me why."

I told her about the image of the old movie villains that came to mind the minute I saw him, but she didn't know what I was talking about. Guess those movies hadn't played in Italy. I tried again. "There is something about him. Something sinister coming off him. It got me right in the gut. Plus, I think he knows more than he's letting on."

"I agree with you. If he doesn't know something for sure, he has a suspicion." She swirled the Scotch around in her glass. "We'll have to work with him. For now, at least.

"What about the kid, Malik?" I asked. "He looked like he was going to wet himself." I smiled. "I might, too, if I knew Mansur was about to kick my ass up and down the coast."

"Adnan didn't know very much about him, other than he'd been at ABH for five years and had a good record. He passed the security vetting process when he started and again when he was assigned to the cloaking team."

"Was Mansur in charge of vetting him?" I asked.

Marina nodded. "Yes, and he passed all the security checks, including a lie detector test when he was promoted to team manager."

"No trouble at work or home?"

"We're looking into that right now. Adnan called his HR department and asked to have Alfarsi's file waiting for him in the morning." She rose and walked to the window with the setting sun casting a golden glow on the water. "We'll start with that and then move on to his personal life. When Latif and Rashid left to go to Janiki, I told Adnan to request their and Mansur's most recent security reviews and lie detector data."

I was surprised by this. "Did he agree?"

"Reluctantly. I told him it was time he let me do my job. If not, I'd be leaving."

"Okay. But you can't think Rashid or Latif had anything to do with Samira's disappearance." I'd never seen two people look so desperate as they did today. Even Mansur had been surprised by Marina's revelation.

"Why didn't you have their files sent to you here? Adnan won't know what to look for."

I moved next to her at the window, and she looked at my reflection as she spoke with a touch of mischief in her voice. "I won't be the one doing the looking."

Before I could respond, the doorbell to the suite rang. "I'll get it. You enjoy the sunset. You earned it today." It rang again, one long, long peal. "I'm coming," I shouted over the clang.

I opened the door, and the rebuke I was ready to offer died on my lips. A young woman covered in an *abaya* with a *hejab* draped around her head, one end held over her face, flew into my arms, and hugged me like crazy.

"What—who are—" I was taken aback until she revealed her face and announced with a grin. "Aren't you glad to see me, Nick?"

I mumbled yes as Ana squashed me in a big bear hug. I looked up at the bellman waiting in the hall with her bags, and all I could do was shrug.

Chapter Forty-Three

I directed the bellman to put Ana's luggage in the suite's second bedroom while she went over to greet Marina.

Ana was just removing the *hejab*, her head scarf, when I walked over to where they were sitting. "Whose idea was this?" I indicated the flowing black outfit and the *abaya* that covered her body.

"Mine," Marina answered. "I asked Ana to wear this on the plane to see if she would look like she fit in here."

"And?"

"It was great. No one gave me a second look. Quite nice, for a change."

Only if you weren't forced to wear one. I gave her a non-committal "hmmm."

"Ana is going undercover at ABH as a temporary assistant to Adnan starting tomorrow. The women who work at the plant dress in traditional style."

I could see why she'd asked Ana to fill this role. With her dark hair, Mediterranean complexion, and British accent, she fit in, more or less. I rolled my eyes. "Are you sure about this? What about her not speaking Arabic?" It was the UAE's official language.

"As you may have noticed, everyone speaks English," Marina countered.

"Yes, because they know we're foreign and don't speak Arabic." I was beginning to get exasperated with Marina and what I now realized was her grand plan.

She continued as if I hadn't interrupted. "So there won't be a problem. Adnan is informing his secretary that Ana, or Anbar, is a distant cousin from London whose parents sent her here to get her away from unsavory elements at home.

"Like Nicolo," Ana piped up.

Marina ignored her and continued. "He'll say he's taking her under his wing and getting her settled. He'll explain that she'll be helping out for a few days on a special project, and he will be giving her paperwork to review and file. She will be reporting directly to him."

"What about El-Hashem? Will Adnan let him know 'Anbar' is one of us?"

Marina shook her head. "There are very few women working at ABH, and HR usually handles their employment process. None of them work in or access the actual labs and production areas or have access to sensitive material, so their security clearance is very low level, which I told him he should review." She shook her head in exasperation. "Our spy could be anyone."

I wondered how ape-shit Mansur would go if he found out about Marina's plan or about her requesting his personnel files. That thought brought a smile to my face. It didn't last long as I imagined what the terrorists would do if they got their hands on another young woman.

"What is it, Nick?" Marina had picked up on my bad vibes.

"Jeez, Marina. I hope you know what you're doing." The words had come out harsher than I meant them. Both women frowned at me. "There's already one young woman whose life is in danger, and you…" The rest of my thoughts lay between us unspoken. I shook my head and turned on my heel. "I'm going for a walk before dinner," I said and marched out the door.

This was a bad idea. I felt it in my bones. When Marina announced Ana was joining us in Dubai, I thought all I had to worry about was Ana being stared at, not being taken hostage by ISIS.

I walked along the path to the shore. Night had fallen, and it was much cooler. That's how it was in the desert, I thought. Broiling hot during the day and freezing at night. Just like my feelings about this case. One minute, all I could think about was getting Samira back, the next packing up, grabbing Marina, and getting out of here. Who was I kidding? Marina wasn't going anywhere until this was over, and neither was I.

I took the path back to the hotel and went up to the suite. Marina had left a note for me. She and Ana were meeting Adnan for dinner in his suite so he could greet his new assistant. I should join them. She signed it with a lipstick kiss.

I went into the enormous bathroom and splashed some water on my face. Then I changed into a clean shirt, slipped on a sports jacket, and left for dinner.

Chapter Forty-Four

The next morning, Marina was up and working when I lurched my way out of bed. When I walked into the living room, she had a steaming cup of coffee and a buttery croissant waiting for me.

The croissant should have been the tip-off that something was afoot. But I was still groggy from the very good wine I had imbibed at dinner last night, so my suspicions didn't register until it was too late.

"Hey," she reached up and kissed me, then handed me my breakfast. "Sleep well?"

"Hmmm," I replied, around a mouth full of coffee. "Where's Ana?" I had expected to see her this morning.

"Already left for work. ABH is about half an hour from here, and they start early. Since Adnan will put it out that she's a distant cousin, he felt she could drive there with him without it appearing suspicious."

"He's the boss. Who's going to question him?"

"Yes, but it should feel as real as possible. He'll tell his secretary it's only for a few days and she doesn't need to put in any paperwork for benefits or salary, whatever their equivalent is to keeping her off the books. The plan is for him to slip her the personnel files I want to see and for her to note anything out of place.

"Why can't she, or you, do that from here on the computer?" I was still worried about Ana being alone at ABH.

"There's too much security for me to access their computers without Adnan's password. Since he never looks at employee files, it might raise a red flag, especially if someone is watching for anything out of the ordinary or has planted any kind of spyware on his computer. We don't want to tip our hand."

"By someone, I take it you mean the mole?"

Marina nodded. "Also, the background reports on employees with a high-security clearance are kept in a paper file. It's a safeguard, so only those who need to, see that information. You can't hack your way into a paper file. Only their most basic information is stored on the computer. Adnan felt it would be safer to examine the paper files at the lab, less danger of tipping off whoever is the spy."

"What about El-Hashem?"

"Adnan sent him to another one of his businesses down the coast in Abu Dhabi. He should be gone all day."

"Are you sure about this? It seems risky to me." I stopped myself from saying, risky for Ana.

"We need to step it up if we want to save Samira. The best way is to find out the Salafi's source. If he's important enough to them, we can use him as a bargaining chip."

It sounded fine when Marina laid it all out like that, but as our good friend Mr. Murphy said: "If anything can go wrong, it will and at the worst possible moment."

Just this once, I hoped he was wrong.

While I bit into my croissant and thought about having another, Marina tucked the handset of the suite's phone between her chin and her ear and was dialing her other assistant, Nikki, who was holding down the London office.

She was the designated information gatherer on the Salafi splinter group. Marina had sent her what she'd uncovered so far and had assigned Nikki to drill down as deep as possible and research the group thoroughly. Not just their actions but also their heritage and their leaders. We already knew their philosophy and goal: world domination and allegiance to hard-core Islam or death.

Nikki was also an extra resource for McCorkendale's crew in Louisville, Kentucky, which concerned me nearly as much as the situation here.

I gave Marina a little wave and mouthed I was going to the bedroom. I held up my coffee and picked up the *International Herald Tribune,* which I tucked under my arm.

Once there, I put the paper and the coffee on the nightstand on my side of the bed and lifted the receiver of the extension phone as quietly as I could.

I knew Marina would fill me in on whatever she and Nikki discussed. Eavesdropping was not something I usually did. I admit it was low, but I was feeling as left out as the guy at the blackjack table with no chips left to play and who could only watch. More importantly, I was becoming paranoid that somehow the Louisville cops would tie Marina and me to Tim Eggers's murder. Or that Lydia would somehow let it slip that I'd fingered Biggie Malatesta. Just thinking about that made me break out in a cold sweat.

So far as I knew, McCorkendale and her team were in Louisville strictly as horsesitters for Devil Wind and didn't know about the murder. I just wanted to be sure. I picked up in the middle of Nikki speaking.

"…she couldn't reach you last night and didn't want to leave a message or email. She doesn't trust the online security in the UAE, so she called the office with an update. She said everything was quiet. Devil Wind was tucked up in his stable, and no one had tried to harm him or any of the other horses. Her teams are ready and in place in case anyone makes a move on the horse or his keepers. She wants to speak to you personally, so she'll ring you back at five p.m. your time."

"Any new developments on the Eggers's murder?" Marina asked, her voice giving away nothing.

Since the murder was related to Adnan's stable and Devil Wind, I knew she'd asked Nikki to keep tabs on this, as well. What Nikki didn't know was how involved Marina and I were.

"Well, I haven't seen anything more about it on the internet. So, I presume things are very much the same as when you left." She paused, and I could hear her typing on her keyboard. "I'm checking now. I'll email you the latest information from the Louisville papers."

"Thanks, Nikki. That'd be great."

I thought so, too.

"Where are we on the Salafi information? Has Nigel sent you anything yet?"

Nigel? Marina was speaking about our pal, Nigel Phillips, who had access to all kinds of goodies we peons didn't. The kind that had kept us from being killed in Monte Carlo. I wasn't surprised that Marina had contacted him; she hadn't mentioned it to me.

"Not yet. He told me he'll try to have something for me by this evening. The Salafi are extremely barbaric. They'd do the world a favor if one of their suicide bombers blew themselves up instead."

I could hear the disgust in her voice.

"They find disillusioned people and entice them to become part of a cause. After a while, they introduce their extremist ideology. They go back quite a way. Right now, I'm looking into the personal histories of the leaders. Some are from Iraq, and some are from Syria and Afghanistan. A regular *Who's Who* of terrorists. I'll send you a report of anything interesting by the end of the day. If Nigel gets back to me, I'll add that in, as well."

"Okay. Sounds good. Bye for now.

"Ta. Talk later."

I waited until I heard Marina replace the receiver before hanging up. Then gave it five minutes before I walked back into the suite's living room. I was hoping she'd mention Nigel. "How's everything in London?" I asked.

"Nikki's on the case. She's digging up all she can find on the Salafi's militant leaders. Ana's looking for any inconsistencies in the background checks of our four suspects." She looked up at me. "I know you don't think Latif or Rashid could ever have been part of this, and hopefully, Ana's search will rule them out. I'm going out to Adnan's stables this morning. Rashid is coming with me to introduce me to the employees who work with the horses. I want to meet whoever was in charge of Devil Spirit when he was maimed. It's all well and good to have files on everyone—" She gestured toward her computer. "—but seeing someone face to face is much better."

"Aha. You're looking for their tell." To a gambler, it was a sign that someone was bluffing, a giveaway like running a hand through their hair or tapping their chin. "Want some help with that?" I asked. "I could tag along if you'd like."

"I'm not so sure you should be anywhere near a stable," she said jokingly, "not after what happened the last time." Marina just stared at me.

I instinctively reached up and touched the spot on my scalp where I'd been hit.

"I'd like to spend some time with Rashid on my own. See if I can determine his true feelings about his family and Adnan."

"Okay. I will go amuse myself after I've had another cup of coffee." I put my wounded ego away, bent down, and kissed the top of her head.

She smiled up at me and then went back to her computer. I noticed she didn't mention anything about Louisville or Eggers's murder either. Another secret she wasn't sharing with me. Was it because she wasn't worried, or just the opposite?

Chapter Forty-Five

Horseracing was the most popular game in town. Except, if you were a gambling man living in the UAE, your betting options were severely limited to none. Gambling wasn't permitted, and if you wanted to place a bet, you had to do so online. I'm sure there were games of chance a person could indulge in privately. I'd been thinking about asking Adnan if he knew of any blackjack games going on in the hotel or nearby. Even though I was just curious and wouldn't have played, given the circumstances, it didn't seem like a good idea.

I'd had my second cup of coffee and, unbeknownst to Marina, who had already departed, eaten another croissant and was considering how to spend the rest of the day. One of the magazines I'd leafed through earlier had an article about the Dubai Racing Club and the Meydan Racecourse, which hosted the Dubai World Cup—a series of six races with nearly thirty million dollars in prize money. It was the richest payday in racing at a track touted as the most luxurious in the world. I was beginning to wonder if everything in this country was "the most fill-in-the-blank" of its kind.

A trip to the track seemed like a good option for this afternoon. It could count as detective work if I poked around and asked a few questions about Devil Spirit and Adnan's other horses. Who knew what I might discover? I'd be on my own, though, without an all-access pass to smooth my way into the private areas.

I decided to speak with our floor concierge—every floor at the Burj al Nomad had one—to ask if he could obtain a ticket for me.

I pressed a button on the house phone and there was a knock at the door almost immediately. When I opened it, I found our concierge standing at attention. Dressed in a black light wool suit with a fitted jacket that looked custom-made over a white collared shirt and black tie, the tall, handsome young man looked more like a Calvin Klein model than a concierge.

"How can I help you, Mister Donahue?" he asked in perfect British English. I was sure he would get Ana's attention if they met. Boulos, as his nametag identified him, had a small leather notebook in one hand and a Mount Blanc pen in the other.

"I was thinking of spending the afternoon at the Meydan Racecourse and perhaps visiting Mr. bin Haddad's horses stabled there."

"Of course." He jotted down what I requested. "Just give me a few minutes, and I will return."

True to his word, Boulos returned a short while later.

"Forgive me for keeping you waiting, sir." He hadn't. "As Mr. bin Haddad's guest, everything has been arranged. Your Meydan host will be waiting when you arrive." He handed me a passport-sized leather folder embossed on the outside with the track's logo. Inside was a full-color brochure describing the racecourse and its history. "As Mr. bin Haddad's guest, he hopes you will enjoy all the facilities at the racecourse with his compliments."

That sounded fine to me.

"Please ring when you are ready to leave, and I will have the Rolls waiting for you in front of the main lobby." He bowed slightly and left.

Well, I'd be traveling in style. At least, I'd start out feeling like a winner.

Twenty minutes later, my driver handed me over to my Meydan host. Short and slightly round through his mid-section, the young man's s smile was so bright, his cheeks bunched up and nearly met his crinkly brown eyes. He introduced himself as Nadim and welcomed me as an honored guest of Mr. bin Haddad.

"I am at your service for your day at our most beautiful racecourse." He raised his arm and gestured toward the huge complex. "I would be delighted to show you all of our magnificent buildings."

I'd read the brochure Boulos had handed me on the ride over, and I thought it would take more than a day to see the whole place, even with Adnan's name opening every door. It was like Churchill Downs all over again, except I hoped, without a bang on the head.

"Would you care for lunch first, Mr. Donahue?"

My stomach was rumbling, and I wondered if Nadim had heard it. Those two croissants I had for breakfast were a long time ago. "That would be good," I replied.

"Excellent. Please come with me."

As we walked, Nadim pointed out the track's main attractions, the grandstand with its crescent-shaped, solar-powered roof and seating for sixty thousand spectators. In the distance, he proudly noted Meydan's grand five-star hotel, a theater, the Meydan Museum and Gallery, and its golf course.

"We can visit each one after lunch if you would like." His smile grew wider if that was physically possible.

Probably not, I thought as I nodded with what I hoped appeared to be enthusiasm. We had arrived at our destination, The Falcon Suite, a restaurant and lounge with its private entrance. Nadim steered me to a table on the balcony with a great view of the track. I invited him to join me, but he declined and said he'd pick me up when I was finished with lunch.

In moments, a waiter appeared with a flute of Champagne. "Compliments of the manager," he said as he placed the glass in front of me on a sparkling white tablecloth set with china and silverware, all bearing the Meydan logo. He handed me a menu and informed me of the chef's special for today, *Al Manshi*, roast lamb stuffed with rice, raisins, onions, and eggs seasoned with many spices. My mouth was watering before he finished describing the dish. And, as I expected, he proclaimed it was 'the best' *Al Manshi* anywhere. I handed back the menu and told him I would enjoy sampling it.

After I finished my main course, which was accompanied by a delicious Montepulciano Rosso, I declined dessert and asked for my check. I should have known better. Lunch was compliments of Mr. bin Haddad, as well.

Just as I folded my napkin and placed it on the table, Nadim appeared.

"So, Mr. Donahue, where shall we go first?" he asked with great anticipation in his voice.

"I would like to visit the stables and Mr. bin Haddad's horses that are running today."

Nadim's smile faded slightly. I think he hoped I'd pick the hotel, "the grandest" hotel in Meydan, instead. "Would you like to motor there—" He gestured to a small fleet of golf carts on the side of the restaurant. "—or walk? The stables are a good distance away."

"Let's walk," I replied. After lunch, I'd just eaten a walk seemed like a good idea, and it wouldn't hurt Nadim to get a little exercise either. "You can show me the other attractions as we go."

His smile perked up a bit at that.

As we passed behind the Grandstand on our way to the stables, Nadim pointed out more interesting facts about the racecourse, including the "most palatial" jockey's changing room.

All these superlatives were beginning to wear a bit thin, and I was happy when we reached our destination.

Two of bin Haddad's horses, Dawar and Bourkan, were running in today's races. Both were in the barns with their grooms and Adnan's head trainer, Sabah Tawfeek.

I introduced myself, and we shook hands.

"Mr. Donahue, welcome. It is a pleasure to meet you. Mr. bin Haddad mentioned that you might stop by."

His greeting seemed warm and genuine. I hoped it meant he'd open up about Devil Spirit.

Since I hadn't mentioned my trip to the track to anyone but Boulos, the concierge, I figured he'd passed the information on to bin Haddad, who in turn told Tawfeek to expect me. So much for operating under the radar. Well, if I judged Tawfeek by his welcome, at least I could ask my questions without being stonewalled.

"Sabah, have you been here all day?" My curiosity got the better of me. He's the one Marina was planning to meet with this morning. I wondered if Rashid hadn't realized he'd be here and not at their Dubai stables.

"Yes," he answered in a puzzled tone. "I am here any day our horses are running."

I'd have to ask Marina who Rashid had taken her to meet at Adnan's stables.

"Would you like to meet the horses now?" There was a good amount of pride in his voice as he asked the question.

I nodded yes and hoped they'd give me a better reception than Devil Wind.

As we entered the stable, two horses poked their heads out of their stalls, "This is our filly, Dawar, and this bad boy here, is Bourkan." Sabah pointed to each horse.

Dawar was a majestic-looking animal with a gleaming chestnut coat that looked as if it had been rubbed with oil. She shook her mane and snickered at our approach.

"She thinks we have a treat for her," Sabah said as he patted the horse affectionately. "Not now, my girl. After your race will be soon enough."

I kept my distance and stayed about a foot behind the trainer, although Dawar seemed not to notice I was even there, which was fine with me.

Bourkan was another story. The horse stamped his hoofs and snorted when he saw us.

"This one, he was named right." Sabah ruffled his mane as he spoke. "His name in English means volcano, and it is as if he is always ready to explode."

I didn't like the sound of that and moved back another step.

"His white face and spots on his coat make him a sabino, an Arabian. And like many racehorses, he seems to be well aware of his pedigree." He gave the horse a rub on his forehead and continued as we left the stable. "These two share the same bloodline and have several champions in their lineage."

We walked out the back of the stables and were standing near the training track. Several horses and their jockeys were riding around, and a few spectators were watching.

"Sabah, I want to ask you about what happened to Devil Spirit."

My words brought a look of pain onto his face. He lowered his head and tried to hide the emotions that came over him. "Yes. Okay."

"Were you here at the time he was attacked?"

He nodded and took a moment before looking up at me and answering. "It was terrible. To do that to a horse...how could anyone..."

I put my hand on his arm. "Please, try and remember exactly what happened."

He took a deep breath. "It was late. The races were done for the day, and most of the horses had been taken home. Devil Spirit had an appointment with the veterinarian. The doctor was detained, and when he arrived, it was so late, I decided to keep Devil Spirit here."

I interrupted. "Was the horse sick?

"No." He shook his head. "He had not been eating well, and I had removed him from the day's racing. The doctor was just going to make sure he was okay so he could race the next day. I planned to stay with him all night and see that he was fit for the morning.

"I only left him for a little while to speak with Rashid about the other horses who would be racing tomorrow and to have some dinner."

"Rashid was here, at Meydan? Rashid Khaleel?"

"Yes." He nodded.

"I thought he'd been in Louisville with Devil Wind."

Sabah shook his head. "No, he had come back to see his family…I don't know why or what for." He paused again and I could see tears forming in his eyes. "When I returned to Devil Spirit's stall, he was lying down on his side, and I thought that his stomach problem had returned. I entered the stall and didn't see what…what had been done to his eyes at first. He was so quiet, I thought he was dead. But we soon realized he had been drugged to keep him silent while they destroyed his eyes."

By now, tears were sliding down his cheeks.

"I called out to the stable hands to find Rashid. I wanted him to help me, but no one could locate him, and I thought he must have already gone. I finally reached him on his cell and asked him to call Mr. bin Haddad. I wanted to stay with Devil Spirit until the doctor could come. By now, the drugs they gave him were wearing off. The horse was in terrible pain, and I knew we had to put him down and end his misery. I could not leave him."

"Did Rashid come back to the stables after he reached Mr. bin Haddad?"

"No. I believe he went to his family's home.

"Did you see anyone around the stables who looked like they didn't belong here?"

"There are so many different people here every day, but no one looked suspicious or out of place. One of the grooms called security while I remained with Devil Spirit. They are supposed to be the best." A look of doubt passed across his face. "Of course, the security people were sure no one who didn't belong here had been admitted to the racecourse.

"Most of the owners are very wealthy and they expect their horses to be protected, almost pampered." He couldn't hide the sarcasm in his words. He realized what he'd said might sound like he was being critical of his boss. "I do not mean Mr. bin Haddad. He truly loves his horses."

"Thank you, Sabah. You've been very helpful. I'm sure Mr. bin Haddad knows how much you care for his horses."

We shook hands, and I walked back to the front of the stables, where Nadim was waiting for me.

"Did you enjoy your tour of the stables, Mr. Donahue?" he asked. "Where shall we visit next?"

I looked around the area in front of the stables and thought I saw Rashid entering the grandstand.

"Let's go back to the grandstand. I'd like to watch one or two of the races from there." I started moving at a fast pace, and Nadim struggled to keep up. It couldn't have been Rashid I'd just seen. He was supposed to be with Marina, not here. Unless they'd finished their visit to Adnan's stables.

"Are you sure, Mr. Donahue? There is the golf course and museum to visit."

I could see that wounded look on his face again.

"Perhaps after the races, Nadim, we can visit the Meydan Hotel."

When we got to the grandstand, Rashid was nowhere to be seen. I probably mistook someone else for him. I shook my head. Talking to Sabah had gotten to me. I honestly lost any desire to remain at the track or see any more of its spectacular sights, but I needed time to think and process what I just heard. The grandstand was as good a place as any. I could pretend to be watching the races while my mind was pretending to solve the case.

Chapter Forty-Six

fter taking in two races which, for all the attention I was paying them, might as well have been toddlers on rocking horses, I begged off any more sightseeing for the day. I thanked Nadim for being such a good host and asked him to please call for the car. If I hadn't been so preoccupied with Devil Spirit, I might have laughed at myself uttering those words. Marina was right: I could get used to this.

I hoped she was back from her meeting with Rashid. I had to ask her what time they'd finished. I was confused about his movements here and in Kentucky.

In the back seat of the Rolls, I pulled out my cell and checked for messages. As if there weren't enough to worry about, there were three messages, all from Lydia. This was not a good sign.

I put the phone to my ear and listened to the first. "Where are you, Nick? Call me." The second one was a little more insistent: "We need to talk about Biggie and Cambiato. The two Louisville cops you met, Harris and Braeton, think you were holding back. Were you, Nick?" And the third was my favorite of all: "The thinking here is that someone else might have gotten to Eggers before Biggie did the deed. Know anything about that? Call me."

Crap. Lydia was wrong. I was *sure* it was Biggie who killed Eggers and no one else. I'd practically seen him do it. Why were the feds still looking for suspects? Had someone seen Marina and me leaving Eggers's place? I felt sweat dripping down my back, even though the air was cranked up. Were we suspects? Jeez. Did we leave anything behind? There was no more putting it off. I was going to have to deal with this. And I had to tell Marina I'd gone to the feds, by which I meant Lydia.

Worrying about the investigation in Louisville had taken my mind off the case here in Dubai. As the Rolls pulled in front of the hotel, I saw Marina standing there looking as grim as a casino owner who just paid out on a break-the-bank jackpot. Something told me things were only going to get worse.

I'd hardly stepped out of the Rolls and thanked the driver when Marina took my arm, sidled up close, and whispered in my ear: "We've got to talk. Upstairs."

We waited for an empty elevator and rode to our suite in silence. Marina shook her head no each time I tried to say something, even though we were all alone. Did she think the elevator was bugged?

Once inside the suite, she let go of my arm and launched into what had made her so furious.

"Ana called earlier from the plant. She was checking back through Malik Alfarsi's references. She called two of the companies he listed and pretended to be a recruiter, verifying his employment dates. The people she spoke with had never heard of him. Ana knew she was onto something and dug deeper into his file and back to his days at Khalifa University of Science, Technology, and Research in Abu Dhabi. She found photos of him in an old yearbook—tagged with a different name." Marina paused, and I could see the fire in her eyes. "He lied to us, Nick. Alfarsi is not his real name. It's al-Badri. When Ana put al-Badri into the search engine, she hit the jackpot, as you might say, and found a nasty family connection. There were a bunch of photos of him with his family. He's the nephew of the late Hathaim al-Badri, the mastermind of the al-Sakari Mosque bombing in two thousand six, an al Qaeda leader, and a brutal and merciless terrorist."

"So. Malik is the mole?

She nodded. "It appears so. Alfarsi is his mother's family name. I expect he realized he'd never be able to infiltrate ABH if they knew his family background. Adnan would never have let someone with known terrorist ties work for him. Especially on the cloaking device project."

My mind flooded with questions. "How did he get the job? Did he have help from inside ABH?"

I couldn't help remembering the story about a family of scammers who did the same kind of thing in a Vegas casino I played in years ago. One person was the dealer, and the other family members were in a group of rotating players who acted like they didn't know each other. It took a long time for the management to catch onto them.

Marina considered the possibility of Malik being linked to someone on the inside. "Maybe. That's what I need to find out. I sent Ana's information to Nikki who is doing more digging into his background." Her lips turned up in a half-smile. "She took the lead from you and is searching through his Facebook friends first. She'll cross-reference them with ABH's list of employees and find out if any one of them quietly recommended him for the job. If she gets stuck, she'll call Nigel for help." She got up and started pacing, her nervous energy evident in every step.

"I didn't know Nigel had agreed to help out." I knew I sounded petulant. "Did you tell him about the project?"

"No. Just that we're looking into the Salafi terrorist cell. The Brits have an interest in them, as well. They've been tied to several ISIS training camps and may be planning to set up one of their own."

"To teach their Jihadists how to use their new cloaking device, no doubt," I added.

Nigel liked to play his cards close to the vest, and I speculated on what he expected to get out of this. He wasn't just "helping" out of the goodness of his heart. Bringing down the Salafi cell would get him a lifetime's worth of brownie points from His Majesty and maybe even a knighthood.

"Have you told Adnan yet?"

"No. I want to wait until I have everything I need to be a hundred percent certain. If Malik is our guy, he's a big fish. One I hope the Salafi won't want to lose." I could see where she was going with this. "We may be able to trade him for Samira."

I hoped she was right. One more question crossed my mind. "How did he get past El-Hashem?" I asked, wondering if the head of security was part of the subterfuge.

Marina stopped moving and looked at me. "That's a very good question, and I can't wait to ask him."

In all the excitement over the discovery of the terrorist spy, Malik al-Badri, I'd forgotten to ask Marina how her meeting with Rashid had gone or mention that he'd been at the Meydan racetrack when Devil Spirit was maimed and not in Louisville. I also wanted to mention I could've sworn I saw him at the track today when he was supposed to be with her.

I'd also neglected to tell her about my messages from Special Agent Lydia Ramos and the ongoing investigation into Eggers's murder. I got up and walked over to the bar. I needed a drink before I trotted out this information and brought a pile of trouble down on my head.

Just as I was about to speak, Marina's cell beeped, and she answered it. I had another reprieve. How long it would last was anybody's bet.

Chapter Forty-Seven

Not long, was the answer.

She rang off and turned to me, fired up by what she had just heard. "That was Nikki, she—"

I put up my hand to stop her speaking. "Marina, wait. Please. There are a few things I have to tell you first." I took her hand, led her to the couch, and sat her down so we were facing each other.

"What have you done now?" Her tone was light, almost teasing.

I shook my head. "It's serious." I watched as her smile faded and her eyes became guarded.

"Before we left for Louisville, I saw Tommy B in New York—twice."

She tensed at the mention of the mobster's name.

"First at the rehearsal dinner, then at the wedding ceremony. I chalked it up to coincidence at first, but then I realized he was keeping tabs on me—on us. When we were in Louisville, I did some sleuthing on my own, hoping to get to the bottom of Tim Eggers's murder."

From there, I proceeded to tell her about my visit to Julie Burnett, her identifying the photo of Biggie Malatesta, and my decision to call Lydia Ramos of the FBI, her team's and the Louisville team's involvement, and my growing suspicion that they were looking at me as a suspect. I ended with the messages I received from Lydia today.

As I was speaking, Marina drew farther and farther away from me. Her face was a canvas of changing emotions that morphed from interest to anger to disappointment. It was the last I had the most trouble dealing with.

"Why didn't you tell me any of this until now? Why keep it all a secret?"

Her arms swept out to illustrate her point.

"If I had told you Tommy B was nosing around us, I was afraid you'd go looking for him." I didn't add that she might get hurt if she got too close.

"And what about the FBI and Lydia Ramos? What's your reasoning for keeping me out of the loop?" Her words were cold and precise.

"Lydia and I…we had a thing a long time ago and…"

"And what? You thought I'd be jealous of some woman halfway around the world?" She shook her head and stood up in front of me, leaning over me like a schoolteacher chastising an errant child. "How could you? I thought we had something better than that. Guess I was wrong." She turned and left the room, leaving me alone and miserable.

She was right. I was a dumb ass jerk, and I was afraid I'd lost her, and her trust, for good.

I sat on my own for a few minutes more, then decided to clear my head with a walk along the beach. It was another beautiful night with the moon, which had just risen, making a path along the water. A shimmering slice of light moving off into infinity teased you into thinking you could flow along with it always.

Somehow, I had to make this up to Marina. She couldn't stay angry with me forever, could she? *Okay,* I told myself, *go back and grovel. Ask, no, beg, for forgiveness, and try to make her understand.*

I started back on the path to the hotel with a purposeful stride, planning my conciliation speech. I hadn't gone more than twenty feet when I heard what sounded like a pop coming from the trees on my right. As I stopped to listen, a figure all in black ran out from the bushes and knocked me to the ground. I staggered to my feet and looked around. He was gone. A low moan came from the garden behind the bushes.

I moved in that direction, not knowing what I'd find. Latif Khaleel lay on the ground. He'd been shot, and a pool of blood was spreading from under his shoulder. I whipped off my jacket and pressed it down on the wound.

"Help," I called as loudly as I could. "Help. Over here. A man has been shot."

Where were all those friggin' security people I'd seen walking the grounds?

Bailing at the first sign of trouble? Finally, two of them came running. They took in the situation in seconds. One spoke into the microphone on his lapel and called for an ambulance, while the other helped staunch the flow of blood.

Latif looked like he was about to pass out or worse.

"Help is on the way," I told him. "Hang in there. You're going to be fine." I squeezed his hand in emphasis. "Do you know who did this to you?"

He tried to speak, his breath a mere whisper. I bent closer to catch his words, but they were a jumble of murmurs I couldn't understand.

Finally, an ambulance arrived, and the EMS team took over. I stood up and watched as they worked on his shoulder. I looked around the walkway and noticed a small group had gathered. Men in dinner jackets and women in evening wear who clutched their shawls tighter around themselves whispered and pointed in my direction. I saw Marina and Rashid rushing toward me. Her face looked sallow and distraught in the pale light. Rashid was shaking all over as he ran to his father. "Baba, baba," he called as he knelt beside his father and grasped his hand. "I am so sorry. So sorry. This is all my fault."

He went on like that until the EMS team gently motioned him aside. They placed Latif on a gurney and were ready to transport him to the hospital. Rashid grasped his father's hand again and stepped into the ambulance with him. Its flashing lights cast a crimson glow over the scene and made the blood on the ground stand out in dark relief. My eyes followed until the ambulance was lost to sight.

When I looked away, Marina was standing next to me. She took my hand in hers. "I forgive you," she said, "but don't think that means this is over."

Chapter Forty-Eight

Adnan was waiting for us in the lobby. The Dubai Police Chief and his deputy were standing next to him. By now, the whole hotel was buzzing with news of the shooting, and people were pointing to me and whispering under their breath. Maybe the dark red bloodstains on my shirt were drawing their attention.

Marina and I walked straight over to Adnan. Calm and in control, he put his hand on my shoulder and nodded to the policemen. "Let us go up to my suite and discuss what has just happened."

The two officers, dressed in a uniform of tan pants and fitted belted jackets with epaulets that made them look as though they were either in the French Foreign Legion or part of the Marrakesh exhibit at Disney World, deferred to Adnan. I expect that the whole police force would do the same if it came down to it. Adnan made the introductions and then gestured for everyone to take a seat.

"Mr. Donahue," began the police chief, "please tell us what you recall of the incident this evening."

I explained what I'd heard and seen. "I'd been walking back to the hotel when I heard a popping sound in the bushes. When I turned in that direction, a man flew past me and knocked me over." I described the shooter as best as I could. I was sure it was a man and that he was about my height but a bit heavier, with broad shoulders. He was dressed in black and wore some kind of mask that covered his face. "I tried to stop the bleeding, and Mr. Khaleel spoke to me, but so softly I couldn't understand what he was saying. I called for help, and the security guards eventually arrived. One attended to Mr.

Khaleel, and the other called for an ambulance. The ambulance arrived a few minutes later, and the EMS people took over and then transported him to the hospital."

I repeated my story several times, and they seemed to be satisfied. Well, at least they weren't looking at me as a suspect. Not yet, anyway.

"Are you sure you didn't understand what Mr. Khaleel was saying?" demanded the police chief once again.

It seemed to be the most important aspect of his questioning, and it piqued my curiosity. Though I doubted it, I wondered if Adnan had mentioned anything about ISIS to him.

"Not a word. His voice was too low. I could barely hear him, and it was all a muddle," I replied.

The police chief closed his notebook and was about to leave.

"I have a question of my own," I said. "Did you find the gun yet? I didn't see a gun in the shooter's hand when he ran past. Maybe he tossed it in the bushes or hid it somewhere on his body."

"Not yet, Mr. Donahue. But we will, and the man responsible for using it, as well." He bowed slightly to us, and then he and his deputy were gone.

Once they left, Adnan rose and went to the bar to pour us all a drink. Marina and I accepted without protest, and I downed mine in one gulp. Adnan gestured that I should fix another if I wanted to, and I did just that.

"What are you thinking, Nick," he asked, "with your question about the gun?"

"Not sure," I replied. "Just wondering how many people on your staff at ABH have a gun. And if any of them had a beef with Latif."

"Do you not think this is yet another message from the Salafi? Wasn't the one this afternoon enough? Did they do this to show me how in control they are?"

"Another?" I repeated.

Marina shook her head slightly at me, and I stopped asking questions.

Adnan's cell beeped. He looked at the message. "I am going to the hospital now. Latif is going into surgery, and I want to be there when it is done. We can talk later or in the morning."

Marina and I left and headed to our suite. I was as exhausted as a poker player on a twenty-four-hour losing streak. I started taking off my clothes the second I opened the door, tossing them to the floor as I made my way to the bedroom.

"You didn't have much to say about the shooting," I said to Marina, who was trailing behind me. "Other than the look you gave me when Adnan mentioned the second message."

"I thought it would be better if I listened to see if anything from the attack offered a lead before I went into what happened earlier today. The Salafi contacted Adnan. They demanded he turn over the cloaking device soon, or they would behead Samira, film her execution, and broadcast it live all over the world. Just as they promised." Marina paused to catch her breath. "And they want the hundred million, as well."

Even though I expected as much, it felt like a blow to my stomach to hear it. "What was Adnan's response?"

"He told them he needed more time. That the machine wasn't ready yet. It must be tested to ensure it would work. They laughed at him and said that he'd better work faster. And they'd be happy to test it for him." She shook her head. "Oh God, I don't know what he's going to do. That's not all of it, Nick. They sent a video. It arrived right after Adnan spoke to them. In it, Samira was bound with her hands tied to a post above her head. They'd removed her clothes and head scarf, and her long hair cascaded over her naked body."

While Marina was speaking, my hands had balled into fists. Those pigs knew that what they were doing dishonored and disgraced Samira. Marina grasped my hand with her own and continued. "They put a knife to her throat and made her beg for them to stop. They just laughed at her pleas and reminded her what they were planning to do to her."

"Kidnapping Samira and shooting Latif were just to prod Adnan into complying, another way of showing him they mean business. Although I'm sure he wasn't doubting it before." I sat, considering the facts. "That's why they haven't killed Samira yet, or hurt her physically. And they only wounded Latif. They know he's the head of the project, and they might need him to help them set up the machine or whatever it is. It's also interesting that they merely said soon and not a specific time or day for Adnan to deliver the cloaking device. Almost as if someone on the inside was providing information that it wasn't ready yet. But they couldn't resist a show of power."

"You might be right." She leveled her gaze at me. "Did you tell the police chief everything?"

"I did." I nodded. "It all happened so fast. One minute I was walking toward the bushes, the next I was on my butt, and the shooter was gone. He was a big guy. Broad through his upper body and solid. There is one thing, though. I thought it was a ski mask covering his face, but thinking about it now, it could have been part of a headdress that he wrapped around his mouth and nose. Like a dessert *Shemagh*."

"A what?" Marina was puzzled.

"It's a traditional headdress men wear in the desert to protect their necks and faces from the sun and sand. I read about it in an article about US troops in Iraq."

"If you say so."

My thinking was getting fuzzy. I needed to rest and tackle it all later. I pulled a pillow up against the headboard and lay back against it. "One more thing, before I forget. How did your meeting with Rashid go?"

"There's something a bit off about him. I just can't put my finger on it."

I nodded in assent. "I know what you mean. How was he at the stables?"

"When we got there, Sabah Tawfek was nowhere to be found."

"I know. He was at Meydan with two of Adnan's horses that were running today. From what he said, Rashid knew that's where he'd be. Later, I even thought I saw Rashid at Meydan in the grandstand but realized I must have been mistaken since he was with you."

Marina got up and started pacing. I knew her brain cells were firing like a rocket about to take off. "Rashid said he forgot Sabah was at the track. Since Sabah is the 'Head Trainer'—" She made air quotes with her fingers. "—he doesn't have to share his schedule with him. He could have gone there after I left."

"Think he's jealous?"

She shrugged. "Could be. But why? Adnan treats him like a prince. Even if on some level he resents it; if anyone has cause to be envious, it should be Tawfek."

"I gotta tell you, that young man loves those horses." I repeated the conversation we had about the night Devil Spirit was maimed and put down. "He also mentioned that Rashid was here and not in Kentucky when Devil Spirit was attacked. Said he came home to see his family."

"That's not the impression I got, not that I asked him where he was. I thought the terrorists sent the ransom note to him in Kentucky."

"What about his family? How does he feel about them? Find any traces of sibling rivalry slipping out from his ego?" I knew she was planning to explore his relationship with his family.

"On one level, he seems to care about them all and, of course, told me how very concerned he is about Samira—and now, his father. However, when he spoke about Latif, there was a definite change in his demeanor, a kind of underlying hostility. I couldn't figure out if it was coming from fear for his father or fear of him." Thinking about Latif seemed to spur Marina into action. "I'm going to phone Adnan and see how Latif's surgery went." She picked up her cell and made for the bedroom door. "I may join him at the hospital if Latif is awake and able to talk."

I stifled a yawn, which made Marina smile. "Sorry," I said with a sheepish grin on my face. "It's not the company."

"I know," she called over her shoulder. "It's hard work being a hero, isn't it? See you later."

"I'm not a hero, just a fall guy. Literally," I shouted at the closing door.

After she left, I realized we never discussed what Nikki had found out about Malik's connections at ABH. It would just have to wait until tomorrow.

Chapter Forty-Nine

Tired as I was, sleep didn't come. Every time I closed my eyes, I saw Latif's ashen face and blood seeping from his wound, staining the ground like a flowing black shadow. I got up and looked at the clock, surprised to see it was only nine in the evening rather than one in the morning it felt like.

What time did that make it in New York? For some reason, I had an irresistible urge to call my dad. With Dubai ahead of New York by nine hours, it was noon in New York. I picked up my cell and then thought better of it. If I told him what was going on, he'd morph from a calm, thoughtful banker to a worried parent before you knew it.

I tossed around calling Lydia back. Her three messages were a sure signal that she'd be on my case until we spoke. With as much trepidation as a blackjack player taking a hit on a thirteen, I picked up my cell and punched in her number.

"Ramos," she answered on the first ring.

"It's Nick."

"I take it you got my messages, all three of them." There it was again, a snarkiness that she couldn't hide.

"This is the first opportunity I've had to call you. There's been a lot going on here."

"I'm not interested in Dubai or horseracing, Nick. I'm interested in putting away that bastard, Tommy B. I don't think this is going to be the case to do it. So, excuse me if I don't sympathize with your 'situation' in the desert."

"I thought the feds in Kentucky were going to move on Biggie and

Cambiato."

"They did. Hauled them in and questioned them. But they couldn't hold them. There was no forensic evidence that they were in the house. No blood. No fibers. No weapons. Not on them, in the house, or their vehicle."

I broke out in a cold sweat. Marina and I had wiped down every surface we touched. At least, I hoped we did. I gulped and prayed Lydia hadn't heard it. "Did they admit to being on his block?"

"Yeah, they did." I could almost see the grin forming on Lydia's face. "Once we showed them the traffic cam footage of their truck turning into the street."

I knew Lydia was expecting me to react but all I managed was a "Hmmm."

"The one thing they did say, Nick, is that they saw you and a red-headed woman leaving Eggers's apartment just when they were about to deliver the wine he'd ordered."

Shit. Had the traffic cam picked us up, as well? "They must be mistaken." I tried to bluff it out. "It wasn't me."

"Don't lie, Nick. You were never any good at it. My colleagues in the Louisville office are very interested in speaking with you." She let that statement hang in the air between us for a minute. "It would be better if you came back to Kentucky now and had a chat with them, then me."

"Look, you know me. You know I didn't shoot Eggers."

"I never said that's how he was killed."

Crap. I fell right into it and gave myself away, just like in a grade-B movie. Lydia was letting me know I was in deep trouble.

"I'll be back soon, as soon as I can."

"Don't leave it too long, Nick. These guys in Louisville want to make this case. They're out for blood, and yours will do just fine. Lest you forget, I'm still out for Tommy B." She hung up without saying another word.

I was as screwed as the guy who lost the rent money betting on a sure thing. I was beginning to think that whoever killed Eggers had nothing to do with the mob. That it was about something else entirely. Now, all I had to do was prove it.

I was wide awake, my eyes open and staring at the ceiling. I tossed and turned for a half hour, then decided I might as well get up and wait for Marina to return. My stomach was rumbling, and I figured I'd hit the outdoor café for a bite to eat. I picked up my blood-stained clothes from where I dropped them and tossed the bundle in the trash. God only knew what happened to my jacket after I used it to staunch the blood pouring from Latif's shoulder. Fortunately, I had my phone and wallet in my pants pocket.

I took a short but very hot shower and tried to wash away my misgivings along with the detritus of the evening. It worked, up to a point. I couldn't get the image of Latif crumbled on the ground out of my mind. I was a gambler, not a detective. To me, the bad guys were casino owners, not shooters.

I dressed in jeans and a pullover sweater and headed for the elevator, wondering how soon it would be before we could leave Dubai. I didn't realize how preoccupied I was until I stepped into the car and saw Mansur standing against the back wall.

He looked about as bad as I felt. I'm sure I must have stiffened at the sight of him. His eyes flicked with a glimmer of satisfaction as if to let me know he still held all the power, then he returned to his usual dark and brooding expression.

"Mansur." I nodded at him. "Any word on Latif?"

"Yes, he is out of surgery and in an intensive care unit."

Marina hadn't called to tell me. Maybe she was waiting until they received an updated prognosis on his condition.

Mansur cleared his throat and put his hand on my arm. I winced instinctively at his touch. This time, however, his eyes were filled with something I couldn't identify at first but soon realized was gratitude.

"Thank you for saving Latif, Mr. Donahue." The words caught in his throat. "He would be dead if weren't for you."

It was an unexpected touch of compassion, and I didn't know how to respond. I just dipped my head in his direction, and he removed his arm. We rode the rest of the way to the lobby in silence.

As we stepped off the elevator, I asked if he wanted to join me for something to eat. I gestured toward the café in the lobby.

"No. Thank you all the same," was his reply. "There is something I must attend to immediately."

He stood a little straighter and strode off in the opposite direction from mine. In the time it takes to flip a card, the old Mansur had returned—steely-eyed, tough as nails, and determined as hell. If his "something to attend to" involved a person, I hoped for their sake, they knew what they were in for.

I took my time over dinner, reviewing the case and trying to come up with a solution that made sense.

While I was dining, the lobby café filled with the rich and famous of Dubai, all dressed to impress. I felt kind of grubby in my pullover and jeans. Every once in a while, I noticed someone discretely looking in my direction and whispering to a companion behind their hand. These people must have witnessed the aftermath of the shooting and seen me with the police. Were they wondering if I was a suspect that the police couldn't hold or some crazy American who got himself into big trouble? Instagram photos and Facebook videos were probably circling the globe right now. I bet the Salafi had already seen them.

In what I assumed was a sort of reverse psychology, none of the gawkers appeared worried another shooter would show up at The Burj Al Nomad to shoot them. They seemed to carry on as usual and had great trust in their exalted presence. After all, who would dare to take a potshot at a well-placed billionaire at dinner?

The waiter arrived with my bill. I added a hefty tip and signed it. It was time to head upstairs to my bed. This time, I'd stay there and hopefully fall asleep in a heartbeat and dream of piles and piles of chips stacked in front of me at my favorite blackjack table.

Chapter Fifty

That was my plan until Marina arrived home. I must have dozed off because she woke me up unceremoniously with a tug on the covers. I grumbled and tried to pull them back on, but she was having none of that.

"There are things I need to tell you, Nick. So, wake up."

I suggested she come to bed instead, but she was having none of that either. "I'll meet you in the living room as soon as you rouse yourself sufficiently."

I gave her a look that said I knew her English was better than that, then rose from our bed and beat a path to the living room.

"How is Latif?" I asked.

"He'll be fine. The bullet hit the fleshy part of his arm and didn't do nearly as much damage as it could have. He was very lucky. They had to repair some of the blood vessels, and there may be slight nerve damage, but he should have full use of his arm. The bullet was a nine-millimeter, probably from a Glock. They haven't found it yet. Or the shooter."

"Did Adnan have anything to add?"

"No. He is so torn about the Salafi's demands that every time his phone rings, he nearly jumps in the air, wondering if it is them with the exact time and place they want the cloaking device."

"Was Latif able to speak?" I was still trying to figure out what he was trying to tell me. Was it a message about the shooter? Or someone else?

"No. After the surgery, they put him into an induced coma. They're afraid he'll become very agitated when he wakes up. They're trying to keep him still. If he has a good night, they'll bring him out of it tomorrow. Adnan is going to stay with him tonight. He insisted that Janiki return here, and Mansur is to look after her."

"I'm sure he'll watch her like a hawk."

"Now, whose English is being purposefully pointed?"

I finally coaxed Marina into bed. Unfortunately for me, now that I was wide awake, she fell asleep the minute her head touched the pillow. I put my insomnia to good use, revisiting everything that had occurred since the night of the bachelor party. To my way of thinking, Eggers being shot and the Salafi's kidnappings and demands were two separate crimes that connected somehow. Was there a common denominator in all of this? I was pretty sure there was. Now, I just needed to figure out what that was. Punching the pillow wasn't helping and neither was tossing and turning.

I got out of bed quietly so as not to wake Marina and went into the suite's living room. We'd left the drapes open, and I sat near the big picture window facing the full moon as it began its descent over the desert trailed by hundreds of twinkling stars. Nature certainly had the power to overwhelm you with the vastness of the universe. It helped put your own problems in perspective. Was there another Nick up there, my doppelgänger, struggling with the same issues I was? I hoped not. I hoped he was tucked up in bed with his own Marina, sleeping in peace.

I let my mind wander back and looked at both cases as if it were a game of Clue I was desperate to win. Just like the Clue playing board, there were different locations or rooms—The Carlyle Hotel, Churchill Downs, Adnan's farm, Devil Wind's stable, Eggers apartment, and The Burj Al Nomad. Then I listed all the people involved so far and the potential ways in which they could do each other in. I moved them around in my mental playing field, placing them in the "rooms" I knew they'd been in and the "weapons" they had access to.

After a while, I began to see a pattern and then what I was beginning to believe was the solution, kind of like Mr. Brown in the Library with the Noose. I was afraid Marina would think I'd gone off the deep end if I tried to explain this to her. I'd probably have to test it out on my own first to see if I hit the mark. We didn't have much time left. The Salafi wouldn't wait much longer for the cloaking device in exchange for Samira if indeed they would let her go.

I tiptoed back to our bedroom but still couldn't fall asleep. All I could see were playing tokens with familiar faces running through my head.

Marina was awake before me and was going back to the hospital to check on Latif. Busy girl that she was, she'd already spoken with Mansur. He'd made sure Janiki had gotten home last evening and was secure, then he went back to the hospital and stationed himself outside Latif's door. Adnan and Rashid were going to be at Adnan's private stable near the Meydan Racecourse to work with some of the younger horses.

"Adnan is trying to make it business as usual. He's adamant he'll race Devil Wind in the Derby. There's no talking him out of it."

"Really?" I couldn't hide the surprise in my voice.

"It appears so."

"What about the Salafi and the cloaking device, not to mention their threats to kill Samira? He can't possibly ignore that."

"He believes we can stop the Salafi."

"Just how does he think we're going to do that?" This was getting too surreal for me. "We still have to find someone to trade for her, someone valuable to them, and even if they go for that, they're still going to want the device."

Marina had been standing next to the bed. Now, she sat on the edge and spoke softly. "I think he'll let them have it."

"I was afraid of that." I shook my head. The idea of those demons winning was revolting.

She nodded her head. "He wants this to be over and everyone to be safe."

"He can't believe they'll honor the deal. They're terrorists. They don't ever tell the truth or play fair. Once they get their hands on the cloaking device, no one will be safe."

I couldn't help thinking about the plan I'd come up with in the middle of the night. I had a few things to work out before I told Marina.

It was a good time to change the subject. "We never did discuss what Nikki uncovered about who recommended Malik al-Badri or Alfarsi, as he calls himself to Adnan and ABH."

Marina clicked on her laptop, which she'd placed on the bedside table. She looked at the screen and then turned it so I could view it. It was a list of Malik's friends who worked at ABH and who were also members of the same mosque. It wasn't a very long list. Just five names. Short, but illuminating.

"Something to think about." Marina pointed at the names. "That's on my list of what I want to discuss when I can speak with Latif."

She stared at the screen for a moment before closing the laptop. We'd both seen the name halfway down the list—the one I was hoping wasn't there. The one I believed was my Mr. Brown.

Chapter Fifty-One

The face looking back at me in the mirror was drawn and pale with valleys below its eyes and a day's worth of stubble along its chin. A few strokes with a razor took care of the stubble. I had to live with the rest until this whole business was over.

I decided to spend the day at the stables with Adnan and Rashid. By now, I was sure the Salafi had people planted in the hotel to monitor all of our activities. With guests from all over the world dressed in clothing that ran the gamut from traditional Arab robes to designer garb, it might be hard to spot a tail. But I was determined to try.

I slung a jacket over the shoulder of my black T-shirt and ambled down to the lobby café like a man without a care in the world.

I ordered my usual croissant and coffee and joked with the waiter, all the while trying to check out anyone who might be interested in me. A man a few tables away was glancing in my direction a little too often, peering over the top of the newspaper he pretended to be reading. I hadn't seen him turn a page since I sat down.

When the waiter placed my check on the table, I pointed to it, as if I were asking a question about the bill. When he leaned over to get a better look, I scribbled a note asking him if there was an exit to the grounds from the kitchen.

Either he was an apt candidate for intrigue, or he'd experienced helping others hightail it out the back way. He bent closer as if explaining what I'd pointed at and whispered that I should go to my left, down the hallway. On the right-hand side were the restrooms and, on the left, a door marked

Private, which led to a short hallway and an outside exit. I nodded and handed him the check with a very generous tip. I got up from the table and left my jacket hanging on the back of my chair, as though I would be returning any moment.

As I started my walk across the café toward the restrooms, I cut my eyes toward the man assigned to watch me. He made as if to get up and follow, then his eyes slid over to my table and the jacket swaying lightly in the breeze. He sat back, satisfied, I presumed, that I was coming back.

I was outside in less than a minute and hailed a cab, leaving the hotel for the ride to Adnan's stable.

The stable was on the same road as the Meydan racetrack about ten minutes past it. Fortunately, the cab driver knew where to go, and the ride, filled with his tourist chatter about Dubai, was quick and easy.

I wondered how long my watcher sat and waited for me to return and what he did when he realized I'd slipped away. Well, that was his problem, not mine.

I was smiling to myself at my successful sleight of hand when we pulled up to the gate at the stable. Two armed guards approached the cab, whose driver suddenly developed a case of lockjaw.

I lowered the window and gave one of the guards my name. He pulled out his cell and spoke quietly into it while the other man stood watch over us. I guess I'd been cleared to go when he nodded at the other guard to unlock the gate.

By now, the cab driver was sweating buckets, and I decided to take pity on him. I paid the fare, added a generous tip, and stepped out.

He did a perfect three-point U-turn and hightailed it back toward town.

The stable was laid out pretty much the same as the one in Louisville, with a barn, exercise paddock, and practice track. As I approached, Adnan came from the back of the barn and greeted me.

"Nick. What are you doing here? Has something happened?" Tension rippled through his body as he spoke.

"No," I reassured him quickly. "Nothing has changed." I paused. "There are a few things I wanted to discuss with you, and Marina mentioned you were here."

"Come. Let us go back to my office." He took my arm and led me along the path on the side of the barn. "Rashid and I have been working with some of the younger horses today." He smiled. "We are testing their mettle you might say, and it is occupying my mind with thoughts other than of the Salafi."

By now we were behind the barn. Adnan pointed to the practice track where Rashid was speaking with one of the stable hands. He must have sensed us looking his way and turned in our direction. He hesitated for a moment, then raised his hand and waved.

"Shall I have Rashid join us?"

I shook my head. "Maybe a little later. I think it'll be better if it's just the two of us for now."

Adnan nodded and led me into his office. It, too, looked and felt very much like his office in Louisville.

He noticed my looking around at the piles of breeding stock books and forms and shook his head. "What can I say? The business of horseracing requires much paperwork. Please sit." He gestured to a chair in front of his desk, then moved behind it to his chair. "What is it you want to discuss?"

I thought about how to begin. What I wanted to tell him wouldn't be easy, and he might not believe me.

"How involved are you with the cloaking device Project Blackout?"

He looked puzzled at my question but answered anyway. "Latif has been briefing me every step of the way. It is a tremendous breakthrough with unlimited potential."

"As a weapon," I added.

"Yes. But there are other scientific uses as well."

Frankly, I didn't see it. Whoever had the device had the power to use it however they wanted. If it fell into the hands of the Salafi...well, we know what they would do with it.

I kept this to myself and continued. "Someone on your team—someone you trust—has given this information to the Salafi. They—"

He interrupted me. "Yes, of course, I know this." His voice rose with every word, and he was becoming agitated. "And when we find out who it is, we will trade him for Samira. That is the plan we discussed, is it not." He said the last more as a statement than a question.

"It might not be as simple as you think." I took a deep breath. "Marina and I believe we've found the spy. Marina is with Mansur at the hospital, and as soon as Latif is able to speak, she'll ask him what he tried to tell me when he was shot." I paused again, collecting my thoughts. "I don't think—"

Just then, both our cell phones rang at the same time. I answered mine, and the words I heard chilled me to the bone. "We have your woman. You will do exactly as we tell you, or she will be beheaded alongside the girl, Samira. Do you understand?"

I tried to keep my voice steady as I replied, but it was difficult. All I envisioned was Marina in the hands of those monsters. "Yes," I finally said. "What is it you want me to do?"

When I looked up, Adnan was standing behind his desk, staring at his phone, ashen and shaken. It was obvious he'd received a similar message from the terrorists. When he spoke, his voice caught in his throat, and it seemed painful for him to utter the words he did.

"Those people, they are at my lab and are threatening to blow it up with all the employees inside." He shook his head. "I cannot let that happen. We must go and give them the cloaking device."

He shook all over and then slowly brought himself back to the present. He nodded his head toward my cell, which I was still holding in my hand. "They have Marina and are bringing her to ABH."

A moment later, we were out the door and into Adnan's Mercedes. He gave his driver instructions to take us to ABH as fast as possible then retreated into his thoughts.

My head was reeling. Thoughts of Marina being held by the Salafi and of Ana in the plant—both of whom could be killed at any moment made me angrier than I had ever been. I tried to channel this anger into a way out of what I was so afraid was going to happen next.

Adnan sighed and, looking straight ahead, spoke to me. "Who is it, Nick? Who has betrayed me?"

The phone calls we received had put off the inevitable. There was no easy way to say it. "Rashid."

I think Adnan stopped breathing for a moment. I knew it hit him hard. To have the man he treated as his son betray him in this way was almost too horrible to contemplate.

"Why? Why would he turn against his own people to be one of those murderers?" His face contorted with fury. When he spoke again, his voice was hard and cold. "Is he responsible for the kidnapping of his sister and for the shooting of his father?"

He was desperate for answers I couldn't give him. "I don't know for sure, but it's likely." I thought of Latif lying in a pool of blood. What was he trying to tell me? Were his whispered words his son's name?

"He was the one who helped Malik Alfarsi secure his job at your lab. It seems they not only attended the same school together but also worshiped at the same mosque, the Sheikh Agba Allah Mosque in Abu Dhabi. Marina just learned of this. We have no more information yet." Saying these words reminded me that Ana, who discovered the connection, was inside the ABH lab.

I considered how Rashid might have become so radicalized as to help kidnap his sister and have his father shot. What had he found in ISIS that had changed him into a crazed terrorist? He had fooled us all, and I wondered if we would ever know.

We had reached the entrance to the lab and passed through security. It was quiet and looked just as it would have on any day. Mansur was waiting for us outside the main entrance. He had several of his men with him, and all were armed with AK-47s, prepared to shoot as necessary.

There were no signs of the terrorists on the grounds. But they wouldn't have to be there, not if they had already planted a bomb they could detonate from afar. I reminded myself they wouldn't—at least not until they got the cloaking device.

Looking at Mansur's calm and collected face brought my ire over Marina's kidnapping to a boiling point. I strode up and spoke just inches from his face. "What happened, Mansur? How did they get their hands on her? She was supposed to be with you." I poked him in the chest, and his men moved closer. He waved them off.

"Ms. DiPietro received a call that she took in the hallway outside Latif's room. When she didn't return after a few minutes, I went to look for her and alerted my men watching the hospital entrances and exits. There was no sign of her." He backed away from me slightly. "Then I received a call of my own to come here." He gestured toward the building.

This had been well planned. We were all exactly where the Salafi wanted us. Rashid was nowhere to be found.

Chapter Fifty-Two

Things were at a stalemate. The three of us remained silent, staring at one another for what seemed like hours, but it was barely a minute. Adnan's phone rang and broke the silence. I could hear the faint voice of the speaker as he listened. When he hung up, he looked at each of us in turn. There was no need to ask who had called.

"I am to go inside and collect the software and the machine for the cloaking device and bring it out here." He gestured to the area where we were standing in front of the lab's entrance. "Once I have done that, they will send someone to retrieve it. When it is in their hands, they will release Samira and Ms. DiPietro."

Mansur stepped in front of him. "I will go instead."

"Thank you, my friend, but no." Adnan put out a hand to stop him. "This is my responsibility, not yours."

We heard the shots before we saw the vehicle. A black SUV with dark-tinted windows blasted its way through the gates, killing the guards and the sentry in the tower as it sped up the driveway that led to the ABH lab. The driver stopped about thirty feet away and revved the motor before coming farther up the macadam. *Trying to let us know who's in charge*, I thought. As if killing the guards hadn't made the point.

Adnan gave the vehicle a long look and then slowly entered the building. The door of the SUV opened, and Rashid stepped out, dressed now in camouflage clothing with a *Shemagh* wrapped around his head and part of his face. That and the Glock in his hand made his transformation from horseman to terrorist complete. Glaring at Mansur and me, he opened the back door and roughly grabbed Marina from inside. She stumbled but he righted her and pulled her close to him, then pointed the gun at her head. I could see she was trying to hold it together, but I knew how terrified she must be inside. Marina understood the threats the Salafi made were real and the horrors they inflicted on their prisoners would have them begging for death.

Moving on auto-pilot, I started for them, until Mansur grabbed me roughly by the arm. He spoke quietly so that only I could hear. "Stop, my friend. Don't give him a reason to kill her." His stone-cold gaze told me he would be ready if we had the chance to act.

In that second, I swore that I would find Rashid wherever he might run to and make him pay, one way or another.

Marina's hands were bound behind her back. Her eyes found mine and seemed to telegraph she was trying to find a way to escape. I felt powerless, standing there with no way to help her, fear gnawing away in my belly with every breath.

Finally, Adnan appeared at the entrance to the lab. He was holding what looked like a small black suitcase. He walked past Mansur and me and placed the suitcase on the ground between us and Rashid and Marina.

"This is what you want. Now, let the women go."

Rashid waved the gun at him and then pushed it back against Marina's head. "Not quite yet, old man." He laughed. "We're not finished here. You, Donahue, bring that closer to me!" He jutted his chin toward the case and emphasized his words by tightening his grip on Marina. "Now."

I did as I was told, picked up the case, and started to move closer to him at an easy pace. My brain was frantically searching for something I could do. If I could distract him in some way, for just a second, I might be able to free Marina.

"Stop there." He pointed at the ground with the gun when I was just a few feet in front of him. Now, might be my chance.

Just as I was about to make my move, another black SUV roared into the driveway. Two men jumped out and grabbed me as Rashid snatched up the case and shoved Marina back into the vehicle. I watched her horrified face as the men forced me toward their vehicle, shackling my hands as they shoved me inside.

In the back, another of the terrorists was waiting with a hypodermic needle in his hand. He laughed as he jabbed it into my arm. "This won't hurt a bit," he said and laughed again as I slumped against the window, Marina's face growing farther and farther away with every breath.

Chapter Fifty-Three

A moonless night had taken over the sky. A layer of gray clouds floated high above me in the deep, inky blackness. I must have dozed off, and I awoke with a start. I was still atop the Burj Khalifa, spent physically and mentally.

I had no way of knowing if what Adnan had handed over to Rashid was the real cloaking device. By now, they would have tried it out. If it hadn't worked, they wouldn't hesitate to take their vengeance out on the women. Even if it had, Marina and Samira could still be dead.

I was filled with rage and howling at the moonless sky when I heard a noise behind me. A hand slid around from behind and covered my mouth and nose. *This is it*, I thought. *I'll never see Marina again.* It was time to fight, as flight didn't seem to be an option. As I struggled, the hand over my face clamped tighter, shutting off my air supply while another brought a cell phone to my ear.

"Donahue. Stop making this harder than it must be. My men are here to rescue you. So be a good lad and go with them. Nod your head to let them know you understand."

I did as the voice told me and the hand was removed from my mouth. I took in a deep gulp of air as I listened to Nigel Phillips. How he knew I was here was a mystery, but there was no time to puzzle it out. The two men, British Special Forces, from the look of their gear, released me and had me inside the building in a flash. Silent and quick, the soldier in the lead put his index finger to his lips, letting me know not to make a sound. I nodded again, and we moved down to what appeared to be a maintenance stairway.

No one had cared how much noise I made when they dragged me up here but if there were any security people on duty now, none of us wanted them to hear us.

A few floors below the rooftop, we stopped. The lead soldier silently opened a door, and we moved outside to a wide, open area on the seaward side of the building. A minute later, I heard the whumping of helicopter blades getting louder as they approached us.

When the chopper was overhead, on stealth mode, three lines snaked down toward us. Before I had a chance to think about it, the second soldier strapped me into a harness attached to the middle line. "Okay, sir?" he asked.

When I nodded, he and his partner grabbed hold of their lines, and he gave a thumbs up. We were lifted into the sky as the chopper banked away from the building.

Relieved as I was to be rescued, I hadn't expected to be airlifted over the Arabian Gulf and soaring around like a seagull. Soon enough, the lines were winched into the belly of the chopper, and we were on safe ground, so to speak.

Another soldier helped me out of my harness and handed me a cell for the second time. "Nigel, you have to find Marina. The Salafi have her and—"

I never got to finish what I was saying. The voice that stopped me was Marina's.

"Nick, it's okay. We're safe. I'll see you as soon as you land."

Marina was alive. Those bastards didn't have her. She was free, but I was still going to make them pay one way or another.

Our reunion took place at the Al Minhad Air Base, about fifteen miles south of Dubai. The base wasn't exactly secret, but the Brits hadn't exactly been advertising they were using it either. Because they'd had men in place, they'd been able to get me out quickly.

Rescuing Marina and Samira was another story. Since we'd gotten to Dubai, Marina had been in contact with Nigel several times. He obviously kept an eye on us. When he heard what was at stake, he pulled a team together and shipped them off to the base, although I doubt the PM or the king knew anything about it.

From there, several soldiers were detailed to extract Samira and Marina, whose up-to-the-minute intelligence reported were also in the hands of the Salafi. The info also specified the group hadn't taken the women to their secret desert camp. Instead, they brought them to a safe house closer to Dubai.

Whatever their reason, it worked to our advantage. Nigel's team moved in fast, executed the Salafi guards watching the women, and got them out.

Unfortunately, Rashid was not among them. Marina told us he'd brought her to their hiding place and left with the cloaking device. Most probably to deliver it to the head of his ISIS cell.

My scenario was slightly different than hers. I figured Rashid left his sister and Marina close at hand in case Adnan needed more persuasion. I have no doubt he would have killed one or both of them and delivered their bodies to Adnan to achieve his goals.

We brought Samira to the hospital to be checked over. She was badly dehydrated, and her wrists were chaffed from being tied, but she wasn't harmed in any other way. She was fortunate she was rescued before the Salafi had gone to work on her.

The employees at ABH were safe, as well. Adnan had gotten everyone out of the lab as soon as the SUVs departed. According to Ana, it was pandemonium. Employees watched in horror as a bomb unit arrived on the scene. Men in protective suits with canines swarmed over the lab. They found several heavy-duty explosive devices scheduled to go off shortly. They had gotten there just in time, and it was a miracle no one was hurt or killed.

Latif, who was still in the hospital, and Janiki were heartbroken at the deceit and perfidy of their son, especially toward a man who had treated him as one of his own.

"It's a matter of honor," Latif whispered to me as he gripped my hand. "We will never be free of this stain our son has placed upon us."

Not to mention, I thought, *he kidnapped his sister and had his own father shot.*

Marina and I had a more private reunion later. "I didn't think I'd ever see you again." I was holding on to her as tight as I could.

"Me neither," she said as she laid her head on my shoulder. "And thank God, Ana was not hurt."

We moved toward our bedroom, still clutching each other. "What do you remember about the house? Were other members of the cell there, as well as the guards?

"I don't know. Rashid blindfolded me as soon as I was in the car." Her eyes were closed as she spoke, seeming to recreate a mental image. "When we got to the house, he flung me into a dark room with no windows and left. I heard a whimpering close to me and called out. The whimpering got louder, and I moved closer. It was Samira. She was bound and gagged, but I managed to get my blindfold off, and working together, we eventually released our bonds." She shuddered. "I've never been so scared. I knew what these people were capable of, and I had no doubts as to what they'd do to both of us."

"That's enough for now." I turned her to face me and kissed her gently. "It's over, and you're safe."

But that bastard Rashid wasn't. I'd find him if it took the rest of my life. You could bet the bank on that.

Chapter Fifty-Four

Louisville:

We were back at Adnan's farm in Louisville, only now, it looked more like an armed camp. Mansur had returned with us and had stationed a cadre of his security people all around the property. Men in black suits with submachine guns paced from the house to the stables. It was an eerie feeling to be surrounded by so much firepower in the hands of men who'd shoot first and ask questions later. Yet, with the Derby just a few days away, he wanted to leave no room for error or a suicide bomber.

Marina had sent Ana back to London. She was pretty shaken up, but trooper that she was, had pleaded to stay. Marina thought one brush with death was enough and the matter was settled. She appeased her by asking her to liaise with Nigel if any other important information on the Salafi should turn up. Not happy, but knowing Marina was the boss, Ana left on the next British Airways flight to Heathrow.

Josef, on the other hand, was not appeased in any way. He was beside himself. With all these people to manage, he didn't know if he was coming or going, unless Marina was in the vicinity, then it was the latter. She tried to keep out of his way but sliding into his path every once in a while and watching him trying to melt into the wall like a copy of Munch's *The Scream* brought a touch of levity to this dire situation.

Latif, Janiki, and Samira were with us, as well. Adnan didn't want them out of his sight until Rashid could be found and prosecuted. Me? I was hoping to be the one to find him, and then there would be no need to take him in for prosecution. The idea of being captor, judge, and jury had a great deal of appeal. The only problem was, I didn't think he'd show his face anywhere around here. If I were him, I'd be long gone into the sirocco, the hot, dust-filled wind that blew across the desert at hurricane speeds.

His problem, as I saw it, was that he let his ISIS masters down. These butchers didn't take kindly to failure or offer up second chances.

When the dust had settled, Mansur and I discussed the bombs that were planted in the lab. It was a sprawling building with separate areas for research labs, production, and shipping. I imagined the main target had been the lab where the cloaking device was being worked on.

"They were Mother of Satan bombs," Mansur said with disgust. "These TATP devices are filled with nails and ball bearings that create fragmentation to do the most amount of damage possible." He was striding around the room as he spoke, eyes blazing. I imagined he was thinking of the carnage such bombs caused.

"I've heard about these bombs before. They've been used in terrorist attacks in the United States."

"You are right. The materials in the bombs, triacetone, and triperoxide, are easily obtained and much easier to acquire than commercial-grade explosives. The only problem, for the bomb makers, is the mixture is very unstable and can blow up at any time. The bombs we found were fifteen kilos each."

That amount of explosives would have obliterated ABH and anyone inside the building. It was a chilling thought.

"Any idea who made the bomb?" I asked. I didn't think Rashid was responsible for this part of the operation.

Mansur stopped pacing and gave me one of his death stares. "Yes."

Okay, that was all he was going to say. And maybe all I needed to know.

Adnan hadn't given the Salafi the real software for the cloaking device. They would never be able to make it work without the special programs and codes from ABH. The Salafi wouldn't be getting them from Malik, either. He was guarding Samira and Marina in the safe house and was killed by the special forces soldiers.

They took the term "take no prisoners" very much to heart.

Their hundred million dollars was off the table, as well. Rashid was so focused on the cloaking device that he most likely forgot about the money for the moment. I'm sure he thought he'd be able to get it at some point. Probably before he killed his sister and Marina.

Before this madness, I'd never heard of the Salafi. Now, I knew way too much. Especially their number one rule: If you're not with them all the way, you're indeniably against them. I'd give odds that Rashid was now firmly in that category. One of us was bound to get him.

I had my continuing problems to sort out now that I was back in Louisville. While everyone was busy securing the farm and Devil Wind, I took the opportunity to slip away and call Lydia.

"You have to come into the Louisville office right now, Donahue. The SAC in charge, Ryan Lederman, wants to talk."

We started right where we'd left off in our last conversation. "You know I didn't have anything to do with Eggers's murder." If I said it enough times, she might believe me. "Trust me on this, Lyd."

"Don't make me laugh. You don't know the meaning of the word." I could see her rolling her eyes in contempt. "Biggie and Cambiato are no longer persons of interest. You on the other hand…" She let her voice trail off.

"I've been doing some thinking and I have an idea who's responsible. I just need a little more time to prove it." I'd figured out who the killer was, but I didn't add that this person was nowhere to be found. Lydia would be taking a leap of faith if she did trust me. "The Derby is in two days. Tell Lederman I'll come in right after the race. I swear."

For what seemed like forever, there was silence on the phone. Finally, she spoke. "Okay. I'll convince him you'll be in to see him. You have until then."

I was off the hook for the moment but like a winning streak at the craps table. I knew it wouldn't last.

Chapter Fifty-Five

Marina and I decided to walk over to Devil Wind's stable and watch his workout. Adnan, Rehan, and Mike were so focused on the horse, they didn't even realize we were there. I'm sure if Devil Wind had gotten my scent, he would have stomped around, making his displeasure known.

Mike was saddling him for a practice lick. This time, he'd be racing against two other horses in the stable. Personally, I didn't think this horse would care if he were racing against a whole brigade of Thoroughbreds. He knew he had whatever it took to beat them all.

We watched as he outpaced the competition and "won" easily. Adnan was smiling. The first smile I'd seen on his face since we left Dubai. As Mike led the horse from the track for his cool-down routine and bath, Adnan noticed us and walked over.

"He's quite an animal, isn't he?" Marina's praise was well-founded.

"I have been raising and racing horses for many years now," Adnan said, "but I truly have never come across one who has so much power and such a will to win." His smile had faded, and his eyes clouded over. "We must keep him safe. We must."

"We will." Marina reached out to him and put her hand on his arm as she spoke. "Nick and I—we won't let anything happen to him."

Just then, Mike called him over, and Adnan left us and walked back into the stable.

We started making our way to the house in silence, each deep in our thoughts.

Finally, I spoke. "I'm worried." I shook my head. "I'd feel so much better if Rashid were in custody."

"Me, too." Marina looked over her shoulder, taking in the stable, the track, and the grounds. "I feel like he's here, Nick, taunting us, just out of reach, and I don't like it one bit."

"I know what you mean." I also had the feeling that we were being watched, that someone was staring at my back. "But Devil Wind is well protected." I gestured to the armed guards we were about to pass on the path. "He'd have to have a secret way in to get by all this security." I stopped dead in my tracks.

"What is it?"

I'd alarmed Marina.

"Nothing. It's nothing." I didn't want to make Marina any more nervous than she was, but maybe Rashid had found a secret way in and was already there. I forced myself to relax and tossed my arm around her shoulder. "Let's have lunch and then maybe a nap." I made my last words sound suggestive, and she reacted as I hoped she would.

"No naps today, buddy," she teased playfully, then swiftly got back to business. "I have too much to do. Mansur and I are meeting to finalize the security protocols for the track. The President of Churchill Downs, James Schimmenti, and the General Manager, Jordan Chase, have made time to see us after the last race of the day. Mansur briefed them on what was going on." She paused to gather her thoughts. "They have a right to know the track could be marked for a terrorist attack. Last year, over one hundred seventy thousand people attended the Derby. "Can you imagine the death and destruction a few of those Mother of Satan bombs would cause?"

I felt a shudder going through her, and I pulled her closer. "Do you think they'd cancel the Derby?" I asked, part of me wishing they would, knowing it was the safer option.

"Not a chance. In its entire history, the race has never been postponed or canceled, not even during World War Two. That's what Lederman told Mansur. I don't think we're going to change his mind, so we need to be prepared with the tightest security plan they've ever seen."

"Just like the Girl Scouts." I kissed the top of her head. I was pretty sure Adnan didn't want the race to be canceled, either. Especially after everything he'd been through.

Since I'd gotten to know him, my respect for him had grown. As my father had told me, he was an honorable man. And, I thought, a brave one, as well. The Salafi had forced his hand, and fortunately, they lost. I was sure it prickled at his conscience that so many lives were at stake when he delivered the incomplete cloaking device plans. But their actions made him understand that hundreds of thousands more could easily die if these terrorists had the device and the limitless possibilities it offered for destruction. It was not an easy choice.

I tuned out while Marina was explaining about the upcoming meeting with the track's head honchos. I murmured a few "um-hums" and "oohs." I was sure her plan was iron-tight.

My mind circled back to Rashid. And the inkling of an idea I had a little while ago came around again. Since we wouldn't be "napping," I decided to go on a reconnaissance mission of my own.

Chapter Fifty-Six

I watched Marina and Mansur slide into Adnan's black Mercedes SUV. Both their faces were grim. I imagined they were preparing for some pushback from the men they were meeting. Having a cadre of outside armed security agents taking over one of the world's most prestigious tracks on the day of its most famous race was a PR nightmare.

If it all sounds as dramatic as a diva refusing to sing, it was. But after the attacks on both own soil and other parts of the world, it was a reality people could not ignore. Having thousands of people blown up by ISIS terrorists was not an acceptable alternative.

Marina had told me the track officials would lobby for the security presence to be unobtrusive, but knowing Marina and Mansur, they'd suggest just the opposite—a show of strength to let the bad guys know they were onto them. I hoped they would work it out.

After the SUV turned onto the long driveway that led to the main road, I stepped through the front door and nodded to the guards stationed there.

I felt their eyes on me as I turned the corner of the house and moved onto the path that led to the stables. Even though they knew me, they weren't taking any chances. While their scrutiny was unnerving, it was good to see how cautious they were.

Instead of taking the short road that branched off and led to Devil Wind's stable, I continued walking straight back, which would bring me to the farthest point of the farm's property.

The path was flat and straight. High grasses on one side partially camouflaged a ten-foot- tall chain link fence topped by a thick coil of barbed wire. A lower, split rail wood fence was meant to keep the horses from straying onto the path following the other side. As I walked along, I could see the fence stretched all the way down to where I was headed.

I decided to check the back perimeter of the property. I thought there might be a gate on that side for easy access to the pasture. Marina and I had driven past this side of the farm, which was separated from the road by a tall stand of oak trees. I'd noticed the fence through the leaves but hadn't given it any more thought until now.

The chain link fence formed three sides of a box, with the main building standing in for the fourth side. It encompassed the whole property except for the driveway and front lawn.

I walked for about half a mile until I came to the end of the path and the back perimeter. I looked down the length of the fence for a gate, but it was solid metal with no place to enter. Unless someone was able to get over the barbed wire, cut the links, or dig underneath. Nothing looked disturbed that I could see, but I decided to examine the fence more closely.

Here, on the back side, there was only the chain link fence. Set in the middle of its length, there was a large water trough resting against it, surrounded by bales of hay piled helter-skelter on top of each other. This was for the horses let out to graze during the day. A few of these working horses, the non-racers that the stable hands used, were in the pasture now. They were far enough away so I didn't have to worry about one of them deciding, like Devil Wind, he didn't like me and trotting over to take a bite out of my hide.

In any event, I wasn't interested in them. It was the fence and the stand of oak trees that bordered it with their leaf-filled branches hanging over that had my attention. None of Mansur's security people were in sight. I know they had checked the entire perimeter of the property and were satisfied that it was secure. I was sure they would be back to check again, but not when.

When I got close to the water trough, I dropped to my knees and started searching around, trying to wedge my hand between the bales of hay and the trough. As usual, I could see that Adnan had spared no expense when it came to his horses. Set into the ground, this trough was about six feet long and three feet high, splaying out at the top. It appeared to be made of solid concrete. I noticed a tap at the top meant to produce a constant supply of fresh water and a drain at the bottom where it should flow out, keeping the water at a level height. The tap was turned off, and the water was not moving, which was surprising since there were horses in the pasture. I looked closer and found that the drain had been plugged. Someone had done a thorough job. I figured the trough weighed about a few thousand pounds, and it would probably take a crane to move it.

From where I knelt, I couldn't see behind it. And because of its V-shaped top, when I stood up, I couldn't see down over the back either. I would have to climb on the bales of hay, which I also couldn't move, then over the fence and its barbed wire if I wanted a closer look at this particular ten or twelve-foot stretch of the back side of the property.

Reaching as high up as I could from my perch on the hay bales, I shimmied up the fence to right underneath the barbed wire. The coils were razor sharp and nasty looking, and I knew if I didn't make it over, I'd be sorry.

I held on to the top pole just under the wire with my left hand and anchored my left foot as deep as it would go into one of the links to my side. Then I swung my body out and up, grabbed onto a low-hanging branch with my right hand, and, using momentum, brought my right foot over and planted it on the oak's trunk. Suspended as I was now, like a dancer doing a mid-air split, I knew I only had one chance to make it over. If I didn't, Marina and I wouldn't be having naptime anytime in the near future. I took a deep breath and went for it, pitching my weight to the right, grabbing onto another branch with my left hand, and bringing my left foot over. I released my right foot and, for a second or two, I swung in the air. Then I dropped to the ground.

When I regained my composure, I started to search and could see the grass and earth behind the trough were trampled. Several of the links on the fence were cut in a vertical line right behind it and then pinched back together. It would have been almost impossible to notice this from my vantage point on the other side. I couldn't figure out why they'd stopped instead of cutting more of the links and shimmying through. Whoever it was must have given up for some reason. My money was on Rashid. I knew in my bones it was him. He had tried to sneak in through the "back door," as I suspected. Fortunately, he hadn't made it.

I stood up and tried to brush off the dirt, grass, and leaves that were clinging to me. I was just turning to go—this time around the outside of the fence—when I noticed a sliver of something shiny half buried in the ground next to the tree I'd used to hoist myself over. I bent down and brushed away the dirt concealing it. It was a can of rat poison with bromethalin, whatever that was. The shiny metal object I thought I'd seen in the barn at the track before I was attacked flashed through my mind. I shook the can and could tell it was empty. I lifted the top off, and it opened gingerly. The can contained some residue, and a stinging odor attacked my nose. I held it as far away from me as possible and closed it.

I looked at the can and then at the water trough and realized I'd gotten it very wrong. Rashid hadn't needed to get onto the grounds to do his dirty work. He only needed enough space to reach his hand through the slit in the fence.

Just then, the horses that had been ignoring me were slowly walking over toward the hay and the water, tails swishing lazily as they moved. I dropped the can and started waving my hands, shaking the fence, and yelling at them. "Go away, Get back. Get. Get." Whatever I could think of to keep them away and stop them from drinking. I scared them sufficiently to make them turn and gallop off. Then I fished out my cell and called Devil Wind's stable. In a matter of minutes, Rehan and several other grooms galloped into the field and started herding the horses back to the barn.

Minutes later, the security guards came rushing through the trees with their guns at the ready. I waved so they could see it was me. The bad guy had come and gone, and we'd missed him again.

Chapter Fifty-Seven

I rode back to Devil Wind's stable with the security guards, and Adnan met me at the door. He looked dreadful, his face ashen, and the smile I'd seen earlier seemingly gone for good.

"My G—God, Nick." He faltered, having trouble speaking. "What next?"

"Let's go inside," I said as I put my hand on his back and gently led him into the stable. I didn't want any of his staff who were settling the horses I'd spooked to overhear our conversation. "I think Rashid poisoned the water for the horses in the pasture." I explained what I thought about my "back door" theory and how it had led me to the trough and the hay.

Adnan sat and listened, his head shaking from side to side and his hands twisting over each other. He finally looked up at me. "Thank you, Nick. Again." He nodded at me.

I shrugged off the thanks. There was nothing I could say to make him feel better. "I'm just glad the horses are safe." Not to mention being relieved the barbed wire hadn't done me in.

We sat there for a moment, neither of us speaking. The same thought was probably going through both of our minds: How were we going to stop Rashid and the Salafi? While we managed to avert a catastrophe and save a few horses, it was the whole Churchill Downs complex and the thousands upon thousands of people attending the Derby who were in danger.

I wasn't sure Rashid had done all the dirty work on his own. He might have accomplices nearby ready, willing, and able to help—and die for their cause. How—or if—we'd find them in time was the real problem.

I told Adnan I was going back to the house to wait for Marina and Mansur and check on how they made out with the track's bigwigs. Adnan said he'd meet us later after he had some time to think. I nodded and left. There was nothing more to say at the moment.

Marina was already back when I walked in the door. She came over and gave me a huge hug. "I heard about what you did, Nick. You saved those horses from a horrible death."

While I was with Adnan at the stable, Rehan came by to thank me. He explained they never kept any kind of rodenticide anywhere near the horses. It would be fatal if they ingested it. That's probably what had happened with Devil Spirit. Sedated him and blinded him with rat poison. It was too much to think about. The metal object I'd seen in Fire Walker's stall could have been a container of rat poison left there by mistake. My attacker must have come to remove it and saw me nosing around.

"How'd it go with Schimmenti and Chase?" I asked, bringing myself back to the present.

Marina took a deep breath. "Well, for starters, they absolutely refuse to cancel the Derby."

"We kind of figured they wouldn't agree to cancel," I replied. "What about your suggestions for security?" I asked, taking in Mansur with my gaze.

"We came to a compromise," Marina said, her tone turning cold. "You know they wanted the security people to be unobtrusive, mixed in with the race day patrons.

"They are stupid people," Mansur added, "for not taking this threat as seriously as they should. Do they not realize what death and destruction a terrorist bomb can cause? Have they not seen the results in Paris, Brussels, and even in the United States?" He paused for a breath. "They think they will be able to catch 'one suicide bomber.' It is—"

Marina interrupted, "With the help of the FBI."

"The FBI?" I asked, my throat closing on the words. Really?" I managed to squeak out.

Marina shot me a look before continuing. "It's a good compromise. The SAC in the Louisville office, Ryan Lederman, is coming over later to finalize the plan. They'll be going over the buildings and grounds tomorrow, making sure it's clear of bombs. They plan to place sharpshooters in some of the towers and have agents mingle amongst the crowd on race day. I've asked Helen McCorkendale and her people to be present as well. They'll dress to blend in with the grooms and stable hands and be positioned near the barns. Mansur had a brilliant idea that would make it plausible for stationing armed men at the entry gates and on the grounds without causing a panic situation." Marina gave a quick nod in his direction. "We're going to float the rumor that some high-up Saudi dignitaries will be attending the race, and the added protection is a precaution for them. It will be a good cover for the beefed-up security, or at least we hope so."

"I still think they should cancel." I recalled the sprawl of buildings that made up Churchill Downs and the huge amount of space it contained. "A bomb, or several of them, if Rashid has helpers, would mean total disaster. Everyone at the track will be in danger."

"Schimmenti and Chase absolutely won't give in to terrorists. They believe that with the FBI on the scene, things will work out. They're prepared to mobilize several hundred agents by race day." I could see Marina wasn't one-hundred percent convinced of what she was saying.

"They've left us no choice unless we catch Rashid before Saturday.

"That doesn't leave us much time to find him." I thought about how crafty he'd been so far.

"Well, now we've got the FBI to help." Marina looked at her watch. "They should be here in about an hour."

"Good. Good," I managed to say as I feverishly cast around for a reason to get out of the house before they arrived. "And make sure to tell them to check the water supply." The can of rat poison came floating into my mind.

Lederman was the Special Agent in Charge of the Louisville Office, the one Lydia had spoken with. As occupied as he might be with Rashid and the Salafi, I was sure he'd remember my name as a person of interest in conjunction with a murder inquiry.

"I think I should go check in with Rehan and see how those horses are getting on. I scared them pretty good," I said and started walking toward the door.

Marina nodded and looked at her watch again. "Well, don't take too long."

As soon as the front door closed behind me, I made a beeline for the garage. I'd discovered there were spare sets of keys for all the cars in a small cabinet at the back. I picked up the set for the Jeep Land Rover and clicked the button. The doors unlocked smoothly, and I hopped inside. I sat there for a few minutes, then started the engine. I had no idea where I was going; I just had to get away before the FBI agents arrived. I'd make up some excuse to tell Marina later.

I pulled out of the garage and circled the top of the driveway. Without really thinking about it, I turned onto the main road and spoke the words "Mulberry Street Wine Distributors" into the GPS. Gretchen, the name I decided to give to the car's female-voiced GPS, answered with directions to the Airport Industrial Center on Rochester Drive. It was a forty-five-minute run from Adnan's villa to the Industrial Center via the Western Kentucky Parkway.

While I was driving, I kept hearing my mother's voice whispering in my ear, "You never could learn to leave well enough alone, could you, Nick?" It was like I was having a bad daymare. I tried to ignore her voice like I usually do, but when I heard my father chime in with the same message, it gave me pause.

Okay, maybe this time, their combined imaginary voices were giving me good advice. Really, what did I hope to find at the distributorship? I agreed with the FBI that Tommy B's boys probably weren't responsible for Eggers's death, but something was drawing me into their orbit. It wasn't just a ploy to avoid the FBI. "Stupidity," Mom would have said, and she'd be right.

Here, I was zipping by 163 Rochester Road and searching for the warehouse with the Mulberry Wine Distributors logo on its front. It wasn't hard to find. It was a large, semi-attached concrete building with pull-down metal garage doors fitted with a small doorway on the side for people going in and out to use.

I pulled the Jeep into a spot across the road and a few buildings down. I was thankful for the tinted windows that let me observe the warehouse without being seen. It appeared closed for the day, as though all the gangsters had holstered their guns and gone home. What *was* I doing here? It was time to leave. I fired up the engine and was just about to pull out when the side doorway opened. A few beefy guys in black leather jackets came out, bouncing on the soles of their feet like gangsters do—at least the ones I knew. They hiked their pants up over their bellies—or was it to adjust their guns—and moved toward a big black Cadillac Escalade. Black Jacket One slipped behind the wheel. Black Jacket Two opened the passenger side back door and waited. A moment later, out came the man himself, Tommy B, dressed in sartorial splendor in a navy suit with silver tie and pocket hankie. I bet his shoes were shined to a high polish he could admire himself in.

I ducked down past the Jeep's steering wheel and let out the breath I'd been holding. What were the chances of seeing him here, in Louisville, I asked myself. Why had I put myself in his path yet again?

My mom was right. Consciously or not, I just couldn't leave it alone, even when the odds were decidedly against me.

Chapter Fifty-Eight

I peeked over the steering wheel and watched the Escalade pull away. When it reached the turn-off for the main road, I sat up and started the engine. I decided to follow. I needed to know where Tommy B was going.

There were, I thought, two reasons he was in Kentucky. The first had to do with racing. Since his inside man, Eggers, was no longer around, he needed someone else to do his bidding at the track. It wouldn't surprise me if he was recruiting a replacement and might be meeting with a few candidates before the Derby.

The second reason was more personal. Call me paranoid, but I thought I might be the reason for his visit, like killing two birds with one stone. The latter bird being me. He had to know Marina and I were in Louisville. Biggie and Vince Cambiato must have recognized me when they drove by. Not to mention, I'd told Lydia about Tommy B's relationship with Eggers, and she sicced the Louisville FBI on his people here. So what if they hadn't done the murder? I'd upset the Zen flow of his thievery and bribery, and now, I had to pay. Again.

My hands were shaking at the wheel, and I couldn't even blame it on the ride, which was smooth and easy. I willed myself to calm down. I stayed three or four cars behind the Escalade until it turned into the driveway to the Brown Hotel Louisville. It was one of the city's top-rated and looked it. I waited until Tommy B exited from the SUV, and a valet walked over to take charge of the luggage. A minute later, the threesome was inside.

I had a decision to make. Did I turn around, head back to Adnan's villa, and face the FBI, or did I brazen it out and go in search of my nemesis and his posse?

My gambler's mojo took over. I fished a coin from my pocket and tossed it in the air. Heads, I go back to the villa. Tails, I tackle the lion in his den.

"You don't have the good sense God gave you." That's another saying my mother is fond of, by the way. And one she would be using if she saw me now.

Tails it was, and off I went. I gave the Jeep over to the parking valet, pocketed my ticket, strode into the lobby of the Brown Hotel, and stopped dead in my tracks. Jeez, I thought the Burj Al Nomad had been over the top. The Brown Hotel was equally extravagant but different. I felt like I was back in the middle of the Renaissance, in some duke's palace where I was waiting for an audience under a coffered gold ceiling as I watched functionaries gliding over polished marble floors. When I pulled up the room rates on my phone, I was surprised to see I could afford to stay there. That was good to know in case Marina booted me out for not showing up to meet the FBI's Special Agent in Charge, Ryan Lederman.

I made a beeline across the floor to the bar and lounge, picking up a local newspaper as I walked. I chose a deep wing chair at a table on the right side of the lounge that gave me a clear view of the bank of three elevators in the lobby. I settled in behind my paper, a surveillance tactic I learned from watching too many TV mysteries.

That was as far as I'd gotten with my plan when a waiter came over to take my order. It was well into cocktail hour, so I ordered Bourbon on the rocks. When I turned back to watching the elevators, the middle one pinged open, and Black Jacket One, who'd escorted Tommy B to the hotel, stepped out. I didn't recognize him from London or New York and figured he was local talent, part of Cambiato's crew. I sank into the wing chair and lifted the newspaper higher to cover my face. I waited a beat, then peeked around the side of the paper to see which way the guy was going.

Crap, he was walking directly toward me. I ducked my head behind the paper and tried to keep it from shaking. Maybe he was heading to the bar at the back of the lounge to get a drink. Or maybe not, I thought, feeling the lump in my stomach growing larger as my mind dredged up my first encounter with Tommy B.

In what felt like an eternity, I slowly lowered the paper down past my eyes and realized he'd walked right by me.

My sigh of relief was probably loud enough for the clerk at the front desk to hear. Slowly, I peeked around the side of the chair and watched as he approached a man sitting at the end of the bar, hunched over his drink, and glancing over his shoulder every few seconds. The guy was dressed in work clothes—well-worn jeans and a tee shirt with a bar's logo on it. He looked nervous and uncomfortable like he didn't belong in such an upscale place. Or maybe it was the idea of taking a meeting with Tommy B and helping to fix races that made him nervous. Could be.

He straightened up as Black Jacket One came into his line of sight. They shook hands and said a few words to each other. The guy downed his drink and followed Tommy B's emissary to the elevators.

I got a good look at his face as they passed by and knew I'd recognize him if I saw him again. Light brown hair fell over his forehead into his brown eyes, a nose that looked like it'd been broken once or twice, and a stocky, powerful-looking build. I pegged him as a stable hand, or at least working in some position at the track. A good bet he was Eggers's replacement.

I watched until they entered the elevator, and its display showed that they were on the top floor. Then I called the waiter over and asked for my check.

While I was waiting, I thought about the information I just gathered. I didn't know what I was going to do with it. I had to tell Marina, and after she chewed me out, we would figure something out. As much as I wanted to get Tommy B for racketeering or race fixing, I knew he didn't have anything to do with the threat to the track, and that was our focus now.

I thought about calling Lydia again, but she probably wouldn't even take the call. She, for sure, wouldn't pass on the information to Lederman, whom I was actively avoiding.

The waiter came back, stood next to my chair, and cleared his throat to get my attention. "Your check's been taken care of, sir, and the gentleman asked me to give this to you."

He handed me a folded note on a small silver tray and walked back to the bar. I unfolded the note slowly, afraid of what I'd find inside. I was right to be nervous.

> *This one's on me, Nick.*
> *See you soon.*
> *Tommy*

Tommy B was toying with me. He'd probably made me outside the warehouse and had a good laugh at my attempts to tail him without being seen. Our paths had crossed again, and this time, it was my fault. I'd tossed my chips into the pot, and now I had to pay the price.

Chapter Fifty-Nine

I headed back to Adnan's, holding on to the one positive thing that had come from my trip to the Mulberry Street Wine Distributors: the replacement guy for Eggers.

Sure, I could offer this up to Marina as my reason for missing the meeting with the FBI; I entered the villa with a purposeful stride and a confident air. It lasted for about a minute, which was as long as it took for Marina to give me the evil eye.

"Come with me," she demanded and jutted her chin to the guest wing.

I guess she didn't want Adnan and Mansur to overhear her reaming me out. I followed her, meekly avoiding eye contact with both men who were probably thinking I was a dumb schmuck.

When we were finally in the suite's living room, Marina turned to face me, arms crossed over her middle, waiting, eyes focused on mine.

I hated to be the one to give in, but some things are more important than pride. Like staying alive. "I'm sorry. Really. I meant to be here. Honestly."

Nothing.

"So," I tried another tack, "how'd it go with the FBI? Are we all set?"

Still nothing.

I was stalling for time trying to work out how to tell her about The Mulberry Street gang without mentioning why I had wanted to avoid Lederman.

Now, tapping her foot impatiently was added to the folded arms and ice-cold eyes. I didn't know what would happen if she ran out of body parts to scold me with.

"Okay, I'll explain, but please hear me out before you say anything." I took a step closer, and she took one back.

"I'm waiting, Nick."

"I had a hunch about the Mulberry Street Wine Distributors, and I decided to follow it." That part, at least, was true, sort of. "I drove over to their warehouse to have a look around." I paused, planning what to say next. "I was just about to come back for the meeting when a group of guys left the building. One of them was Tommy B."

"He's here?" she asked. "What the hell is he doing here?" She shook her head in frustration. "He's one more headache we don't need right now."

"I think he was here to meet Tim Eggers's replacement."

Now, I had her full attention. I told her about following the mobster to the hotel and everything that happened after, including the love note I received, which I pulled from my pants pocket and handed over.

She read it quickly, then crumpled it in her hand, an unsatisfying substitute for the man himself. I know he'd affected her sense of self badly, and she wasn't over it yet.

"I got a good look at the new guy. I'm sure I can identify him if I see him again." I paused for a beat. "I'm sorry if I messed things up with the FBI meeting."

She sighed, took my hand, and led me to the couch. "You didn't. Not really. Although it would have been good to have another set of ears listening."

"I'm sorry," I said. This time, I truly was. Especially since now, we were on Tommy B's radar, and it was my fault.

"Like I said, Mr. Bonnannaio is going to have to take a back seat to the terrorists. But—" A wicked smile spread across her lips. "—I'll be happy to point the FBI in his direction the moment I see him. They can decide what to do about him and his new inside man."

If only it were that easy, I thought. If the authorities came looking for him, he'd reciprocate and come looking for us. Maybe I was correct in thinking I was part of the reason he was here. Marina was putting up a brave front, whether for me or herself, I wasn't sure.

"C'mon." Marina rose from the couch, pulling me up with her. "Let's get back to Adnan and Mansur before they send in their security guys to rescue you."

Chapter Sixty

Even when you knew it was coming, derailing a terrorist attack was a nearly impossible feat. With less than forty-eight hours until post time, every minute counted, and Marina and Mansur were determined to make the most of them.

Schimmenti and Chase had agreed to close the track the day before the Derby, which had never been done previously. They told the press they were adding security personnel to make sure the track was secure for the Saudi dignitaries who would be attending, intimating that there were concerns regarding the Saudi party, without ever coming out and saying it. They took Mansur's idea and used it to ensure the racegoers would understand the presence of men in black with guns. It was a good move and gave everyone the breathing room they needed to prepare.

We arrived at Churchill Downs at seven in the morning. Marina and Mansur were off and running like Thoroughbreds out of the gate. They gathered all those who would have a role in protecting the track, its horses, and the patrons during the Derby and began delegating assignments. There were several hundred people involved, including Feebies from Louisville and Lexington with bomb-sniffing dogs and sharpshooters. Everyone was given a photo of Rashid to compare to anyone entering the grounds.

The dogs and their trainers needed to cover every inch of each building, including the clubhouse, the grandstand, barns, and tunnels, as well as the paddock and the grounds, before anyone would be let in for tomorrow's race, and they got right to it.

The SWAT team was deployed to the top of the grandstand and clubhouse.

They measured angles and distances to ensure there was a clear line of sight for every area of the track and the infield. They checked their communications and stationed themselves so a member of the team would be in a position to fire at the target if need be.

McCorkendale's New York crew was joined by Louisville undercover police, who determined which areas of the track would allow maximum crowd visibility. Churchill Downs's security staff would man the eighteen entrance gates.

Several other FBI operatives were vetting the track employees from Schimmenti and Chase on down. They were looking at the owners, trainers, jockeys, and stable hands who would be present for the race.

To make things even more complicated, the groundskeepers were out in force, pruning, watering, and setting up colorful banks of flowers and shrubs.

It was a monumental task. And tomorrow, it had to appear as if it was business as usual.

Since Adnan and I were not part of these plans, we took ourselves to the barn to check on Devil Wind in his stall. Rehan and several of the grooms had transported the horse from Adnan's stable to the track. They were armed and would keep watch all night to keep Devil Wind safe from harm.

Adnan was looking marginally better than he had over the last few days. His eyes lit up at the sight of his favorite horse. Devil Wind snickered when he saw his master and stuck his head over the stall's door to get closer. Adnan obliged by rubbing the Thoroughbred's head and speaking to him softly.

I, on the other hand, kept my distance from my nemesis. "I'll stay over here." I nodded to a spot several feet away. "I don't want him to get over-excited."

Rehan tossed me a sly smile. He knew I meant I didn't want Devil Wind to bare his teeth and lunge for me.

After Adnan finished his heart-to-heart with Devil Wind, we left the barn area and walked around the back end of the track to the clubhouse. We rode the elevator to the second floor of the Trackside Café, which had remained open to feed everyone working today. We sat at a table overlooking the oval and ordered coffee.

"When I asked you and Marina to help, I had no idea what was involved." Adnan toyed with his cup as he spoke. "I'm sorry, Nick. You two shouldn't have had to be thrust into the path of the Salafi."

I could hear the exasperation in his voice. "No one could have known it would come to this." I tried to assuage his guilt. *No one*, I thought, *except Rashid*.

As if he could read my mind, Adnan spoke while looking into the distance. "I should have seen what was happening in my company right in front of my eyes." He turned to me. "I trusted Rashid like a son." He shook his head and looked down at the table. "Now, he has betrayed everyone."

Just as I was about to reply, one of Mansur's people approached and asked to speak to Adnan. I took the hint and excused myself.

As I walked toward the café's exit and glanced down at the oval, I had an idea about how to make myself useful. I was the only one who had seen Eggers's replacement as Tommy B's inside man. Now, it was time to go find him.

Chapter Sixty-One

Outside, I watched Marina and Lederman, heads together, poring over several maps and papers spread out on a folding table. She looked up and pointed to a space on the other side of the grandstand, and Lederman nodded his head.

I was lucky she was occupied and wouldn't notice me skulking around the barns, which were where I had decided to look for the new fixer. By now, I was very familiar with the area, and I moved quickly along the path. Several security people were stationed along the way, and I nodded at them. They'd seen me with Lederman and Marina, so they let me pass unchallenged.

Several horses running in the Derby were already on the premises with their entourage of trainers, riders, and grooms. They'd come from their home barns, many of which were out of state and couldn't be turned away. Their trainers were given the same story about the Saudi bigwigs as a reason for closing the track today, and they were asked to cooperate with the security personnel. A few of the mounts were taking their afternoon jogs, and from what I could see, it looked like Devil Wind was facing some tough competition, including Petrocelli's Night Music.

I wandered around and took a good look at every man I passed. Nothing. If the inside man was here, I didn't see him.

I was just about to give up when I decided to check out the dormitory. A long, low building with a hall down the middle and rooms on each side, it was located on the backside of the track a little way from the barn. A group of men were milling around in front of the entrance as I approached, talking quietly amongst themselves. I looked at each one, smiling to mask my interest. All were dressed in jeans and T-shirts, and I figured they were the grooms and stable hands who did the grunt work.

I sauntered up to them, trying to think of a ruse that would get me inside the building. I was just about to ask if anyone knew where I could find Rehan when another man stepped into the open doorway, head bent down to light the prohibited cigarette in his hand.

"Can you believe all the crap they're doin' for a few friggin' Saudis," he complained, flipping his lighter closed and looking up as he took a drag.

That's when he saw me look from his face to his hand holding the lighter and bolted. He tossed his cigarette on the ground and stepped back through the door, slamming it behind him just as I started to enter. I flung the door open and dashed inside, leaving the other men bewildered. By the time my eyes adjusted to the dimly lit interior, he was gone. Crap. He must have seen me in the hotel lobby when he met with Tommy B and realized I was the guy he banged on the head in Fire Walker's stall, and I recognized his jailhouse tattoo.

I moved down the hallway cautiously, half expecting him to jump out and attack me again. A door at the end of the hall was closed, and I opened it to find an empty kitchen with a screen door open to the outside swinging back and forth. I pushed it and heard it bang against the frame as I ran out, but the guy was nowhere to be seen. I looked left and right, but he had disappeared. He might have made it over the fence onto the road beyond. I jogged around to the front of the building to see if maybe he'd come this way. All I saw was the same group of guys from a few minutes ago; now all turned in my direction with perplexed looks on their faces.

"The guy that just ran into the house, what's his name?" I asked. They all looked down at the ground, shuffling their feet, ignoring my question and me. "If that's the way you want to play it, I'll call the security guys, and you can explain your silence to them."

Even though they were low men on the track's race card, they all knew that something serious was going on with security. I suspected they wouldn't want to lose their jobs. I reached for my cell phone and started pushing the buttons.

Finally, one of them spoke. "He's Caleb Fillmore. Does some work for O'Rourke's mounts."

O'Rourke's stable hand and Tommy B's new inside man? Jeez, I thought. It was worse than I thought.

Chapter Sixty-Two

Even if I spent the rest of the day looking for Caleb Filmore, I'd probably never find him. But I could put him on Marina's radar.

I jogged over to the clubhouse and the "command center." Marina was standing there, hands on her hips, staring into space. There seemed to be a lot of that going around today.

"Hey." I leaned in and kissed her. "Everything all right?" A dumb question, given the reason we were all here, but her beautiful green eyes looked so clouded with worry and dejection that I couldn't help but ask.

"Better now that you're here." A small smile played across her lips. "I'm just afraid none of this—" She spread her arms to encompass the people moving all over the grounds. "—will do any good."

Maybe now was not the best time to tell her I'd found and lost Tommy B's new inside man. I knew she wanted to deal with that situation later after we captured Rashid.

I put on my most positive expression—the one I save just to annoy pit bosses—and took her hand in mine, squeezing it gently. "You'll find and stop Rashid. I'm sure of it."

I wasn't so sure. He was so devious and calculating we might never get him. Horrible but possible.

I changed my mind and decided to tell her about my run-in with Caleb Filmore if only to distract her for a moment or two. "He took off like an antelope being chased by a lion. I have no idea where he went, and I don't think the rest of that crew would tell me, even if they knew. The good news is—" I lifted my eyebrows skyward for emphasis. "—he won't be fixing any races for Tommy B, at least not now."

Marina tensed at the mention of the mobster's name. No matter how long ago it was, being kidnapped by him was something that made her both furious and, I suspected, a little afraid all at once. Maybe I was right in thinking part of the reason he was here was because of us, or me, and my meddling ways.

"As soon as this is over, I swear, I'll get him, and his new toady," was all she said and then changed the subject back to the problem at hand. "So far, no one's found anything out of the ordinary."

"That's kind of what you expected, isn't it?

Marina nodded. "I believe Rashid will try and slip in tomorrow using the press of the crowd to conceal himself. By now, he must be going crazy knowing that he failed the Salafi and that we're onto him, as well." She bit the corner of her lip, a habit she had when thinking, then continued. "His monumental ego won't let him stop, though. He'll want to prove to his masters he can get the job done. He'll be here all right, and we'll be waiting."

There wasn't much I could add to what Marina had said. I agreed about Rashid showing up, but I wasn't as certain we could stop him. Lady Luck is a fickle friend. I was hoping she'd be on our side for this confrontation.

Marina and I chatted for a few more minutes, and I saw Lederman heading our way. It was time to make myself scarce. I was sure he knew who I was from his conversation with Lydia. He also probably figured out I skipped the meeting last night on purpose. I wasn't ready to discuss it, or Tommy B, right now.

I looked at my watch then gave Marina a quick kiss goodbye. "I'm going to meet Adnan and check on a few things."

She nodded her head and turned toward Lederman. I turned and walked away at a slow and even pace. I knew the Feebie was staring at me, and I swear I could feel his eyes boring into my back like steel blades. Like Marina, he had more important things on his mind right now. He was probably planning to skewer me after the Derby. My reprieve wouldn't last long.

I took another walk around the track, hoping that Filmore might have returned by now. No luck with that, either. I hung around for a few more hours, then told Marina I was going back to the villa. There's nothing more superfluous than a gambler who was out of chips standing around watching all the other players.

By the time we got to bed, it was well past midnight. Marina and Adnan had come home around eleven, and I joined them as they reviewed the preparations for tomorrow. Marina looked beat, her eyes anxious, her face ashen, and her posture dejected. My woman was worried, and I was worried for her.

Adnan hadn't fared much better. He was a man stripped of all self-assuredness, not the billionaire titan he was just weeks ago. He slumped into an easy chair, and Josef hovered over him, waiting to fulfill his every command. Adnan just motioned him away.

"Did you finalize all the plans?" I asked.

"We've done all we could," Marina answered, looking at me and then turned her gaze toward Adnan. "I think we should get some rest," she added, "tomorrow is going to be a long, long day."

Chapter Sixty-Three

The smell of freshly brewed coffee woke me, and I turned to put my arm over Marina, only to find she wasn't there. When I checked the clock, I groaned. It was barely five. Wiping the sleep from my half-closed eyes, I forced myself to stand and move. The promise of the coffee wafting toward me was an added incentive.

I tossed on some jeans and a sweater and moved into the suite's kitchen. Marina was sitting at the table with her laptop open in front of her. She smiled when she saw me, a much more hopeful look than last night's.

"Anything new?" I asked.

"No. I'm just checking in with Ana and Nikki. Nigel's been keeping them up to date on the Salafi's movements. He received information they moved into an old Libyan training camp set up by Khadaffi. So far, it doesn't appear that any of the members from Rashid's Syrian cell are here in the States." She paused. "But, he may have contacts who will help him."

Unless the Salafi had made him persona nongratia for his monumental failure, I thought. *Then he'd be totally on his own.* I stepped behind her, put my hands on her shoulders, and rested my chin on her head. "You'll find him," I said with what I hoped was conviction while a little part of me was thinking, *maybe not.*

Marina tilted into me, moving her head so it rested on my shoulder. She looked up and grinned. "Mr. Optimist," she said, then turned and kissed me. "I'm heading to the track in about fifteen minutes. You can come later if you prefer."

I shook my head. "No. Now's good. Just let me shower and change." I grabbed a mug from the counter and filled it with the strong black coffee that had drawn me in with its aroma. "I'll be back in a few."

While I showered, I mentally reviewed where we were. Derby Day. A hundred thousand-plus people crowding every inch of the track to watch The Run for The Roses. One, or possibly more, crazed terrorists armed with a bomb, planning to blow everything and everyone to kingdom come. And then there was Tommy B's guy, Caleb Filmore. *Who knows what he's up to and how will it affect the race?* I stepped out of the shower and dried off. Not the odds I'd have chosen but the ones I had to live with.

I walked back into the kitchen and Marina was waiting. She picked up her laptop and a tote bag filled with papers, and we left the villa. I said I'd drive, and we hopped in the Jeep I had used the day before.

"Should we wait for Adnan?" I asked.

"He left earlier; he wanted to check on Devil Wind before the race."

"I saw Fire Walker working out yesterday on the practice track. I think he might give Devil Wind a run for the money, as they say."

"Devil Wind is the favorite. There's going to be a lot of money bet on him. I think he'll take the race." I could hear Marina's admiration for the horse in her voice.

"Do you know how the term favorite came to be used in horseracing?" I asked.

"No," she smiled, "but I'm sure you'll tell me."

"It started in the Middle Ages during jousting tournaments. Before the match began, the queen or lady of the manor gave her scarf, her colors, to the knight she favored, hoping he'd return to her after he won." I glanced over at her. "The idea of a favorite stuck and eventually was used to describe the horse rather than the competitor."

"You're a fountain of knowledge, Nick." She gently cuffed me on the arm. "I don't know what I'd do without you."

The last was said more with seriousness than playfulness. I took my hand off the wheel for a moment to squeeze hers.

A few minutes later, we arrived at the track and entered via the service road on Longfield Avenue. Security people checked inside the Jeep and slid a mirror under it to look for hidden explosives. They'd be checking the cars in the parking lots, as well.

Entering right behind us was a truck filled with bales of hay. They were getting the same going over as we had. "What are those guys doing here today?" I asked.

Marina turned and looked over her shoulder. "They're the landscaping people, finishing up from yesterday. They're setting up bales of hay around several areas, including a stage in the infield. One of the local bands is scheduled to perform between races, and the hay bales will keep the crowd from bumping into the stage."

I steered the car toward the barn area and parked as close as I could to Devil Wind's stall. It was much quieter at the track than yesterday. The mood was subdued because of the importance of the race, or the fear of what might go wrong, I couldn't tell you.

Chapter Sixty-Four

I knew some of the track personnel weren't buying the Saudi dignitary story, even though Schimmenti and Chase had set up a secure space in the Finish Line Suites on the fifth floor of the clubhouse as a ruse and stationed security people there.

Adnan was in front of Devil Wind's stall, speaking with Rehan and a slight young man in riding boots and the stables' purple and blue silks, whom I assumed was the jockey.

We joined them, and Adnan introduced us. "Marina, Nick, this is Gabe Purcell, the jockey who will take Devil Wind to victory."

You couldn't mistake the pride in his voice for his horse and his jockey. I'd heard of Purcell through Mad Mel as part of my instant racing education. Mel had mentioned him along with a few other jockeys who were slated to ride in the Derby. Purcell had an impressive record for someone so young and had won at many of the tracks across the country.

We shook hands all around, and then Marina excused herself. "I'm going to catch up with Mansur and double-check a few things before the gates open."

I stayed behind listening to what Adnan was telling the jockey about his mount, not that I understood most of it, except "let him have his head on the home stretch." I didn't think Devil Wind would have it any other way.

Purcell appeared calm and engaged in Adnan's instructions, and I wager he hadn't been told about the potential threat. Even for someone with nerves of steel—something you had to have to sit atop over two thousand pounds of thundering horseflesh—the idea of terrorists waiting at the next turn would be daunting.

It was just after six and the barn area was filled with horses, their keepers, and their jockeys. There were several races before the big event and many of these horses in them. Maybe it was my mood, but I sensed an underlying tension in the horses I passed. Shaking their manes, clomping their hooves in the dirt, and whinnying for no apparent reason, they seemed disturbed and on edge. Were they picking it up from their owners and trainers, or did these big, beautiful animals have some sort of second sight? I shook off the feeling. *Nick, stop being weird.*

The gates would open to racegoers at eight. I decided to take one more turn around the track to see if I could sniff out Caleb Filmore. I took my time, peering into every building I passed. There was no sign of him anywhere. I figured he might be laying low until it was closer to post time. His dorm mates had mentioned he did pick up work for O'Rourke, but I hadn't seen him anywhere near Fire Walker. I wasn't giving up, though. I'd check back periodically during the day.

In the next hour, the pace picked up, and the tension mounted. People were busier and brusque in anticipation of the big race. The gates would open soon, and in a matter of a few hours or so, the track would be filled to capacity. Unlike the owners and bigwigs, those who had to watch from the grandstand and rail were claiming their spots early.

The infield was already packed with people, as well. Bars and food stands were serving race day fare and the ubiquitous mint juleps. The landscapers had left, and the band was tuning up.

Marina was with Mansur in the security office. They were double-checking communications with all the teams and channeling through the closed-circuit TV monitors. I said I'd be with Adnan for a while and be back before post-time for the Derby. Marina nodded absently at me, intent on the monitors and the security team riffling through the bags of the people who were now starting to pour in.

After I made another loop looking for Filmore and Rashid, I caught up with Adnan in the Triple Crown Room, where we'd watched the races a few weeks ago. He was sitting by himself at a table facing the track. His hands were wrapped around a mug of coffee, and the remnants of a mostly untouched breakfast were spread before him.

He appeared to be fixated on a point far in the distance. Maybe he was running the race in his head, seeing Devil Wind thundering down the track, muscles straining, legs pumping, head pointed forward, pulling out front in the home stretch to take the lead and win by a mile, well, several furlongs, and securing the first leg of The Triple Crown.

He didn't hear me approach, and I cleared my throat to let him know I was there.

"Nick, sit. Please, have some breakfast. Whatever you like." He summoned the waiter to take my order.

I have to admit I was starving. Sitting at a blackjack table was a sedentary occupation, and I hadn't done this much walking in quite a while. I ordered eggs, bacon, toast, and a large coffee, which the waiter delivered immediately.

"So, where are we, Nick?" he asked. "Will this be a day that goes down in history for the wrong reasons?"

I sipped my coffee before answering. "We've done everything we can. If Rashid tries to slip in with a bomb, we'll get him." I'd filled my voice with confidence and hoped it hadn't rung false.

The first race was about to start, and I thought I'd sit here and watch it with him.

It got off without a hitch, and the long shot came in, paying a nice twelve to one. The band in the infield started strumming their guitars and banjos, and the crowd responded to the music, cheering and clapping. *What would they do*, I wondered, *if they knew the potential danger they were in?*

Chapter Sixty-Five

The day seemed to go on forever. Everyone on the team looked exhausted. The Derby was the last race and was coming up in about half an hour. Churchill Downs was a madhouse. From women and men dressed to the nines to track regulars in more ordinary attire, it was a riot of color, of wall-to-wall people, over one hundred thousand strong.

Champagne, mint juleps, and Bourbon were flowing. Everybody was having a high old time, except those of us who knew the danger we were facing. I'd been through the crowd several times, looking for Rashid. Moving through the racegoers was difficult, and I tried to look at every male who was the same height and build as Rashid. I thought I'd seen him once or twice, but each time, it was a false alarm. The two men I'd grabbed by the arm and spun around hadn't appreciated my actions, and I apologized as quickly as I could, saying I thought they were someone else.

Marina's nerves were frayed to the breaking point. I spoke with her several times.

"Anything yet?" she asked, the worry seeping through my cell like water through a dam about to burst.

Each time, my answer was the same. "No."

Time was running out. The trumpeter called the horses to the track. The University of Louisville Marching Band had started to play my "Old Kentucky Home."

I craned my neck and peered at everyone. It was no good. It was like finding a needle in a haystack.

Suddenly, it hit me. I knew where the bomb was, and I knew Rashid was there to set it off.

Chapter Sixty-Six

All the horses were on the track. Their jockeys had trotted them a few furlongs to warm them up, and now they were slowly making their way to the starting gate, giving the folks along the fence a good look at each of them.

The crowd was up and cheering, hollering at their favorites, raising their drinks, and having a high old time. I had to get to the infield before the race began, and I wouldn't be able to cross the track. There was a wide strip of green turf separating it from the dirt track. I flew across both and slipped under the infield fence, close to the band and those bales of hay surrounding their stage. I pushed and shoved my way through a mass of people, ignoring the dirty looks and drunken slurs tossed at me.

Somehow, I knew that's where Rashid had stashed the bomb he smuggled in with the hay. He'd want to be close enough to check it one more time, then move out of range and detonate it at just the right moment. I was sure he planned to survive the blast so he could laugh in our faces and seek redemption from his Salafi masters.

That's when I spotted him. He'd changed his appearance, lightened his hair, added glasses and a mustache, and was dressed in a sports jacket. Somehow, he made it past security. I inched my way closer, not wanting him to see me, and set off the bomb before I could subdue him. If that happened, we'd all be dead. I ducked behind two smiling women in big floppy hats who thought I was trying to photo-bomb the photo another woman was taking of them.

"C'mon, sugar," one of them said, "we'd love to have you in our picture."

I smiled and moved on, hearing one of them whisper, "Oh, he's no fun."

While I was inching up on Rashid, the race started. I couldn't figure out what he was playing at. He moved toward the edge of the infield when I noticed the satchel he had in his hand. He had removed it from the hay, and it had to contain the bomb. If he set it off now, he couldn't save himself. Unless I was wrong and getting out alive wasn't on his agenda.

I sped up my pursuit and called out to him. "Rashid." If I could get to him, I might be able to grab the bag and the detonator I knew in my gut he was holding. He turned at the sound of his name and took off for the fence and the turf beyond it.

The crowd was on its feet, screaming and yelling at the horses galloping down the track for all they were worth. Getting out of the infield and across the track was a near impossibility.

All this was going through my mind as Rashid slipped under the fence, separating the infield from the turf. He looked to his right to where the horses were bunched close together, coming around the far turn, and started to run closer to the rail.

I'd have to do the same if I was going to stop him in time.

People had started to notice us and were pointing at the two crazy men running on the turf. I could hear the horses' hooves beating as fast as my heart.

"Rashid!" I called out. "Stop. Don't do this."

He was in the middle of the turf now, his gait slowing, waiting for the horses to get closer. He meant to make sure they died, as well.

"Donahue, you bastard. You'll get what you deserve. The fire of Allah will rain down on you and the rest of these heathens."

In another ten seconds, the horses would be right next to us. I watched as Rashid took a cell phone out of his pocket and started punching in a number. I made one last effort to reach him and lunged just as the first horse flew by. We tumbled to the ground as I tried to wrest the phone from him.

By now, those thundering hooves of the rest of the pack were just a few furlongs away. As we struggled, we rolled closer and closer to the track. I managed to grab his arm and knock the phone free. Several of the horses were past us now, leaving the rest of the field to follow. Rashid kept trying to drag us closer to the rail and onto the track, which would have meant certain death for the horses and us. Gripping him with all the strength I had left, I yanked the bag from his hand and watched the horses gallop toward the finish line.

My breath was coming in quick rasps, and my body was shaking as I realized what had just happened. I let go of the bag and scuttled a few feet backward, dragging Rashid with me. He started to stir, and I punched him in his jaw to keep him down. I figured I earned that right. And one more for good measure. Then, I sat up and waited for the cavalry to come. Thankfully, it didn't take long.

Chapter Sixty-Seven

To say that things at Churchill Downs were a little wild is putting it mildly. Before I knew what was happening, several FBI agents swarmed across the track onto the turf and pulled both of us off and into the security office. They cuffed Rashid and took him away as soon as Lederman arrived to take charge.

As I stood there covered in dirt from head to toe, Marina ran up to me and put both her hands on my face. "*Ti uomo pazzo,*" she said, in the Italian she sometimes reverted to during times of stress, then kissed me hard.

What I'd done was a little crazy, but if I'd stopped to think about it, I would probably have had a very different outcome.

Fortunately, the racegoers didn't have a clue about what had happened—the mint juleps might have had something to do with that. It would have been too late to evacuate the track. Rashid had timed it perfectly and was on track to blow us to kingdom come until I interfered.

The track officials put out an announcement that two of the guests had had an altercation and neither one had been hurt. They asked the people in the infield to clear the area so that the police could investigate and sent out two bomb guys dressed in police uniforms to secure the area and check for any other bombs. As we suspected, there were none. If there had been, they'd have done their damage by now.

We were lucky. The bomb captured from Rashid wasn't a Mother of Satan powerhouse. He really must have been on his own and made the bomb himself. It was much smaller than the bombs found at the ABH labs, but could still have caused a great deal of misery. That catastrophe had been avoided.

Devil Wind won the Derby and the first leg of the Triple Crown. Unofficially, that is. There was a steward's inquiry, which meant he couldn't officially be declared the winner until they reviewed the footage of the race.

Of course, the owner of every horse running complained that it wasn't a fair race, based on what they witnessed. They claimed the two men fighting was distracting.

The stewards did their job and declared that none of the horses were interfered with, and Devil Wind was the winner.

The closing ceremony went on as scheduled. Devil Wind received his blanket of roses and Purcell his accolades. Adnan was smiling for real, and, for once, even Mansur looked pleased.

Of course, this wasn't over, not by a long shot, except for Marina and me. We'd done our job—saved Devil Wind and stopped the Salafi in their tracks—and were happy to be heading home as soon as possible.

It was a different story for Adnan. He broke away from the well-wishers who had surrounded him and found us on the edge of the crowd. "How can I ever explain this to Latif and Janiki?" he asked. The muscles in his face looked as if they were welded together, and his eyes were dark and impenetrable.

"You can tell them at least he's alive," Marina answered, gently putting her hand on his arm. "If we hadn't caught him, it would only have been a matter of time until the Salafi found him and—"

He put up his hand to stop her from uttering the words he knew she was going to. "Yes, you are right. At least he is alive."

"And the cloaking device is safe," I added while thinking, *Better if it had never been created.*

There was still a small crowd surrounding Devil Wind, Purcell, and Rehan. Marina gave him one of her brilliant, gorgeous smiles. "Go back to Devil Wind and his admirers. Enjoy the moment. You earned the right to do so."

Adnan took her hand and brought it to his lips. He kissed her gently, then turned and made his way to his majestic champion.

There was just one more thing I had to clear up before I left Louisville. I noticed Lederman conferring with some of his men and called him over. I explained why I told Lydia that the mob had killed Eggers, but I realized I was wrong. I was pretty sure Rashid was responsible. Eggers had probably figured out what Rashid was up to, but Rashid silenced him permanently.

"I could bring you in for this," he said. "Not only did you leave the scene of a crime, but you also obstructed my investigation." Lederman just scowled, disgust written all over his face. "Lydia said you could be a dumbass jerk. She was right." He turned his back and walked away.

He was pissed, but I knew he wouldn't do anything about it. He was just angry he hadn't been able to nail Tommy B.

I knew Lederman would get the truth from Rashid, and I didn't think he'd worry too much about how he obtained it.

I walked up to Marina and took her hand. "Are we done here?" I asked, smiling. "Now that I know for sure horse racing isn't my game—" I patted my jacket, and a cloud of dirt blew out. "—I think I'll stick with blackjack."

The next day, we were back in New York at the Carlyle, getting ready for our flight home to London. Alex and Simone had returned from their honeymoon, beaming rays of happiness like a shining disco ball. We met them at Mom and Dad's apartment and filled them in on our case in Kentucky. Most of it, anyway. I didn't want Mom to have a coronary in the middle of dinner. Dad raised his eyebrow quizzically in my direction, and I nodded to let him know I'd tell him all about it later.

Before we said our goodbyes, I presented Alex and Simone with their wedding present. I'd finally come up with the perfect gift, something I was positive they didn't have: a racehorse.

Adnan had given Marina and me a bonus, an ownership share in the first foal sired by Devil Wind. With his blessing, we re-gifted this unusual present to the happy couple who loved the idea of owning a future racehorse. I reminded Alex not to forget his generous brother if and when this future racehorse won.

Marina and I ambled back to the hotel, enjoying the feeling of just *being*.

The clerk at the front desk turned over our key and a small package. "Mr. Donahue, this was left for you."

I thanked him and took it up to our room. My name was written on the front and there was nothing that identified who it was from.

"Open it, Nick," Marina demanded like a small child. "Maybe it's something from Adnan."

"I think the fee he paid us, and our bonus, was probably more than enough without him sending a gift," I replied as I undid the wrapping. My heart stopped for a minute, and I felt the heat rising in my face as I read the note inside the package.

Nick,
    Sorry we didn't have a chance to catch up in Louisville.
    Plan to get together the next time I'm in London.
    You owe me one, you know.
    Tommy B

Inside the box was a five-hundred-pound chip from my favorite casino in London. Marina looked at me with a puzzled expression. All I could do was shake my head and whisper to myself, *Just when you thought it was safe.*

The End

Acknowledgements

I'm so happy that Nick Donahue, one of my favorite characters, is back in the game! Many thanks to my publishers, Level Best Books, aka The Dames of Detection, Verena Main Rose and Shawn Reilly Simmons, and her superpower editing. Thanks also to all the friends whose names I appropriated for this novel. You all just seemed to fit. Thanks to my sibs in Sisters in Crime NY/Tri-State for always having my back. Thanks to Neil Petrocelli, whose knowledge of and insights into the world of horseracing was incredibly helpful. All the mistakes are mine. Thanks to my nephew, Ben Stoler, who gave me the inspiration for the perfect weapon of mass destruction when he told me about a cloaking device that actually exists. And, thanks to my family who always support me—my husband Paul, daughter Lauren, son-in-law, Mike, and newest member, Madison Grace.

About the Author

Cathi Stoler, a native New Yorker, drew on her travels to interesting and exotic places to write two new mystery suspense novels, *Nick of Time*, and *Out of Time*, featuring professional Blackjack player, Nick Donahue.

Her suspense novels, *Bar None, Last Call, Straight Up,* and *With A Twist, The Murder on the Rocks Mysteries*, are set on the Lower East Side of New York City and feature The Corner Lounge owner, Jude Dillane. She is also the author of the three-volume Laurel & Helen New York Mystery series, which includes *Telling Lies, Keeping Secrets,* and *The Hard Way*.

Stoler is a three-time finalist and the winner of the Derringer for Best Short Story "The Kaluki Kings of Queens." Her Murder on the Rocks novels have been nominated for several awards. She is a board member of Sisters in Crime New York/Tri-State, and a member of Mystery Writers of America and International Thriller Writers. She lives in New York City with her husband. You can find her at www.cathistoler.com.

SOCIAL MEDIA HANDLES:

https://twitter.com/cathistoler
https://www.facebook.com/CathiStolerAuthor
https://www.instagram.com/cathistolerauthor/
https://www.goodreads.com/author/show/4807990.Cathi_Stoler

AUTHOR WEBSITE:
www.cathistoler.com

Also by Cathi Stoler

The Nick Donahue Adventures
Nick of Time

The Murder on The Rocks Series
Bar None (#1)
Last Call (#2)
Straight Up (#3)
With A Twist (#4)

Laurel and Helen New York Mysteries
Telling Lies (#1)
Keeping Secrets (#2)
The Hard Way (#3)